Working It

An It Girl Novel

Leah Marie Brown

LYRICAL PRESS
Kensington Publishing Corp.
www.kensingtonbooks.com

First Electronic Edition: June 2016
eISBN-13: 978-1-61650-811-1
eISBN-10: 1-61650-811-6

First Print Edition: June 2016
ISBN-13: 978-1-61650-815-9
ISBN-10: 1-61650-815-9

Printed in the United States of America

Falling in love is always in fashion....

With her trust fund and coveted job at Christian Dior, Fanny Moreau believes she has it all. But when her best friend finds a fulfilling new career abroad—and a dreamy relationship with a great guy, Fanny's fabulous life suddenly feels empty. Inspired to find her true purpose, she trades her cushy lifestyle in San Francisco for an adventure in the Alaskan wilderness.

Everyone thinks Fanny has gone off the deep end. What's a girl with a Ph.D in Prada doing teaching in an Inuit village? Even Fanny is wondering, especially when she comes face to face with Calder MacFarlane. The Scottish search and rescue pilot is everything Fanny is not—selfless, heroic, and used to living on the edge. He's also the man who once loved her best friend. Yet something in Calder's sexy gaze has her believing that she's a woman capable of great things—a woman who might just find her own happily-ever-after, in a place where she least expects it....

"Leah Marie Brown has a wily way of bringing her stories to life with sharp dialogue and drop-dead sexy characters."
—Cindy Miles, National Bestselling Author

"When it comes to crafting clever, intelligent, wonderful escapist fiction with a heroine every woman wants to know, Leah Marie Brown is a new voice to watch. Prepare to fall in love!"
—Renee Ryan, Daphne du Maurier Award-Winning Author

Books by Leah Marie Brown

The It Girl Series
Faking It
Finding It
Working It

Published by Kensington Publishing Corporation

We all need two a.m. friends – people we can call late at night, when the world is dark, and we need a little light. Thank you to a few of my two a.m. friends:

Kurt Bauer, who reads everything I write and declares it brilliant. I am glad you have stayed in fashion far longer than lady loafers. Lori Lee Bacon, who is the most uplifting and reliable person I know. Trevin Larkin and Ernie DiDomizio, my beloved brothas from otha mothas. Robert Hurst, who doesn't do meth, but would definitely shank a man for me.

Author's Foreword

I am Live Out Loud kinda gal. I frequently update my social media accounts and blogs with random trivia about my life. If you follow any of my accounts, you might have noticed Vivia and I share a few personality quirks: we both enjoy champagne cocktails on the beach, brushes with celebrities, and rock music. We both love the color pink, sometimes speak without thinking, and have best friends named Stéphanie. The similarities end there.

It would be ridiculous for me to say that Fanny Moreau is a figment of my imagination. I based Vivia's sophisticated BFF on one of my BFFs, Stéphanie Mounts. Both are competitive, sharp-witted Frenchwomen who adore adventure, counting calories, and their slightly-outré best friends. The fictitious Fanny Moreau's resemblance to my very real Fanny ends there. They have had different journeys. Stéphanie Mounts' journey is very much her own – except the bits she has been generous enough to share with me.

Stéphanie Moreau's journey, on the other hand, is very much public. I hope you enjoy embarking on Fanny Moreau's journey as much as I have enjoyed sharing Fanny Mounts' journey.

Part One

A woman's perfume tells more about her than her handwriting.
Christian Dior

Chapter 1

A Stinky Pussycat

The worst day of my life started with an unfortunate spritz of perfume.

Every tragedy can be traced back to one fatal mistake, one seemingly insignificant miscalculation that sets into motion a series of small blunders resulting in utter catastrophe.

Take James Cameron winning the Oscar for *Titanic* over Gus Van Sant for *Good Will Hunting*. If the Titanic's wireless operator had known how to work the Marconi efficiently, he might have translated the warning messages about ice in the area, the unsinkable ship would have remained afloat, and James Cameron wouldn't have won the Oscar for a hopelessly insipid movie.

If Christian Lacroix had added jet beads to his pared-back coat dresses and peplum skirts, his '09 Fall Collection might have been the buzz of the season; instead, fashion editors and snarky bloggers lamented the loss of his talent.

One seemingly insignificant snowball-sized mistake starts its journey down the mountain, and before you know it, a shit avalanche is descending upon you.

My best friend, Vivian—her name is Vivia, but I call her Vivian because it's more glam—coined the phrase "shit avalanche." It's an unpalatably graphic and overblown phrase and not one I use often, but it superbly describes my situation.

My shit avalanche started with an unwelcome spritz of Kitty Kat's Purrfect. Kitty Kat, the bubblegum pop singing phenom, might know a thing or two about writing hit songs, but she doesn't know a thing about the delicate art of blending scents to create an intoxicating perfume.

How could a spritz of perfume cause a disaster?

I will start at the awful beginning, but only because I hope my tragic story will serve as a cautionary tale. The *Titanic*. James Cameron.

Christian Lacroix. Stéphanie Moreau. The world has suffered enough disasters. Read and learn, *mon amie*.

Chapter 2

Moonlight as a Tranny Hooker

Text to Vivia Perpetua Grant:
Help! I am wrapped in an unfashionable cloak of ennui. Bored with my job, my nonexistent love life, myself…San Francisco isn't the same since you left.

Text from Vivia Perpetua Grant:
Girl, you need to shake up your life like a snow globe.

"What is that ghastly stench?"

Several of my subordinates perform discreet pit checks, sniffing their shoulders, but I keep my gaze fixed on my boss. I am the offender, and I know it. It's only a matter of time before my boss knows it, too.

My boss, Nicola Salupo, is the Executive Vice President for Aurèle L'Heure, Inc., North American Division. She's chic, clever, driven, and a complete *salope*—that's French for bitch. She thrives on humiliation—not her own, mind you, but on the utter mortification of her subordinates. Nicola feeds on humiliation the way vegans feast on tofu burgers.

She begins walking around the Lucite conference table, slowly, like a vulture circling road kill. People shift in their seats, a timid intern dabs beads of perspiration from her upper lip, but I keep my chin lifted and my gaze fastened on the vulture in couture.

"Someone reeks of"—she lifts her cosmetically sculpted nose high in the air and sniffs—"dimestore desperation."

She stops walking directly across from me and pierces me with her glacial blue gaze.

"Mademoiselle Moreau?"

"*Oui?*"

"Either you've been moonlighting in the Tenderloin or you have grossly neglected your personal hygiene this morning." She sniffs again and wrinkles her nose as if catching a whiff of a putrefied cadaver. "What is that stench?"

"Kitty Kat's Purrfect."

"Kitty Kat's Purrfect?" She looks around the conference table with wide eyes. "Did I miss the memo? Has L'Heure Cosmetics created a line of fragrances for tranny-hookers?"

Salope.

I consider telling her my miserable tale—about how a snotty kid on the bus dropped his backpack on my foot and broke the transparent heel of my thirteen-hundred-dollar Dior calfskin pumps, how I had to superglue the heel while standing at the cosmetics counter in Walgreens, and how the salesgirl spritzed me with Purrfect—but Nicola is more of a bullet points person.

"I had an unfortunate collision with an overeager salesgirl in Walgreens this morning."

"Walgreens?" Nicola gasps. "I always thought your makeup looked a little… I had no idea you purchased your cosmetics at Walgreens."

Salope. Salope. Salope.

"I don't purchase my cosmetics at Walgreens."

"Anyway," Nicola continues as if I haven't said a word, "it is a violation of corporate policy to wear competitor's fragrances."

I snort. "I would hardly call Kitty Kat a competitor of Aurèle L'Heure."

The nervous intern chuckles.

Nicola narrows her gaze.

"You have violated corporate policy. I have no choice but to draft a formal letter of reprimand and attach it to your personnel file. In the meantime, you are relieved of your duties today."

"But, I am presenting my projection report to Monsieur Henri this afternoon."

"I'll present your report."

Of course you will.

Monsieur Henri Bousson is a veritable god in the L'Heure Universe. Impress Monsieur Henri, and your future in fashion is as solid gold as Louboutin's lock on the luxury high heel market. Since he is based out of Paris and rarely makes it to California, this might be my only opportunity to impress him.

"I worked hard on my presentation. I conducted independent market research, gathered supportive data for my forecasts…."

I don't bother saying that impressing Monsieur Henri is just one more step in my climb up the career ladder toward a position at my dream house, Christian Dior, and I would shank Nicola with L'Heure's Divine Eyeliner before I would let her knock me off my wrung.

Nicola stares at me coldly, unmoved by my appeal.

"What about my sketches?"

"Email them to me along with your presentation."

Putain!

In the last few months, I have logged over two hundred unpaid overtime hours, working on sketches of shoes, purses, coats—original designs—in the hopes of impressing Monsieur Henri enough to offer me a position on his Parisian-based design team. Now, a stupid Walgreens employee and her tawdry perfume sample are threatening to knock me out of the running as I make my final lap toward the finish line. A promotion at L'Heure would pretty much guarantee me a position at Dior, and working at Christian Dior's head offices in Paris has been my dream since I was old enough to play dress up in my grandmère's closet.

"Go home and clean up, Mademoiselle Moreau."

"This is ridiculous. It was one spritz."

"Be gone, Mademoiselle." Nicola waves her hand in a dismissive gesture. "Be gone."

I consider snapping my translucent heel off my shoe and repeatedly jamming it into her eye socket until she stops looking at me with her patronizing expression, but I have sacrificed too much to risk an assault and battery charge. So I gather my notebook, stand, and walk out of the conference room with my head held high.

Chapter 3

Cunning Linguistics

Thirty minutes later, I have returned several phone calls, drafted a memo, and grudgingly emailed my presentation to Nicola. I am standing outside the sleek frosted glass Aurèle L'Heure Flagship Store in Union Square, staring up at a vertiginous network of scaffolds. The ten thousand-square-foot store is still under construction, but when it opens later this year, it will contain luxury items from one of the most iconic couturiers in the world.

It's a jewel box of a building, and it's my job to fill it with treasures to delight discerning fashion-savvy consumers.

I shift my gaze to the crane hoisting a shiny gold "L'Heure" sign onto the roof, and a coagulated lump forms in my throat.

What is the matter with me? Why am I letting Nicola *Salope* and her petty maneuverings get in my head?

Because you worked your ass off to become the Regional Director of Aurèle L'Heure Boutiques and she just marginalized you in front of your new staff.

And because, deep down, you're not as happy as you thought you would be.

My Blackberry begins vibrating. I pull it out of my trench coat and stare at the small photograph above the words *Incoming Call from Vivian*. The image is of my best friend standing in a stream in Scotland, the water spilling over the tops of her pink Wellies, a beaming grin plastered across her pretty freckled face. The lump in my throat thickens.

"*Coucou*, Vivian." I have always called her Vivian because I think she is as glamorous as an old-time movie star and Vivia Perpetua is just not glam. "*Comment ça va?*"

"What's wrong?"

"*En français*, Vivian!"

"*Que pasa?*"

"That's Spanish."

"*Merde!*"

"*Voila.*" I try to laugh, but the lump makes it come out as a croak. "Now, you're speaking French."

"French-schmench. What's up? You sound sad."

"I'm fine."

"Bull *merde*. You don't fool me—"

The line crackles and I lose some of her words.

"—about your presentation. Chill, girl. You got this one. You got this one like Andrew Neiman had 'Caravan.'"

"Yeah, I have no idea what you're talking about."

"*Whiplash.*"

"Whip what?"

"*Whiplash.*" She exhales audibly. "Academy Award-Winning film about Andrew Neiman, an ambitious, talented young drummer attending a prestigious music school who is harassed by his professor."

"Ooo-kay."

"The professor kept making Andrew play this difficult piece of music—'Caravan'—and even though he mastered it, the D-bag rode the kid like Kim Kardashian riding Kanye in the Bound2 vid."

I shake my head and blink my eyes. I feel as if I have just tumbled down the rabbit hole and am lost in Wonderland. It's a sensation I experience often when I listen to Vivian speak. I head west down Post Street, toward Union Square Park.

"Fanny? Are you still there?"

"*Oui,*" I say, rubbing my temples. "I am trying to get my bearings in this conversation, but I fear I am hopelessly lost, way back on Andrew Newman."

"Neiman," she sighs. "I am saying you have mad skills, girlfriend. You pick up those drumsticks and bang your little heart out because you got this one. Okay?"

"Thanks, but..." My voice catches and I pause to swallow the ever growing lump.

"What's going on? You're starting to freak me out."

I enter the park, take a seat on an empty bench, and tell my best friend about my mangled heel, the rancid spritz girl, and Nicola's bitchy attack.

Vivian whistles. "Man, I was on target with my *Whiplash* analogy. You've got a Fletcher."

"No more movie analogies, Vivian, *s'il vous plâit.*"

"Fletcher, the brutal professor," she says, ignoring my heartfelt plea. "Nicola the *Salope* is a Fletcher. She's abusing her power to subjugate and humiliate you, because she is secretly threatened by your brilliance."

"Or she's just a *salope*."

"Or she's a *salope*. A soulless plastic-nosed *über-salope* who probably spends her free hours cruising the Tenderloin in Forever 21 daisy dukes. Mama's gotta pay for the Botox somehow, right?"

"Ouch. That's brutal."

"Sorry, nobody fucks with my best friend. You're Type-A, got it all together, competitive, self-contained Fanny. It's freaking me out to hear you so…"

"So what?"

"Vulnerable."

I inhale and square my shoulders. "I am not vulnerable."

"You sound vulnerable."

"Well, I'm not."

Yes, I am.

"Yes, you are," she astutely argues. "You worked your size-two Armani-clad ass off on your Monsieur Henri presentation because you hoped it would gain you the recognition you deserve, and your boss just took that hope, squatted down, and shat all over it. You're allowed to be sad, Fanny."

And that, *Mesdames et Messieurs*, is why Vivian Perpetua Grant is my best friend. Her colorful, free-flowing language, often peppered with random pop-culture references, and open, affectionate nature is in complete contrast to my reserved speech and manner. Vivian views every stranger as a potential friend and every friend as family. She smiles, laughs, and hugs freely. She has a bonhomie that is infectious. I grew up in an affection vacuum and am, by nature, more reserved. Vivian is the yin to my yang.

"I'll be fine." I glance at my watch. It's only 8:46. What am I supposed to do for the rest of the day? "That is, if I can figure out what to do now."

"Where are you now?"

"Union Square Park."

"Ooo! I know!" Vivian half murmurs, half moans into the phone. "Go to Bitchin' Baklava!"

"What?"

"Bitchin' Baklava, on Balboa. They make the best dark chocolate almond baklavas. One bite and you will forget all about Nicola the Salope."

"Do you know how many calories are in baklava?" I stretch my legs out in front of me and flex my calf muscles. "I don't want to be miserable and fat."

I have never told Vivian that I was overweight as a child, that the girls at my boarding school called me Éléphanny, and made stomping sounds whenever I walked by. Boom. Boom. Some secrets must be kept hidden away, like a bad boob job, even from best friends.

"Okay, no baklava." Vivian sighs. "You could go to Tuescher Chocolatier and have one-eighth of a champagne truffle."

"I could go to the gym. I think they offer a noon-time Body Combat—"

"Boring," Vivian interrupts. "Go see the new Colin Farrell movie, hang out in that music café near Leaning Tower of Pizza, or get a massage so you're nice and relaxed for your date tonight."

"*Putain!* I forgot about my date. I am going to cancel."

"You can't cancel this late. It would be rude."

"Look, Vivian, even on my best days I am woefully inadequate when it comes to small talk."

"True, but meaningful relationships start with small talk. Luc and I started out talking about fast food and cowboy movies."

Vivian is engaged to her dream man, Jean Luc de Caumont, a witty, kind romantic literature professor and former Tour de France cyclist. We met Jean-Luc on a bike tour through Provence and Tuscany. Actually, it was supposed to be Vivian's honeymoon, but her priggish ex-fiancé dumped her after he found out she had lied about her virginity. Vivian is the only woman I know who could go from jilted bride to long-distance lover in two weeks. She's the absolute master at flipping the script, and I envy her for it. She is overdramatic—über-dramatic is the word she would use—and moans about every setback as if it were fatal and final, yet she always manages to turn it around.

"I wish you were here" —I sigh—"or I were there. I miss France."

"What? I thought you loved California."

"I loved it when you were here and we could get into mischief."

"You mean I got into mischief and you got me out."

I laugh because Vivian has never said a truer statement. She does have a penchant for misadventure.

"It will all work out, Fanny. I just know it. You are too organized, talented, and driven not to succeed."

"I don't feel driven." I lean back against the park bench and exhale. "My internal drive mechanism seems to be malfunctioning. You think I have it all together. I thought I had it all together. But I am not so sure anymore. I don't know what I am doing with my life."

"You could always move back to France. I'll bet Philippe would hire you as one of his bike guides."

We laugh. Philippe is Jean-Luc's brother, and he owns a thriving bike tour company.

"Enough about me. How are you? How's nearly-married life? Get the minivan yet?"

"Ha-ha. Actually, I bought a zippy little Fiat convertible…"

I only half listen as Vivian tells me about the article she is writing for her magazine column, her hunt for the perfect "muffin top-concealing" wedding gown, and her struggle to adapt to life in France, because I am brainstorming ways to make the store's grand opening the most successful in L'Heure history. That would surely net me another shot at impressing Monsieur Henri.

"…Hello? Fanny? Damn mobile connection."

"I'm here! The line just dropped off for a few seconds."

"Thank God!"

I lied because I can't exactly tell my best friend that listening to details about her happy life is making me feel worse, that I would prefer to talk to someone with a crappy life so I can feel better about my own.

"This call is going to cost you a fortune." I look at my Blackberry screen. "We've been talking for thirty-six minutes already."

"Shit! Are you serious? I better go, then. Cheer up and have fun on your date. Text me when you get home tonight, unless you invite him back to your place. If that happens, skip the text and send me selfies instead."

"Vivian!

"Kidding."

"*Au revoir*, Vivian."

"*Hasta la vista*, baby!"

The line goes dead. Ten seconds later, I get a text.

Text from Vivia Perpetua Grant:
I forgot to tell you. Fiona and Angus are coming to the wedding. If Calder comes, you could be his date. Think about it.

Fiona and Angus operate the sheep farm Vivian and I visited when we went to Scotland last year. Calder is Angus's slightly sexy, completely arrogant brother.

Text to Vivia Perpetua Grant:
So not gonna happen. He was into you, remember?

Chapter 4

Balling

I arrive at Snob, an artsy wine bar not too far from my apartment, take a seat at the counter, and order a glass of my favorite red wine while I wait for Morph2Perfection, also known as Ethan DuBois.

I "met" Ethan in an online dating site's chat room. He is a software developer with a "passion for rock climbing, fine wine, and foreign languages." Apparently, he developed some unusual software program and is now Zuckerberg rich. He didn't tell me that last part. I Googled him.

"Waiting for someone?" the bartender asks.

"A date." Nerves tickle my belly. "First date."

"Nice."

"I met him online."

He whistles. "Hope you don't get catfished."

I don't watch a lot of television, but I get the reference. "Me too."

The bartender smiles and moves down the bar to greet a new wave of customers.

Honestly? I've been so wrapped up in the fall-out of the Kitty Kat Purrfect debacle, I haven't considered the possibility that Morph2Perfection might have lied on his dating profile. I am not a religious person, but I suddenly feel the need to pray.

Please, Higher Power and Goddess of First Dates, please don't let Ethan be a catfish. Please no finger-sniffing, overweight, balding, middle-aged men.

I finish my wine and order another glass.

Nothing wrong with courage by Cabernet, is there?

We agreed to meet at seven o'clock. Ethan walks in the door at six fifty-nine.

Punctual. Score one for Ethan.

He looks just like his profile photo—tall, lean, with sandy brown hair that points in all directions, like he just ran his hand through it. He's cute, in a slightly disheveled absent-minded professor kind of way. He doesn't hesitate in the doorway but walks right over to me.

Confident. I like that. Score another point.

"Stéphanie?"

"Ethan?"

"*Enchanté*, Mademoiselle Moreau," he says, grabbing my hand and pressing a kiss to the back of it. "You're even more beautiful in person than you are on your profile photo. How is that possible?"

Perfect French accent and charming compliment. Score two more points for Ethan.

"*Merci.*"

"Shall we move to a table?"

I pick up my glass and follow him to a small table situated in a partially-curtained alcove. He doesn't pull out my chair.

Minus one for Ethan. Fortunately, he's still up three points.

We spend the next fifteen minutes making polite chitchat. I use a trick I learned from watching Vivian in action and ask him an open-ended question about his job. People love talking about themselves, even on awkward first dates. Ethan is not the exception. Using technical programming jargon, he tells me about an exciting new program he's developing for a government contractor that will revolutionize battlefield tactics.

"That sounds exciting. You're a regular Q."

He stares at me. "Q?"

"James Bond." I smile. The head of research and development for MI-5."

How can a geek not know that?

"Ah." He leans back in his chair. "Except Q was an industrial scientist who developed hardware that could be used in the field, and I am a computer engineer who develops software. Not quite the same, technically speaking."

"Right."

An awkward silence stretches between us. Is he always a stickler for precise language?

"So you work in a clothing store?"

"Not exactly. I work for L'Heure."

"Isn't that a clothing store?"

"Boutique. Yes, but the phrase 'work in a clothing store' implies a sales position. I am a regional manager, responsible for several boutiques." I grin. "Not quite the same, technically speaking."

He continues to stare at me, and a wicked little voice in my head whispers, *Does not compute.* My playful jab simply does not register.

Sorry, Ethan. Half a point docked for inability to detect sarcasm. I am French. Sarcasm is an inherited trait. It's in our DNA.

"So," I say, changing the subject, "how long did you live in Paris?"

"Twelve weeks and two days."

"That's all?"

"I attended a language immersion course."

Three months? A three month language immersion course hardly qualifies. Minus two, Ethan.

If I can't date a Frenchman, I at least want to date someone with an understanding and appreciation of my culture. Acid churns in my belly. Clearly, disappointment and wine do not mix.

The bartender arrives, hands Ethan the wine list, and promises to return in a few minutes. Ethan studies the list for several seconds. He frowns and his brow knits together, as if the menu were written in Greek. He looks over the top of the menu at me.

"What are you drinking?"

"Chateau de Beaucastel Coudoulet Rouge. It's a Rhône Valley red. It has notes of plum and blackberry."

"Is it good?"

"*Oui!*"

"Can I try a sip?"

And just like that Ethan, morphs from a great catch into a catfish.

The uncouth creature reaches for my glass, and I have to quell a sudden impulse to slap his hand away. I stare at his lips pressed against the rim of the glass and wonder if he brushed his teeth. He finishes swigging my pricey pick and hands me the empty.

"Huh," he says, smacking his lips. "It tastes a little…gamey. Like the grapes were stomped on by a herd of wild boar."

C'est quoi ce bordel?

English translation: What the fuck?

"Perhaps that's the truffle."

"Truffle? As in mushroom?"

Wine connoisseur, my ass. Minus one. Game over, Ethan. You lose.

"Chateau de Beaucastel Coudoulet Rouge is made with Mourvèdre grapes, which take on a certain earthy flavor as they age."

He raises his hand in the air and snaps his fingers.

I am cringing. Inwardly. Outwardly. Cringing. Who does that?

Nobody.

Next, he will be saying, "Oh gar-son."

The bartender hurries over.

"I'll take a glass of the Yellow Tail Sparkling Rosé."

Cringing. Again.

Yellow Tail? Sparkling Rosé? I look around to see if anyone else heard Ethan order. Maybe this is an elaborate prank. Maybe Vivian met Ashton Kutcher and talked him into punking me.

I was stuck in an airport lounge in Omaha once, and the televisions were set to a *Punk'd* marathon. Yeah, my idea of hell is being stuck in Nebraska and forced to sip Yellow Tail Sparkling Rosé while watching endless loops of *Punk'd*.

The bartender looks at me, widens his eyes a fraction, and returns to the bar.

If Vivian were here, she would say, "*Ain't no shame in drinking pink wine.*" I would vehemently disagree. Pink is *not* the new white.

"So, Ethan"—I plaster a fake smile on my face—"what do you do in your free time, that is, when you're not developing James Bond software?"

"I volunteer at a soup kitchen near the Tenderloin."

Tenderloin? His mention of that seedy area reminds me of Nicola and her snarky comment implying I worked it in the red light district.

I groan.

"Not into volunteering?"

"What?"

"You groaned when I said I volunteer at a soup kitchen."

"Sorry." I wrap my fingers around the stem of my wineglass and tip it back and forth. The residual wine moves like a tiny claret wave. "Your comment just reminded me of something my boss said about the Tenderloin—"

The bartender returns with Ethan's sparkling wine, rescuing me from having to lie or recount my most humiliating professional encounter.

Ethan takes the glass from the bartender, lifts it in the air, studies the streaming legs in the light, brings the glass to his nose, sniffs, and then takes a sip, swishing the pink wine around in his mouth as if it were Listerine.

I would cringe, but I am all out of cringes. So I decide to keep the conversation rolling until I can toss my catfish back in the dating pond and forget I ever snagged him.

"I read in your dating profile that you are an avid rock climber."

"Yeah, I am."

"I love climbing. Do you have any climbs planned?"

He grabs his right shoulder and rotates his arm, groaning. "I'd love to, but I messed up my shoulder 'balling with some college buddies last week."

"Balling?" I smile. "You play basketball?"

"What?" He frowns and then chuckles. "No."

"What is balling then?"

"Paintball."

Putain!

What do you even say to that?

Somewhere, out there in the vast sea of people, there is a paintball-playing, soup-ladling, Rosé-swilling female just yearning to catch this catfish. I am not that woman. No yearning going on here.

Somehow, I keep the conversation going for another hour before offering a flimsy excuse about needing to be up early for an important meeting.

Ethan looks genuinely disappointed, which perplexes me. There has been no connection here. Zero. I haven't even felt the tiniest jolt of sexual electricity flowing between us. Is it possible he has?

"I am so glad we did this," he says, smiling. "I really feel a connection."

He stares at me. I stare back.

What is wrong with me? Why aren't I racked with guilt or suffering the pin-pricks of embarrassment?

"I brought you a little something," he says, reaching into his jacket. "A first date gift."

"Oh, that's okay."

"It's just a little something I made for you."

Please, please tell me he didn't knit me a paintball jersey.

He pulls out a folded square of papers, unfolds them, and hands them to me.

I take the papers and stare at the images of two mutant looking children, a boy and a girl. They have big brown eyes—like those Japanese cartoon characters—and pouty expressions. The girl has a sharply angled asymmetrical bob, curiously like my own.

I look at him, frowning.

"They're our children."

"Excuse me?" Bile bubbles up my throat.

"I morphed your profile picture with mine." He grins. "This is what our children would look like."

"What? How?" I drop the papers onto the table. "Why would you...?"

My mouth suddenly feels dry and my thoughts fuzzy, like someone shoved cotton in my head, like I drank too much cheap pink wine.

Leah Marie Brown

"I developed a software program that analyzes the genetic history and images of two people and digitally recreates their offspring."

"Morphing?"

"Technically, yes. But Morphenetics is far more complicated than the average morphing software, which merely takes two shapes and morphs them into one image, often accomplished by utilizing cross-fading film techniques." He leans forward, resting his arms on the table. "Morphenetics analyzes multiple faces, scans them for commonalities, and comes up with a complex mathematical algorithm that results in the creation of a new face. It's a sort of digital DNA. Just as geneticists have been able to analyze and isolate DNA to detect the probability of a person inheriting certain diseases, my program analyzes and isolates facial DNA to detect the probability of a person inheriting a particular hair color, eye shape, moles, dimples—"

"Wait a minute. You said multiple images. How were you able to come up with this"—I point to the image of the wide-eyed mutant girl-child—"*this* if you only used my profile photo?"

"I didn't only use your profile photo. I used several of your photos, as well as photos of your father and cousins."

C'est quoi ce bordel?

"I only loaded one photo onto the dating site."

Ethan grins. "I was able to access your Facebook photo albums and downloaded images of your family. You don't have many pictures of your family in your albums. I couldn't find one of your mother."

Ma mère.

An invisible band tightens around my chest, violently pushing the air from my lungs. Several seconds pass before I am able to inhale.

I am not sure what pisses me off the most: that this freaky little catfish accessed my personal photo albums, that he mentioned my mother, or that he exercised tremendous presumption in assuming I would ever want to commingle our DNA—sexually or digitally!

I open my mouth to speak, but close it again for fear I will lacerate him with the full force of my sharp tongue. I don't care that his software is being used by law enforcement agencies all around the world to track missing and abducted children. I don't care that he was punctual, effusive in his compliment of my appearance, and eager to meet again. My skin is crawling. He could have said he was a foot-fetishist or that he loves anal sex, and I wouldn't have been more creeped out than I am right now. I've been there, done that with dates who confess freaky predilections, but never with one who got off on morphing my face.

I simply reach into my purse, pull out a twenty dollar bill, toss it on the table, and walk out of Snob, leaving Morph2Perfection without even saying, "*Adieu*, Freak Show."

Chapter 5

Drunk Dial

What do you do with the rest of your evening after a crap-crap-crappy day at work, and a crap-crap-crappy date? Drink wine, *bien sûr!*

After leaving Snob, I grab some comfort food from Happy Bamboo, my favorite vegetarian restaurant, and two bottles of wine, and head back to my place.

I am halfway through my Pho Rice Noodle Soup and Seaweed Salad when I remember I promised to text Vivian about my date.

Text to Vivia Perpetua Grant:
Home. Alone. My date morphed our profile photos & brought pictures of what our children would look like.

Text from Vivia Perpetua Grant:
Jesus, Mary, and John Wayne Gacy!

Text to Vivia Perpetua Grant:
Who is John Wayne Gacy?

Text from Vivia Perpetua Grant:
Was. Serial killer. The kind that dressed in clown costumes and chopped up little boys. He probably would have morphed photos—if the technology would have existed. I am totally creeped out.

Vivian sends another text before I have a chance to respond to her first one.

Text from Vivia Perpetua Grant:

Unless you liked getting photos of your future offspring…and then I am not totally creeped out, just a little creeped. (Please tell me you didn't like it.)

Text to Vivia Perpetua Grant:
Loathed it. Loathed him. Loathe kids. Loathe clowns. It's early there, what are you doing?

Text from Vivia Perpetua Grant:
Working on my book.

Text to Vivia Perpetua Grant:
Then, stop texting me & write that bestseller!

I mute my ringer and toss my phone on the table. I have a queasy, greasy feeling in my stomach, and it's not from the Pho Noodles.

I am jealous of my best friend. It's the ugly kind of jealousy, too. The kind of jealousy that makes me secretly wish something a little bad would happen to her, something that would tip her scale from über-happy to mildly content.

C'est tout simplement horrible. Je suis horrible!

I push the soup bowl away, too sick with shame to eat another noodle. What kind of person wishes ill-luck on her best friend?

The worst kind.

I empty the contents of the first bottle of wine into my glass, lift the crystal glass to my lips, and finish it in one gauche gulp. It takes a lot of wine to get me drunk. Fortunately, I have a lot of wine.

Halfway through the second bottle, I take my Pinot-fueled pity party into my living room, collapse on my expensive but uncomfortable leather couch, and stare out the window at the amber lights of the Golden Gate Bridge reflected in the smooth black waters of the Bay.

I have a penthouse apartment with a killer view, a heavily padded trust fund, a great job, a couture wardrobe, a loyal best friend, yet…

Yet I am not happy. I do not feel fulfilled. Something is missing from my life, but I don't know what.

I finish the second bottle of wine, and I don't even care that I will have to pound the treadmill for one hundred and seventy three minutes at six miles per hour to burn off the calories I've consumed tonight in wine alone. I am *that* miserable.

I came to the United States ten years ago to attend Parsons School of Design, but I hated New York so I transferred to the Art Academy of Fashion in San Francisco. I felt lonely during those first few months at the Academy. My comprehension of American slang was embarrassingly deficient, and my finishing school manners gave me a haughty air—or so I was told. I felt as isolated as an Ebola patient. In a rare moment of vulnerability, I asked a girl in my History of Costume class why the other students didn't approach me.

She had this whole rockabilly thing going on—kohl-lined eyes, sausage roll bangs, bandana tied around her artfully pin-curled raven hair, and a swingy polka dot dress.

She tilted her head and pouted her crimson-painted lips, staring at me through her narrowed cat eyes. Then she shrugged and said, "It's probably because you have resting bitch face."

I graduated with a dual degree in Business Management and Apparel Technical Design and started working for LVMH the very next day. I kept myself so busy grasping for each new rung of the corporate ladder, I had little time to feel lonely.

This is the first time I have ever felt completely, pathetically alone. I feel like a cinder, lacking substance, just waiting for the first breeze to send me floating away.

I return to the couch, grab my phone, and scroll through my contacts, desperate to find some two a.m. friends. Two a.m. friends are the kind of friends you can call in an emergency in the middle of night and you know they will pick up.

Adriana Adams

Nicole Apodaca

Lena Bacon

Curtis Bower

Elizabeth Berg

Victoria Brandt

Nancy Bromley

I keep scrolling, down, down, down, past Happy Bamboo and Ho Min Drycleaners, until I get to the last name in my contacts: World Fitness. Other than Vivian, I don't have a single two a.m. friend.

I scroll through the list again, and this time I see a potential two a.m. friend: Ashleigh Pratt.

Yes! Of course! Ashleigh Pratt. How could I have forgotten about Ashleigh? She's totally a two a.m. friend.

I select her name to dial her number and press the phone to my ear. It rings four times before someone picks up.

"Hello?"

"*Coucou*, Ashleigh!"

"Who is this?"

Her question comes out as a croak.

"It's me, Stéphanie," I say, only slightly slurring my words. "Your good friend, Stéphanie."

"Stéphanie?"

"*Oui!*"

"Stéphanie, who?" She lowers her voice. "Look, I think you must have the wrong Ashleigh."

"Stéphanie who?" Suddenly, I get why she's whispering. I lower my voice. "Oh, you dirty tramp! You've got some hot guy in bed with you. That's why you're whispering, isn't it? You dirty, dirty *shlut*."

I laugh at my slurred word, but Ashleigh doesn't.

"Stéphanie? Is this Stéphanie Moreau?"

"*Bien sûr!* Why are you acting so surprised? We're good friends, aren't we? Two a.m. friends?"

"No," she snaps. "We are definitely *not* two a.m. friends."

I swallow past a thick lump in my throat. "Why not?"

"Why not?" She chuckles softly, though not kindly. "Because we haven't spoken in six years, remember?"

"What?" I stare out the window and then close my eyes when the lights in the Bay start spinning like a disco ball. "It hasn't been that long."

"Yes, it has," she hisses. "We stopped talking six years ago."

"Are you sure?"

"Yes. Very sure. We stopped talking right after the birth of my first child because you said that baby talk bored you, and you just didn't see how we could keep our friendship vibrant when we were pursuing such different life paths."

"I said that?"

"Yes, you did."

An infant begins wailing in the background, an ear-piercing, shrill cry.

Ashleigh sighs. "I don't know why you are calling, but I want you to know that I have no hard feelings. We *were* on different paths. I hope your path has brought you as much joy as mine has. Gotta go. Take care."

The line goes dead. I open my eyes again and stare out at the lights until hot tears prick my eyelids, until I think I am going to be sick.

That's it. I finally know what is missing from my life: joy. I am joyless. Joyless Fanny, plodding down the career path with a Blackberry full of meaningless contacts.

Chapter 6
Googling for Pleasure

I wonder if Tiffany and Company sells joy tucked into one of their iconic Tiffany blue boxes and wrapped with a white satin bow. If only it were that simple.

I half-roll, half-hoist myself off the couch and stagger toward my bedroom, shedding my clothes along the way.

Once in bed, cocooned between my eighteen hundred thread count sheets and silk duvet, I reach for my iPad on my nightstand and type "joy" into the Google search box.

The search returns 650,000,000 hits, including a link to an IMDB page for the new movie *Joy* starring Jennifer Lawrence. Ugh. I am not taking life lessons from a woman who can't even manage a red carpet walk. First, she face plants in the auditorium on the way to collect her coveted Oscar, and then she pulls a repeat performance the following year, tripping on the red carpet—while wearing a fab strapless Dior original and three million dollars' worth of Neil Lane jewels. She's so not BCBG. (The BCBG to which I am referring is the French slang for *Bon Chic, Bon Genre*, which means a person possessing good taste and a refined style, not the moderately-priced chain store selling truly uninspired garments. J-Law is très BCBG, the store.)

I search again, this time using the phrase "how to find joy" and am pleased when it returns only 366,000,000 hits.

I spend the next hour reading articles about how to find lasting happiness on tinybuddha.com, treehugger.com, meaningfulhappiness. com, and ohmmm.net, until I come to an article titled The Power to Change by Father True Allight. That I am even entertaining notions espoused by a New Age guru—a man named Father True Allight—tells me how very low I have sunk.

The Power to Change

by Father True Allight

Andrew was a handsome young man with a successful career in Finance, a vacation home in Aspen, a vigorous social life, and a pervasive desire to take his own life. Six days after ingesting a bottle of opiates, he sat in my office, his head in his hands, repeatedly asking me what he could do to feel joy.

He said, "I've made millions of dollars, bought a warehouse full of sports cars, taken the most luxurious vacations, but I have never felt true happiness. Why? What's the matter with me?"

I look away from my iPad to the ceiling, staring into the darkness, feeling Andrew's pain. I've never tried to commit suicide—never would—but I understand the hollowness that might drive someone to commit such a desperate act.

I groan.

Or maybe consuming two bottles of wine on a nearly empty stomach has made me as emotional as Nicholas Sparks's legion of weepy Kleenex-clutching readers.

Still, I am curious to know what wisdom Papa Light dispensed to keep Andrew from swallowing a fistful of Vicodin.

My answer was simple. I told Andrew that joy is not found in the pursuit of fame and riches. True happiness can only be experienced by those who live spherically, those who possess a sense of purpose beyond selfish pleasure, pursue their passions with enthusiasm, demonstrate compassion for those less fortunate, and actively seek to spread joy...

I stop reading and consider whether I meet Papa Light's criterion for living a joyful life.

Do I possess a sense of purpose beyond selfish pleasure? Not really. Work is my only purpose. Working hard enough to become a luminary in the L'Heure Universe.

Do I pursue my passions with pleasure? Passions? What passions? Do I even have passions? I drop my iPad onto my chest and press my fingertips against my eyelids. *Think, Fanny. Think! You must have passions. Passions. Passions. Fashions.* Yes! I am passionate about fashion. I pursue sample sales and fashion trends with great passion. Somehow, I don't think this is what Papa Light meant when he wrote about pursuing one's passions.

Do I demonstrate compassion to those less fortunate and seek to spread joy? I might not have ever volunteered at a soup kitchen like Ethan Catfish

Dubois, but I have demonstrated compassion. I have. Just last week, my assistant came to work complaining about having a splitting migraine, and I let him leave an hour early—with pay. Never mind that someone would have to bury a hatchet in my skull before I would leave work early, he was in pain and I demonstrated compassion-like behavior.

Didn't I?

I imagine Ethan working in a dirty, smelly kitchen, ladling out canned soup to dirty, smelly homeless people, and I suddenly feel less proud of my random act of kindness. Spreading joy and oozing compassion is just not my forte. It doesn't come naturally to me like it does for people like Ethan and Mother Theresa and...Vivian.

A memory sparks to life in my wine muddle brain of our trip last year to a Scottish sheep farm. One of the guests at the farm was a young mother, a cancer survivor named Lisa. Lisa admired Vivian's shiny pink rain boots, so do you know what Vivian did? Before the end of our trip, she went into town and bought Lisa a pair of pink rubber boots. Not the cheap Hunter knock-offs, but an authentic pair of Hunter Wellingtons. Vivian's bank account is Nicole Richie thin. I am talking sadly, perpetually anorexic. That's just Vivian, though. A people-pleaser who lives spherically, spreading joy and pursuing her passions.

I need to be more like Vivian and Mother Theresa. I need to live spherically. I need a purpose beyond pleasure.

That's it! Maybe I am without joy because I spend my days pursuing hollow pleasures. My very job is about manufacturing and marketing materialistic pleasures—beautiful but unnecessary luxuries.

What if I just stopped? Stopped pursuing worthless goals, like raising sales, lowering the profit-loss margin, building brand awareness, and shifted my efforts to expanding L'Heure's philanthropic pursuits.

Last year, L'Heure posted profits in excess of eight billion dollars. That's enough money to keep the Campbell's flowing in every soup kitchen in the country. And L'Heure is merely one company in a vast luxury empire owned by the French billionaire Bernard Arnault. Louis Vuitton, Dior, Marc Jacobs, Givenchy, Fendi, Pucci, Donna Karan—they're all vassals in service to our Lord and Master Arnault.

That's it. I have found my purpose. I will give the L'Heure Flagship Store at Union Square a new passion: philanthropy over profits. No more selling empty overpriced designer bags to empty souls just to meet sales quotas. I am going to rebrand L'Heure as the designer with heart. We could even rework the L'Heure logo by replacing the E with a big pink heart.

We could give gently-used handbags to women reentering the workforce, shoes to Africans displaced by tribal wars, or perfume to impoverished Indians.

I sit up, invigorated by my new sense of purpose, but the room begins to spin, so I lie back down, open my word processing app, and begin drafting a mission statement.

An hour later, I have crafted an inspiring three thousand-word mission statement promising to put an end to rampant corporate greed and the wanton neglect of the community beyond L'Heure's privileged clientele. My plan is simple: We donate fifteen percent of our annual proceeds to a local charity and encourage our employees to become more civic-minded through the implementation of an employee-volunteer savings program. When an employee volunteers, L'Heure pays them their hourly rate by depositing the wages directly into a retirement account.

It is a revolutionary business model. It is socially aware and fiscally responsible. It is the sort of plan that will grab old Monsieur Henri by his tortoiseshell bifocals and force him to focus his rheumy gaze on me, Stéphanie Moreau.

I Google San Francisco-based charities and stop when I come to Each One, Teach One, a non-profit organization "committed to eradicating financial, spiritual, and intellectual poverty in communities worldwide through the application of mentoring and vocational rehabilitation."

Parfait!

I could be a mentor. Everyone in my store could be mentors. Before doubt sets in, I click the contact button, fill out the form, and tick the box next to "Yes, I want to help the downtrodden and disenfranchised by sharing my talents."

My eyelids feel too heavy to keep open, so I copy and paste my mission statement into an email, choose all of my work contacts, and save it as a draft.

Then, I close my eyes and sink into a heavy wine-and-good-works contented sleep.

Chapter 7

One Painful Aha

My phone is ringing, but I am buried beneath a mountain of discarded gowns, shoes, and handbags and can't reach it. I writhe around, struggling to extricate my arm from the smooth leather straps of a Diorific bag, but my Blackberry keeps ringing, ringing, ringing. When I am finally able to pull my arm free, I reach for my phone, my fingertips barely making contact with the slender plastic device. I jab the answer button and say hello. It's Anna Wintour calling. Vogue wants me to be on the cover of their annual tribute to Leaders of Fashion for my resounding success in rebranding L'Heure as the designer with heart. "Thank you," Anna says, "for giving us a new reason to say, 'J'adore L'Heure.'"

The mournful opening guitar plucks of Lana Del Rey's "Blue Jeans,' followed by Lana singing about her blue jeans and white T-shirt-wearing James Dean-like lover, play over and over, blaring out of my Blackberry, until I blink heavy lids and squint at the ceiling.

Foutre! My hair aches. Literally aches. I drank way too much wine. Years ago in France, someone who drank too much *eau de vie* and woke up hungover would have said he suffered from a *mal aux cheveux*, literally a hair-ache. Today, the phrase isn't used by anyone under fifty. I don't know why, because it works. I close my eyes and clutch my head. It *really* works.

Lana is still singing, her desolate voice echoing in my empty apartment, making me sincerely regret choosing her song as my ringtone. I have always loved Lana Del Rey. Now, caught in the brutal clutches of a hangover, suffering from the worst kind of *mal aux cheveux*, I hate Lana Del Rey.

Keeping my eyes closed, I reach for the ends of my pillow and press them against my ears. Lana will not be so easily silenced, though. She keeps on singing, a muffled, melancholy moaning. I am just about to get out of bed and search for my Blackberry when Lana stops singing.

I let go of the pillow, roll over, pull the covers over my head, and am almost asleep when Lana starts again. I throw back the covers and do the blind's man shuffle into the living room, eyes closed, arms outstretched, until I locate my Blackberry. I crack one eye open, jab the answer button, and switch it to speakerphone.

"Hello?"

I close my eyes.

"Mademoiselle Moreau?"

Oh, no. God, no.

"*Bonjour*, Mademoiselle Salupo." I really hate that Nicola insists on using French forms of address when she's not even fluent in the language. "*Comment ça va?*"

Nicola doesn't answer. I wait several seconds.

"Hello?"

Squinting, I look at my Blackberry. The screen is black. I jab the power button, but the screen stays black. My battery is dead.

I grab my phone, blind man shuffle back to my bedroom, plug it in, and fall back into bed, pulling the covers over my head.

When I finally drag myself out of bed and take a shower, the sun is low in the sky and my aching hair aches a little less. I dry off, slather my skin with *Panier des Sens*, an organic olive oil-based body butter I order from Provence, and slip on a robe.

I have cleaned up the evidence of my Pinot pity party and am arranging a handful of multigrain crackers and some apple slices on a plate when my Blackberry begins chirping. I carry the plate back into my bedroom, deposit it on my nightstand, and curl up on my bed.

That's when I suddenly remember Nicola's phone call.

Merde! Merde!

I grab my Blackberry from the nightstand. I have thirty-four new text messages and—wait a minute, that can't be right—ninety-seven new emails. I hope there hasn't been some kind of emergency at the store.

Text from Nicola Salupo:

I need you to return the keys to the store, your laptop, and Blackberry as soon as possible.

Wait, what? There's only one reason Nicola would be asking for my keys, laptop, and Blackberry. She's dismissing me. No. No. That's ridiculous. She can't dismiss me because I wore cheap perfume to a staff meeting.

Text to Nicola Salupo:
Over a spritz of perfume? You must be joking?

Text from Nicola Salupo:
A spritz of perfume? YOU must be joking.

I am so confused. Is Nicola dismissing me or not?
Text to Nicola Salupo:
Are you dismissing me?

I hold my breath and wait for Nicola's response. I don't have to hold my breath for long. Nicola's one word text hits my phone with terrifying speed.

Text from Nicola Salupo:
Oui.

Salope. She's really going to fire me for some minor corporate violation? That's ridiculous, even for her. If she thinks I am going to lie down and let her walk all over me in her hideous freakishly large pumps, she's as bat shit crazy as she looks.

I start jabbing the screen and have nearly finished composing a strongly worded text when my Blackberry chirps again.
Text from Nicola Salupo:
Check your email for a termination letter and details from HR about your benefits package, severance pay, et al.

Molten acid is churning inside my stomach and bubbling up my throat. *La Vache!* This isn't happening. This is *not* happening. I am not being dismissed from L'Heure.

I open my email box and begin scrolling through my new messages. The first fifty or so are from fashion bloggers and style reporters. This doesn't surprise me. My inbox has been jammed with interview requests from local media outlets, fashion magazines, and bloggers ever since we announced the date of the grand opening. I keep scrolling until I come to an email from Nicola Salupo.

I think I might be sick. The subject line reads: Employment Contract Termination. I try to inhale, but choke on the acid burbling up my throat.

Stéphanie Moreau
2200 Sacramento Avenue, 1906
San Francisco, CA 94109

Dear Ms. Moreau:

This letter is to formally announce that your position with Aurèle L'Heure, a division of the LVMH Group, has been terminated, effective immediately.

You are being terminated, per company policy, for exposing L'HEURE to public censure and embarrassment through the distribution of an unauthorized press release (See attached). After lengthy consultations about your performance with LVMH Group's Human Resources and Legal Departments, it was determined that termination was the only option.

Your final pay will be direct-deposited to your checking account of record. You will receive any accrued vacation time in the form of a check within fourteen days of your termination. Please contact me to arrange the return of your company cell phone, laptop, and passkeys. HR will be sending you a package regarding severance eligibility and health insurance costs, if you would like to continue your coverage. Otherwise, all benefits will be terminated thirty days after your termination date.

If you have any questions about this letter of termination, call Human Resources at ext. 9424.

Best regards,

Nicola Salupo

Unauthorized press release? The last press release I distributed was about the store's unique architecture and unrivaled square footage of retail space. There wasn't a single word that could have opened L'Heure to censure and ridicule. The Botox must have migrated from Nicola's forehead to her brain. What other explanation could there be for her mentally retarded behavior?

I open the second attachment, titled Mission Statement, and begin reading. The words are only slightly familiar, so I keep reading, and then I remember, in a mortifying, blinding flash. The wine. Father True Allight's article about finding joy. My email about giving L'Heure a purpose beyond profit. But wait! I saved that email as a draft, didn't I? So how did Nicola get a copy?

I click back into my email box and open my sent folder. The last email sent was at 1:16 this morning and carried the subject line: A New Reason to Adore L'Heure. The room tilts so precariously, I have to concentrate to keep from falling off the bed.

I open the email and am horrified to discover I blasted it to every store manager in North America, as well as my press contacts at *Women's Wear Daily, Marie Claire, Vogue, InStyle, San Francisco Magazine,* and dozens of newspapers.

Putain!

My phone chirps, alerting me to a new text message. It's from my assistant. Former assistant.

Text from Curtis Bower:
I read your Mission Statement this morning. Ohmygod! It was brill. Insane, but absolutely brilliant.

Text to Curtis Bower:
Thanks. Unfortunately, Nicola didn't think it was that brill. She fired me.

Text from Curtis Bower:
I know. She is losing her f***ing mind. She called us all into the office this morning for "damage control duty."

Text from Curtis Bower:
Check Twitter. You're already a hashtag.

Text to Curtis Bower:
What do you mean I am a hashtag?

Text from Curtis Bower:
Read this: http://bling-bling.com/moreau

I click on the link and wait for my browser to open the page. It directs me to the latest article posted on the popular fashion blog, Bling.

A Moment of Silence, s'il vous plait
By Candace Shannon

Gather round, fellow Fashionistas, and let us bow our heads in a moment of silence for one of our fallen comrades. Stéphanie Moreau, once a bright and shiny star in the L'Heure firmament, committed #CareerSuicide early this morning when she distributed a press release ridiculing LVMH Global's...

I stop reading and stare at the artwork embedded within the article. It's an animated .gif of a fashionably dressed girl with a rope around her neck jumping off the L'Heure sign. Jump. Dangle. Jump. Dangle. The awful cartoon image just keeps looping. Jump. Dangle.

Ohmygod. Please don't let this be as bad as the Dolce and Gabbana scandal. Please.

The Dolce and Gabbana scandal happened when Domenico Dolce and Stefano Gabbana made public statements against in vitro fertilization. They said infants born as a result of in vitro fertilization were "synthetic children." The backlash was immediate and brutal. Sir Elton John took to Twitter to criticize the designers for their insensitive comment. Numerous celebrities returned their Dolce and Gabbana frocks, the designer's stock dropped, and #BoycottDolceAndGabbana became one of the most popular hashtags on Twitter for weeks.

Text to Curtis Bower:
Be honest. How bad is this?

Text from Curtis Bower:
Bad. Like, Daniel Radcliffe rapping on Jimmy Fallon bad.

I've never heard the Harry Potter kid rap, but commonsense tells me it can't be good.

Text to Curtis Bower:
Worse than the car crash ad boycott?

A few years ago, a small band of consumers called for a boycott of Christian Dior products over a magazine advertisement featuring a model clutching a Dior bag to her chest, her limbs contorted in unnatural angles, her eyes rolled back in her head, motor oil streaking her face. The advertisement was supposed to depict a woman resting after having fixed her car, but some consumers thought it looked like a police photo of an accident scene.

Text from Curtis Bower:
For you, maybe. Nicola is spinning it to look like you're a disgruntled employee who abused her authority to push her own personal political agenda. She said the closest you will get to working in the fashion industry is selling Dickies at Walmart. GTG, but good luck.

Of course Nicola is spinning it to make me look like a lunatic. I wouldn't be surprised if she tipped off the Bling blogger. She probably even suggested the headline and the brutal career suicide hashtag.

Salope!

I go back to my internet browser and click on the #CareerSuicide link in the Bling article. It directs me to the Twitter feed listing all of the tweets containing #CareerSuicide. There are dozens of tweets by headhunters on how to avoid making career-killer mistakes and just as many about a London-based heavy metal band named Career Suicide, but only one tweet referencing me directly, posted by a Bling blogger.

The picture of Vivian standing in the stream in Scotland flashes on my screen and Lana begins singing "Blue Jeans" again.

I am seriously starting to hate that song.

"*Bonjour*, Vivian."

"What's up with the Bling piece?"

"How do you know about that?"

Vivian is half a world away, living in a small village in the South of France, but the news of my humiliating professional defeat has already made it to her. *Incroyable.*

"Google Alerts," she says. "I set up a Google Alert to notify me of any news about your store. Is it true? Did you write that mission statement?"

"Yes."

"That's awesome!"

"Awesome? Awesome? Nicola sent me a termination letter this morning. I've been fired...from L'Heure!" My hand trembles. I switch to speakerphone. "It is not awesome."

"It's awesome, because you've realized your purpose is greater than just selling handbags, because you demonstrated compassion and caring."

"You make it sound like I am unfeeling."

A long, painful silence stretches between us. Finally, Vivian breaks the silence by asking me what prompted my midnight mission statement. I tell her about feeling blue and scrolling through my contacts to find a two a.m. friend.

"I am your two a.m. friend."

"Besides you."

"And?" she whispers.

"And I didn't find one."

"Shut up."

"I am serious." My voice wavers. "You're my only real friend, Vivian. Since coming to America, I've channeled most of my energy into my career. Having a healthy, active social life takes a lot of work."

"When have you ever been afraid of hard work?" She mimics a buzzer sound. "Wrong answer. Try again."

"I don't know." I sigh. "I am not like you, Vivian. I don't care what people think about me. I don't need to make everyone my BFF."

"And that's why you don't have any two a.m. friends." She waits several seconds before speaking again. "Look, Fanny, you know I love you more than my flat iron."

"Thanks."

Vivian hates her naturally wavy red hair and keeps a portable flat iron in her purse the way most women keep lipstick. You know the game where you name three things you would grab if you were in a house fire? Well, Vivian would definitely grab her flat iron.

"It's just..." she begins again. "You have all of these big, impenetrable walls around you. I am talking medieval castle walls. Some people might interpret that as aloof or snooty."

"That's not..."

I am about to protest when I remember our trip to Scotland last year. By the time we finished our stay at the sheep farm, Vivian had made a dozen new friends. Not me. I hadn't even bothered to learn the other guest's names.

"It sounds to me like you had an aha moment?" Her voice is low, her tone gentle. "You should go with it."

"A what?"

"An aha moment. Haven't you ever heard of the Eureka Effect?"

"No, I haven't."

"An aha moment is that moment when you suddenly understand a previously incomprehensible concept."

"An epiphany?"

"Exactly."

"I would rather be like some ignorant Neanderthal squatting in a dark cave, too stupid to rub two sticks together to start a fire." I wipe a stray tear from my cheek. "Aha moments hurt."

"Don't be ridiculous!" Her voice rises with excitement. "You *were* that caveman, last year when we were in Scotland, remember? You felt sad and angry and hollow, and you didn't know why. You're out of the dark now, Chaka."

"Who is Chaka?"

"A cave boy on an old Saturday morning television—" She sighs. "It doesn't really matter. What matters is that you've stepped out of the darkness and into the light."

I stifle a groan. Vivian's new-agey pep talks are way too upbeat, too positive for my natural negative state.

"Great! I am basking in the light, a spiritually-enlightened cave girl. So what do I do now?"

"What do you want to do?"

"I don't know." The truth of that admission hits me like a speeding Mercedes. "Nicola seems to think I am going to end up selling Dickies at Walmart."

"Fuck Nicola," Vivian shouts. "She is not the master of your fate. You are. What do you want to do?"

Fresh tears fill my eyes, and the molten acid begins churning in my stomach again. For the first time in my life, I don't know what to do. Not knowing fills me panic.

"You're the list girl," Vivian says in an encouraging voice, talking me down off my mental ledge. "Make a list."

"Of what?"

"Of everything you have ever wanted to do."

"Working at Dior is all I have ever wanted to do."

"That's not an option. So what's next?"

"I don't know," I snap. "I don't have a Plan B."

"Bullshit! You always have a Plan B, and a Plan C and D and…." There's silence, and then I hear her snap her fingers. "What about that charity?"

"What charity?"

"The one you mentioned in your mission statement."

"Each One, Teach One? What about it?"

"Why not work for them?"

"Doing what? What could I possibly have to offer a charity?" I laugh ruefully. "I know, I could teach impoverished Somalians how to tie a Zara scarf or how to spot a fake Hermès. Useful skills."

Vivian doesn't respond, and I worry we've had a dropped call. It's not like her to be so quiet for so long.

"Vivian?"

"Are you finished?" Comes her immediate response. "Because if you want to keep holding that shitty pity party for one, I will just put the phone down and go do something important, like buff my nails or organize my paperclips…"

"I am finished."

"*Bon*," she says. "Remember what you told me after Nathan broke up with me?"

"Don't fall in love with another sanctimonious douchebag?"

"No."

"Keep the ring? Take the honeymoon? What?"

"You told me that I set my price tag too low, and now it is time for me to return that sage advice by telling you that you have set your price tag too low. Like, Dollar General low. Like, Salvation Army low. Each One, Teach One would be lucky to hook a catch as smart and capable as you. See what I did there…with the reference to fishing?"

"Yes, Vivian." I chuckle, despite the churning acid in my belly and the panic squeezing my chest like an iron band. "I see what you did there."

"Call them."

"*Au revoir*, Vivian."

"Wait!" She cries. "Fanny?"

"Yes."

"You've helped me pick up the pieces of my shattered life twice. I owe you big time. If you need me to fly back to San Francisco, I'm just a G6 away. I gotcher back, Boo."

"I'm good," I lie. "But you can do me one favor."

"Name it, girl!"

"Stay away from Urban Dictionary."

She laughs. "Don't be a hater."

After we hang up, my best friend's final words replay in my head, like a bad *Punk'd* marathon. *Don't be a hater. Don't be a hater. Don't be a hater.*

Chapter 8

Work Those Dickies

Text from Vivia Perpetua Grant:
Did you know Christian Dior's sister fought in the French Resistance?
He was designing gowns for the wives of Nazi officers while she was
fighting to liberate their country from tyranny. Call me crazy, but I think
Sister had her priorities right. Forget Dior. Find your purpose.

Monday morning dawns gray and watery, with thick fog circling the
bridge and hanging low over the Bay. The melancholy scene reminds
me of the cheap watercolor paintings hawked by street vendors outside
Ghirardelli Square. It's bleak and tragic, like a Brontë novel, like my life.

I am reaching for the remote that operates my electric blinds, when I
remember the list I made after talking to Vivian. Taking my best friend's
advice, I made a list of things I have always wanted to do, like open
a boutique, fall in love, make friends, deepen my relationship with
my dad, push my boundaries, go on an adventure, and be buried in a
vintage Dior gown.

The weak, whiny side of me wants to close the blinds, pull the covers
over my head, and sink into the oblivion of sleep, but the tougher,
no-time-for-tears side knows I'll never achieve my goals if I hide
out in my bedroom.

So I sit up, reach for my iPad, open my lists app, and make a To Do list.

To Do:
1. Exercise.
2. Return laptop, Blackberry, and keys to store.
3. Resist the urge to go to Walgreens, buy a bottle of Purrfect, and
liberally spritz perfume in Nicola's air vents.
4. Buy new cell phone.

5.   Forget L'Heure and Dior.

6.   Find my purpose.

* * * *

Three and a half hours later, I have checked the first four items off my list and am feeling surprisingly empowered.

Returning to the store was every bit as excruciating as I had imagined it would be, but I walked in with my head held high and looked Nicola in the eyes as I handed her my keys and Blackberry.

On the way out, Curtis gave me a hug and his "You Better Work It, Bitch" coffee mug. He snagged the mug from the craft service cart when he was a contestant on Project Runway. It's one of his prize possessions.

"Girl, don't you dare cry," he said, handing me the mug. "I have constructed a world with you as a ferocious diva. Shattering that illusion would just be cruel. Besides, you don't want to look like a hot tranny mess with makeup running down your face."

Curtis's unexpected praise and generous gift did bring tears to my eyes.

"Thank you, Curtis," I said, taking the mug and cradling it against my chest. "You are a terrific assistant. I will miss you."

"Uh-uh," he said, wagging his finger. "I am not last season's lady loafers. You can't get rid of me that easy."

I left L'Heure happy in the knowledge that Curtis just might be an enduring trend in my life. He might even become a two a.m. friend.

* * * *

Fuelled by an intense desire to prove Nicola wrong, a need to be productive, and three espressos, I return to my apartment and spend the afternoon submitting resumes to all of the major couturiers, as well as half a dozen corporate head hunters in Paris and New York.

When I finally turn off my computer, it is dusk. Outside my window, the San Francisco Bay is as black as the heavens, the distant silvery lights of Sausalito winking like stars on the placid surface.

I am too exhausted to go out to dinner and too hungry to wait for Happy Bamboo to deliver an order of their delightful green noodles, so I pour some Muselix into a bowl, add a splash of almond milk, and eat standing at the window, staring into the darkness.

For the first time, I feel like my future is as murky as the flat cloud-blackened sky outside my window. What if nobody wants to hire me? What if my father was right? What if I have squandered my familial connections and expensive education simply to become a bourgeois salesperson?

I walk back to the kitchen, wash my bowl and spoon in the sink, dry them off, and put them back into the cupboard. Then, I strip off my clothes and fall into bed.

The last thought to flitter through my brain before I fall asleep is: What if I end up selling Dickies at Walmart?

Chapter 9

Big Girls Swallow

Text from Vivia Perpetua Grant:
Did you know that Coco Chanel's father sent her to live in a convent for orphans? Talk about not having any two a.m. friends! Yet she went on to build one of the most influential fashion houses in the world. Don your Coco pearls and find your purpose. You got this one.

The first thing I do after waking up and reading Vivian's motivating text—the first text received on my new iPhone—is to check my email.

The first email is from my father.

Á: Stéphanie Moreau
De: Guillaume Moreau
Objet: Visite

Mon Cher Fanny,
J'ai dû annuler mon voyage à San Francisco. Kaliyah se passe en Suisse pour une procédure médicale peu...

I hit delete before I have finished reading my father's email because his opening lines told me all I need to know. He's canceling his trip to San Francisco—again—because his obscenely younger girlfriend is going to a medical spa in Switzerland to have silicone injected into her boobs or butt or brain. Nipping and tucking is Kaliyah's favorite hobby.

Don't get me wrong. I am not opposed to a little medical maintenance. I have even had some myself. When I lost my Éléphanny weight, I lost what little I had going on in my Wonderbra. I was embarrassingly flat-chested. Remember when Gwyneth Paltrow wore that pink taffeta Ralph Lauren ballerina gown to the Oscars—the year she won Best Actress for

Shakespeare in Love? Yeah, she made me look buxom. I understand she was going for that whole waif princess look, but I wasn't.

So my father would rather play recovery nurse to his pin-tucked paramour than visit me. *C'est la vie.*

Continuing to scroll through my inbox, I skip over the notification from *GoGirl!* Magazine alerting me of Vivian's latest article about her tour of the Lindt Chocolate Factory in Germany, spam from various fashion magazines, more interview requests from bloggers, until I come to the first in a series of form rejection letters.

Donna Karan. Valentino. Hermès. Chanel.

Rejection. Rejection. Rejection. Rejection.

I can't help but wince as I read the canned phrases: *Not hiring. We will keep your resume on file. We will not be able to offer you a position. We wish you every success in your job search.*

I open the email from the head of Human Resources at Bautista, read the first line thanking me for applying, and my heart skips a beat. It is not a form letter.

Bautista! As in, Cristóbal Bautista, the fiercely talented Spanish designer who sketched his way from the Basque Country to Paris. The creator of the cocoon coat and sack dresses. Bautista's 2015 Fall Collection—the cigarette pants, mink trimmed gowns, and bubble skirts—was inspired. In-spired. I love Bautista! I love the Basque Country.

Dear Stéphanie,

I was pleasantly surprised to find your resume in my inbox. I immediately recalled meeting you at the Versace show during Mercedes Benz Fashion Week and how much you impressed me with your observations about the influences on Versace's 2014 collection.

Yes! I love Bautista. I do a few fist pumps and continue reading the email.

I was prepared to offer you a position at Bautista. However, I am sorry to say that your references didn't support you. I wish you the best of luck in your job search...

My references didn't support me? Bullshit.

Nicola the *Salope* didn't support me. My previous boss at Louis Vuitton loved me and would have given a glowing review.

I hate Bautista. I hate sack dresses and cocoon coats. Who puts jodhpurs on the runway, anyway? And nobody ever looked good hobbling along in a hobble skirt. I hate the Basque Country.

Leah Marie Brown

At this point, I have two options open to me: drink my way through Snob's collection of Burgundy wines or hit the elliptical and try to think of a way to continue my career in the fashion industry that doesn't include selling oversized utilitarian coveralls at a sad discount store.

I am halfway through my workout, dripping perspiration, and no closer to finding a way to save my dying career, when Florence and the Machine start singing "Shake it Out."

I changed my ringtone when I got my new phone. Lana's mournful song matches my present ennui, but Florence reminds me that it is always darkest before the dawn, that my depression is transitory.

I stop running, swipe the perspiration from my forehead, and reach for my iPhone. I don't recognize the caller.

"Hello?"

"Hello, is this Ms. Moreau?" asks the female voice.

"Yes."

"Ms. Stéphanie Moreau?"

"Yes. Who is this?"

"Thank goodness." She sighs. "This is Rachel Mills, Vice President of International Development with Each One, Teach One. I have had quite a time finding you. You must have entered the wrong number on your application, because it was a non-functioning line. I had to call L'Heure to get this number."

Merde! I completely forgot about filling out Each One, Teach One's volunteer application. As if getting fired wasn't bad enough, now I have to rescind L'Heure's offer to help a worthy charity. Maybe a generous donation will smooth things over.

"You called L'Heure?"

"Yes, I spoke with your assistant, and he gave me this number."

Ouch. Being reminded I no longer have an assistant feels like a hatpin to the heart.

"How may I help you Ms. Mills?"

"Rachel, please. We operate on a first name only basis at TTF."

"How may I help you, Rachel?"

"I was hoping you might be available this afternoon to discuss an exciting opportunity with our organization."

In the last seventy-two hours, I have been catfished, fired from my dream job, ridiculed by bloggers, and abandoned by my father. A painful series of pride-swallowing events. And now I get to take one more gulp. *Salut, Stéphanie!*

"I am terribly sorry, Ms. Mills, but I am afraid L'Heure won't be able to participate in your worthy program." I consider pretending we have a bad connection and disconnecting, but a woman working for a charity deserves better than a flimsy brush off. "The thing is…I didn't have the authority to commit L'Heure's resources, and now, I don't even…"

My throat closes when I try to say the words "work for L'Heure anymore."

"I believe we might still be able to help each other, Ms. Moreau," she says in a soft, reassuring voice. "Would you be available to meet with us this afternoon?"

"Us?"

"Finn Thompson, the Founder and President of Each One, Teach One, will be joining us. How does three sound?"

I can't imagine why the president of a non-profit organization wants to meet me, the Immaterial Girl. There's little I can bring to his conference table.

"Are you sure you have the right person? Did you mean to call Stéphanie Moreau, French-born, graduate of Fashion Institute of Design and Merchandising?"

"Yes." She chuckles softly. "Shall I put you down for three, then?"

This girl is determined.

"Rachel, something tells me your talents are being wasted working for a non-profit. You should get into sales. You'd make a fortune in commissions."

"Thanks," she says, chuckling again. "I will text you our address. See you at three."

"Yes, three."

"See you soon."

"Bye."

I have barely disconnected when my iPhone chimes and Rachel's text pops up on my screen. I stare at the address, a skyscraper in the Financial District, and wonder what one wears to meet the VP of a non-profit. Something tells me I will look a bit out of place in my Armani suits. Maybe a trip to Walmart is in order. I wonder if Dickies makes power suits?

Chapter 10

Something Smells Fishy

Text from Vivian Perpetua Grant:
Did you know Jimmy Choo's business partner wanted to take the company global, but Jimmy wanted to focus on quality and knew mass producing his product would sacrifice quality? Jimmy stuck to his principles, selling his half of the business to a huge conglomerate. Today, he makes shoes in his original London shop and teaches apprentices. Now that's a purpose beyond profit.

An organization like Each One, Teach One should be located in one of the converted warehouses that have transformed the Mission District from rundown ghetto to mod 'hood for the eco set, but it's not. Each One, Teach One is located in a sleek chrome and glass high rise on the fringes of Chinatown.

My Louboutin stilettos echo in the lobby like rapid-fire bullets ricocheting off the black granite floor and glass walls. The security guard checks my name against a register, gives me a passkey, and directs me to take the express elevator to the twenty-eighth floor.

When the doors open, I step out of the elevator into a sleek reception area with floor-to-ceiling windows and panoramic views of the city and bay.

The receptionist is wearing a Bluetooth earpiece and seated at a Lucite desk with a computer monitor built into the top. It's very Tony Stark-ish. I am not a big movie-goer, but a date took me to see *Avengers* and I've been crushing on Robert Downey, Jr. ever since.

She smiles at me and taps the computer screen.

"Good afternoon, and thank you for calling Each One, Teach One. How may I help you?"

She pauses. I use the opportunity to study the picture on the wall behind her of African teens constructing an elaborate pipeline-like structure. The picture dissolves and is replaced by another—grinning school children in a thatched hut in Panama or Guatemala or Honduras. *La Vache!* That is so cool. A hidden laser is projecting the images onto the glass. Totally slick. Totally Stark Industries.

"Yes, sir," the receptionist says, pressing her finger to her earpiece. "I would be happy to announce your call. Will you hold, please?"

She taps the tabletop screen and then looks at me.

"You must be Ms. Moreau."

"Yes."

"Won't you please have a seat?"

She nods her head at the low-slung white leather sofas arranged in a U behind me. I take a seat, cross my legs at the ankles, and casually stare out the window at the clouds in the wide blue sky, as if I am not completely impressed by this *trop stylé* office.

"Evan," the receptionist says, in a low modulated voice. "Mr. Eggum is calling with Feed the World. Shall I put him through?" She taps the screen two times and says, "Rachel, Ms. Moreau has arrived."

A moment later, the receptionist is standing in front of me.

"Ms. Moreau, if you follow me"—she gestures for me to follow—"I will show you to the conference room."

I stand and follow her down a hallway of opaque windows until we come to a large conference room with a sleek circular mosaic glass table. I take a seat in one of the white leather chairs and rest my hands on the arms.

"Finn and Rachel will be with you in a moment. In the meantime, can I offer you some *jugo de papayo?*"

I frown.

"It's a South American juice. We make it fresh each morning using pawpaw, lime, and carambola." She smiles. "It's quite delicious."

"It sounds delicious." I return her smile. "I would love some, thank you."

Each One, Teach One has this whole Tony Stark meets Deepak Chopra vibe going that totally bewilders me. Should I take my shoes off and sit cross-legged, forearms resting on my knees, thumbs and index fingers touching to form circles? Or should I play it cool and unfazed, as if their slick offices and laser beam photographs are unimpressive, almost passé?

I opt for cool and unimpressed, because it is closer to my natural state and takes far less effort than attempting to pull off the New Age-y thing.

Once, Vivian forced me to visit a Neoplatonism practitioner with her for an article she was writing about the art of meditation. We were shown into a dimly lit room—the Golden Temple of the Etheric—where we were instructed to lie on mats. A tall, gangly man with a long, dirty gray beard promised us he would be our guide on a mind-bending out of body experience that he called astral flight. Yeah, it was utterly *outré*. Beyond bizarre. Vivian thought it was relaxing and said she thought her soul might have left her body for a few minutes—that she heard fiddle music and saw herself floating over the Irish countryside. I thought it was complete bullshit. And Vivian's out of body experience? It was probably due to our having consumed a copious amount of Magners Irish Hard Cider while watching a Colin Farrell movie before our visit to the Golden Temple.

The receptionist returns with my juice. "Let me know if there's anything else you need."

"Thank you."

I am sipping the neon orange juice when two people enter the conference room—a tall, wiry blonde in a White House Black Market dress, and a taller handsome man wearing impeccably tailored Canali trousers and vest with a pair of leather mandals. Ugh! The last man to work a pair of mandals was Julius Caesar—and look how things turned out for him.

"Stéphanie," the woman says, walking toward me with her arms out. "We spoke earlier today. I am Rachel Mills."

I quickly stand and hold my hand out. Instead of shaking my hand, Rachel hugs me like we are giddy pre-teen BFFs meeting at the mall. I am not a hugger. I stand there with my arms locked at my sides until she steps back.

"And this is Finn Thompson"—she beams up at Mandals—"founder and President of Each One, Teach One."

"*Bonjour* Mademoiselle Moreau," Mandals says, grabbing me by the shoulders and kissing both my cheeks *a la* Parisian greeting. "*C'est un plaisir de vous rencontrer. Vous remercie d'être venus.*"

"*Merci.*"

Finn Thompson, with his shaggy sun-tipped California surfer hair and expensive Italian trousers, is as perplexing as his office.

"How was my accent?" he asks, grinning. "Hopefully, not too atrocious."

"*Parfait.*" I switch to English because I am not sure if Rachel understands French. "You speak like a native. Did you live in France?"

"Briefly." He pulls my chair out and gestures for me to be seated. "When I was in college, I spent a summer in the Oisans working as a volunteer on a mountain biodiversity project."

"Which village?"

"Villard-Reculas."

"Really?"

"Yes." Finn walks around the table and takes a seat opposite me. "Do you know it?"

"My mother was born nearby, in La Garde."

"*C'est un petit monde!*"

"Yes, a very small world!"

During my loneliest and lowest moments at boarding school, like when the other girls snatched my bath towel and pushed me out into the hallway, naked and wet, I wished God would send my mother back to earth to be my guardian angel. I am not a superstitious person—the French are too practical to be superstitious—but I wonder if this is an omen.

"Are you all right?" Finn asks.

My cheeks flush with heat. I have been staring at Finn. I nod.

"Are you sure? You suddenly looked sad."

I can't very well say, "I have felt hopelessly lost for days, but I think my dead mother just sent me the message that I should be working for your company." So I employ one of my classic avoidance maneuvers and change the subject.

"Your offices are spectacular." I run my hands over the smooth mosaic glass tabletop. "I like this table."

"Thank you." Finn narrows his gaze just enough to let me know that he is wise to my avoidance maneuver. "All of the furniture in the room has been made with reclaimed items."

"Really?"

"The table was made in Mexico, using repurposed soda and beer bottles," he says, smiling. "The covers on these chairs and the sofas in the lobby are Eco-friendly sustainable leather, made using bark cloth from mutuba trees in Uganda. In fact, they were made by students at our edification centers."

"Edification centers?"

"Some would call them schools," Rachel explains. "We prefer to call them edification centers because we believe our mission is to educate, elevate, and enlighten. We don't just teach the impoverished a trade. We restore their sense of self-worth through close mentoring."

"That sounds inspiring."

"I am glad you think so, because we believe you would be a splendid asset to TTF."

"We read your mission statement," Finn interjects. "We were very impressed."

"Thank you," I say, my cheeks flushing with heat. "Unfortunately, my boss wasn't as impressed."

"I know you were terminated."

"How?" I blink. "How did you know?"

"We read *San Francisco Magazine's* editorial piece."

Wait. *What?*

"What piece?"

Rachel slides a thick manila folder to Finn. He opens the folder, removes the first piece of paper, and pushes it across the table to me.

San Francisco Magazine's banner stretches across the top of the page, and just below it, the words Aurèle L'Horreur in big, bold block letters. The perversion of L'Heure's name—from *the golden hour* to *the horror* - makes me cringe. As I scan the text, the acid lying dormant in the pit of my stomach begins roiling. It is an op-ed piece criticizing capitalism and unchecked corporate greed. The editor—Roberta Buelher—mentions me by name and calls on her readers to boycott luxury brands like L'Heure until they "stop violating the fundamental, puritanical principles that are the cornerstones of this great nation." It's an articulate, scathing indictment against a company I respect. The final paragraph is brutal.

"Ms. Moreau's mission statement might not have been fiscally responsible, but it was uncommonly socially aware. Corporations like LVMH Global have become the tyrants of our generation, selling their over-priced, unobtainable luxury items and fomenting deep discontent among the less-than-privileged classes. L'Heure is like Louis XVI, bloated by profits earned from a slender segment of society, while ignoring the suffering of the masses. It is time for a Revolution—in fashion and finance. Let the masses no longer cry, 'J'adore L'Heure!' Let them firmly assert, 'J'abhor L'Horreur and unchecked corporate greed.'"

"You've spawned a movement," Rachel says, smiling. "Soon, J'abhor L'Horreur will be the mantra on every consumer's lips."

I can't speak. The moment is too surreal.

"J'abhor L'Horreur," Finn repeats. "It's the new catch phrase for those opposed to wanton corporate greed. J'abhor L'Horreur."

I wince. Finn and Rachel might be impressed with the op-ed piece, but I see it for precisely what it is: another nail in the coffin containing my mortally wounded career. J'abhor L'Horreur? Roberta Buehler's article effectively destroyed my chances of ever getting hired by another major couturier.

"Look," I say, turning the article over and sliding it away from me. "When I wrote that mission statement, I was…"

Drunk. I can't very well tell these radical touchy feely do-gooders I got sloppy-drunk and had an epiphany.

"Yes?" Finn encourages. "You were what?"

"When I wrote that mission statement, I wasn't intending to smear L'Heure or spawn a movement. I loved working at L'Heure and am horrified my mission statement has caused the company embarrassment."

"Which speaks highly of your character, Ms. Moreau."

"Thank you, but I am not worthy of such praise."

An awkward silence stretches between us. I want to slide off my sustainable leather chair and curl up in the fetal position beneath their recycled *cerveza* bottle table until the world forgets my name and my stupid mission statement. I don't want these two tree-hugging do-gooders grinning at me like I singlehandedly settled the crisis in Darfur or negotiated peace between North and South Korea. *Foutre!* I wrote a mission statement. A stupid, ill-conceived, pity-fueled mission statement.

"Yes, well," Rachel says, clearing her throat. "We reviewed your application and believe we have the perfect position for you here at Each One, Teach One."

What the what? Did she just offer me a job? I look at her White House Black Market dress and boring chin-length bob and wonder if she wants me to be her personal stylist. What would a recruiter at a non-profit need with a stylist?

Maybe they were so blown away by my rousing mission statement that they want to offer me a position working in their PR department. That must be it.

I can't keep from grinning because we have moved into comfortable territory. I am a highly adept negotiator, having honed my skills in the Beijing markets. When I was a teenager, my father took me on a few of his business trips to China. He would hand me a wad of yuan, and I would spend the day haggling for cashmere pashminas, bolts of shantung silk, and strands of pearls.

"I am intrigued," I say, keeping my tone appropriately bland and leaning back in my chair. "What did you have in mind?"

"We believe you would be perfect as a community outreach educator."

I knew it. They want me to do PR. They probably want me to let the community know about their good deeds by writing press releases. I can do that. It's not fashion, but it would be something to do while I get my life back together.

Finn turns to face Rachel. "This might be a good time to show Ms. Moreau your presentation."

"Of course."

Rachel pulls a small remote out of her pocket and pushes a button. The overhead lights dim, and blinds lower from the ceiling to conceal the windows. She presses another button, and a laser picture of teenagers weaving palm fronds on a white sandy beach materializes on the far wall. It is the first picture in a slide show featuring smiling children in exotic locales around the world.

"Each One, Teach One is a non-profit organization that empowers the world's poorest citizens to reach their full potential through vocational training and life mentoring," Rachel says, her voice low and serious. "Each One, Teach One outreach workers have helped three point two million people around the world gain the skills necessary to lead them out of poverty...."

Rachel continues her impressive sales pitch for several minutes, matching her most salient points with powerful, striking images. Her presentation is so inspiring, I am mentally writing a generous check to Each One, Teach One.

"In 2015, we opened the Sitka Edification Center." She presses the remote and a picture of a small coastal village nestled between two snowcapped mountains materializes on the far wall. "Sitka, as you may know, is a city located on Baranof Island, one of several islands that make up an archipelago off the coast of Alaska."

She presses the button, and a picture of a rambling three-story log cabin, the night sky above strangely aglow with wavy green lights materializes. I catch my breath.

"Our Sitka center offers vocational training to the citizens of Baranof Island, particularly Native Alaskans." Rachel presses the remote, raising the lights. "We would like to offer you a position as an educational outreach worker at our center in Sitka."

Chapter 11

Working Knit

Text from Vivia Perpetua Grant:
Did you know R. H. Macy failed at seven business before finally making bank with his New York City department store? If Macy can do it, Moreau can, too!

"Sitka? This is a joke, right? It has to be a joke because nobody willingly moves to the middle of Nowhere, Alaska, except maybe hairy, toothless fisherman eager to risk their lives for a net full of stinky king crab." Vivian gasps. "Ohmygod! Please tell me you didn't audition to be on the Deadliest Catch."

"What is—"

"The Deadliest Catch," Vivian interrupts. "It's an awful reality TV show on the Discovery Channel that follows a crew as they risk life and limb fishing for Alaskan king crab in the Bering Sea."

The reality of my new anything-but-a-sitcom life is starting to sink in. I am moving to Sitka to teach natives about fashion design and sewing. Sitka. Alaska. I look around my modern posh apartment. What the fuck had I been thinking when I signed my name on the dotted line on a Each One, Teach One volunteer contract?

"Remember that non-profit organization I mentioned in my mission statement? Each One, Teach One?"

"Yes."

"Well, I met with them today." My voice suddenly wavers. "They asked me to become a community outreach something-or-other in Sitka, Alaska and I agreed."

"What does that even mean? What does a community outreach something-or-other do?"

"I will be empowering Sitka's poorest citizens to reach their full potential through vocational training and life mentoring," I say, parroting Rachel. "I will teach them about fashion design and sewing."

"So no catching king crab?"

"No."

"That is freaking awesome, Fanny!" Vivian cries. "I am so proud of you."

"You are?"

"Yes!"

"Why?"

"Because you bounced, girl. You bounced in a big way."

"What does that even mean?"

"It means you could have let your termination deflate your spirit, but you didn't. You bounced. You set aside your pain and found a worthier purpose than hocking pricey purses." Vivian draws in a deep breath. "Do you realize what you have done? You have slipped the shackles of your materialistic life by agreeing to exchange your luxury apartment, designer wardrobe, posh city life, for an über-humble existence helping others. That is so on fleek."

Panic seizes me like a bride clutching a gown at a Vera Wang sample sale. "Ohmygod! What have I done?" I gasp. "I can't go to Alaska. What will I wear? Armani suits and Louboutins?"

"You will just have to go shopping for a new wardrobe."

"Where? Cabela's?"

"Hang on." I can hear Vivian tapping on her keyboard, and I know she is probably googling Alaskan Attire. "No worries. There are six clothing stores in Sitka."

"Please tell me one of those stores is Stefan Kaelin Luxury Ski Wear."

"Nope," Vivian laughs. "No Stefan Kaelin, but you do have your choice of fine attire from Fur Sure, Sitka Outfitters, Make Knit Work, Barren Land Surplus, Alaskan Bush Company, and One-Eyed Jack."

"I am not buying clothes from someone named One-Eyed Jack."

"Don't be a hater," Vivian admonishes. "One-Eyed Jack could be an inspired designer."

"I doubt it."

"You never know. Look at Karl Lagerfeld."

"What about him?"

"He's a big designer, and he's blind."

"Karl Lagerfeld is not blind."

"Really?"

"Really."

"Then why does he wear dark sunglasses all of the time?"

"It's his fashion statement."

"Get out," Vivian cries. "Who does that? Nobody wears Ray Charles sunglasses day and night unless they're high or blind."

"Roy Orbison wore them."

"Roy suffered from crippling stage fright. His glasses helped him cope. It's not the same, at all."

I laugh and shake my head. This is classic Vivian. Frequently random and off-topic. Lost in her own stream of consciousness. She is perpetually, irrepressibly upbeat, and she can find the humor in any situation. I love that about her.

"You're going to be okay, Fanny," Vivian whispers. "I promise."

Emotion clogs my throat. I wish I had my best friend's optimism, but I am terrified that I am about to prove my father's dire predictions right by becoming an embarrassing failure. Unrealized potential. That's what he said after I told him I planned on pursuing a career in fashion. *Fanny, my dear, you are a tragic example of unrealized potential. You've been afforded the benefit of a superior lineage and an exclusive education, and this is what you do with it, become a bourgeois merchant of frocks?*

"I wish I had some of your optimism, Vivian."

"Ain't nothing but a thing, girl," Vivian says. "I have enough optimism for both of us. When you feel the negativity closing in, just call me. I gotcher six."

A bubble of laughter pushes past the thick emotion clogging my throat. *"En Anglais, s'il vous plaît."*

"I told you." Vivian sighs. "I gotcher six means I have your back. I am protecting your most vulnerable spots."

"Thank you, Vivian."

"Do you want me to join you in Alaska? I have Kayak open right now. A couple of clicks and I will be winging my way to Sitka for a little QT with my best girl."

"Thanks, but I think I need to do this alone."

"You sure?"

"Yes." I am not sure. Not one bit. But asking Vivian to join me in Alaska would be admitting a vulnerability, and vulnerability is not my default mode. "Besides, I don't want you wasting your frequent flier miles on a trip to boring old Sitka."

"Are you kidding?" Vivian protests. "I would gladly sacrifice my miles if it meant embarking on another adventure with my best friend."

I laugh. "Scotland was adventure enough for a lifetime."

"Pfft. That was nothing."

"Nothing?" I laugh again, but this time it is an incredulous laugh. "You fell off a mountain. You had to be rescued by a Coast Guard helicopter. That is hardly nothing."

"A mere trifling thing."

"You were hospitalized for days."

"True," Vivian sniffs. "But it made for one helluva vacay story, didn't it?"

"It did."

"The thing is, Fanny, you can try to organize and manage your life, but it's the unpredictable, messy bits that bring you the most growth and joy. If I hadn't fallen off that mountain, I wouldn't have had my epiphany about marrying Luc."

"So what are you saying? That I should fall off a mountain?"

"I wouldn't recommend that," Vivian says, uncharacteristically serious. "I am saying you should let go, Miss Type A. Stop trying to force your life to follow an unnaturally controlled path. You're going through an unpredictable, messy bit right now. I know it's frightening, but have courage. This time next year, you just might find yourself traveling in a new, happier direction."

"I hope you're right."

"Trust me, a lot can happen in a year."

Chapter 12

Bottoms Up

Text from Vivia Perpetua Grant:
When Vera Wang failed to make the U.S. Olympic figure-skating team, she made alterations to her dream (See what I did there?) by becoming an editor at Vogue. Then, after being passed over for promotions, she became a designer. Alter your dream and make it work, girl!

"Anchorage has changed."

"Too many damned Californians. Too built up."

"We should call it Los Anchorage."

"Bahaha!" Sardonic laughter explodes from my lips, and the chatty passengers behind me finally fall silent. I have been listening to their less-than-scintillating conversation—about hunting for caribou, the salmon run, the best home-brewed beer, the unusually cold spring—for the last two hours. I really don't know how much more I can take.

"Did you hear we are getting a Target?"

I groan and press my fingers to my temples, rubbing in vigorous circles. The flight attendant comes over.

"Headache?"

I nod.

He pats my shoulder. "Would two aspirin help?"

"Only if you bring a very large glass of wine to chase them with."

"Be right back," he says, winking.

The loquacious Alaskans aren't the sole cause of my foul mood. When I picked up my itinerary and travel orders from Each One, Teach One yesterday, Rachel told me I would be meeting another outreacher at the hotel in Anchorage. Apparently, we are traveling from Anchorage to Sitka together. Her name is Delaney Brooks, and she is going to be my suite mate.

I hate meeting new people. I hate sharing my space with anyone—
let alone some crunchy-granola environmental educator from
Boulder, Colorado.

I stretch my legs, looking down at my high-heeled leather
Burberry Finway boots.

Vivian would laugh if she could see me in these boots. She would tell
me how impractical they were and insist I buy a pair of those hideous
sheepskin boots she always wears with her jeans and band T-shirts. Uggs.
They are truly the ugliest boots ever mass produced.

The flight attendant returns with my aspirin and wine. I pop the pills
in my mouth and nearly drain my glass in one swallow. The lady sitting
across the aisle looks at me, one eyebrow raised in silent judgment, her
lips pressed together in a grim, sanctimonious line.

I raise my glass and smile. *"Salut!"*

I defiantly tip the rest of the wine into my mouth. She picks up her
book, *Tea with Jesus: Morning Devotions for the Baptist Woman*, and
begins reading, turning the cover so it's facing me.

The ridiculous almost-farcical nature of this moment is not lost on me.
I am moving to a cultural wasteland. A place where people get excited
over a Target store opening. If the passengers seated around me are any
indication of what Alaskans are like, I am going to be a fish out of water.
I don't hunt. I don't drink beer, unless it's from Belgium. I don't read
religious books. The only thing I have ever purchased from Target was a
box of tampons.

I order another glass of wine, pop a pair of earplugs into my ears, and
pretend I am winging my way to Milan.

* * * *

By the time we touch down at Ted Stevens International Airport in
sunny Los Anchorage, I am working a pretty good buzz. The kind of buzz
that makes me feel like I am wrapped in a cocoon as warm and fuzzy as
Vivian's hideous, trendy sheepskin-lined Uggs.

Pulling my rolling carryon behind me, I follow the crush of passengers
down the boarding ramp and through the terminal. I am not sure what I
expected the Anchorage Airport to look like—perhaps a World War II era
Quonset hut filled with cheap plastic chairs and vending machines—but I
never expected it to be a sleek, modern facility with local artwork hanging
on the walls and massive windows offering panoramic views of distant
snowcapped mountains.

I roll past a glass case displaying shaman masks, sealskin boots,
and fur parkas. I pause when I come to a second display case, this one

containing the stuffed carcass of the largest Kodiak bear ever killed by a human being. The bear has been posed in an attack stance, standing on its hind legs, gigantic paws outstretched, claws poised to rip flesh from bone. The wooden plaque affixed to the display case lets curious onlookers know that this dead beast has a thirty and twelve-sixteenth skull score. Whatever that means.

"Awesome, isn't he?"

I turn and find Ms. Los Anchorage, the chatty passenger seated behind me during the flight, standing beside me, staring up at the stuffed bear.

"He certainly is," I say, looking back at the plaque. "It says this bear was 'harvested in Anchorage in 1997.' That must have been when the city was still relatively small and less developed. You probably don't see bears in Anchorage anymore, do you?"

"Twenty years ago, the hills around Anchorage were filled with moose, dall sheep, red fox, black bears, and brown bears, especially in the spring when the lingonberries and blueberries were ripe for the picking"—she sighs heavily and shakes her head—"but that was before the snowbirds arrived."

"Snowbirds?"

"People from the lower forty-eight," she says. "They watch those damned reality TV shows—*Alaska State Troopers, Deadliest Catch, Man Versus Nature*—and then they move here, their heads filled with silly romantic notions about living in the last frontier. They bring their fancy SUVs and Starbucks."

Thank you, snowbirds! "The snowbirds came and all of the bear left. Is that it?"

"Well, now," she says, chuckling. "I wouldn't say that. It's still Alaska."

An icy finger trails down my spine. I am spending the night in Anchorage. Should I be concerned? Should I arm myself with some bear spray or a bazooka?

"But I won't see bears here in Anchorage, will I?"

"You might." She shifts the strap of her steel-framed backpack from one shoulder to the other. "A mountain biker was mauled at Russian Jack just last month."

"Russian Jack?" I consider asking if he is related to One-Eyed Jack, but figure the sarcasm will be lost on this woman.

"Russian Jack Springs. It's a park."

"How far is it from Anchorage?"

"What do you mean, how far is it?" She grumbles, frowning. "Russian Jack Springs is *in* Anchorage. It's only about eight miles from here, just down Minnesota Drive to Fifteenth."

I swallow, one of those cartoon character audible swallows.

"I…I didn't realize."

"Relax, snowbird." She looks at my raccoon-trimmed Sônia Bogner parka, my high-heeled boots, and my Louis Vuitton Pegase carryon, and smiles. "There's never been a bear sighting in the Hilton."

"Thanks," I mumble.

She starts to walk away, and then stops and looks over her shoulder at me. "You might want to reconsider wearing that tonic."

"Excuse me?" Tonic? I am not wearing hair tonic. "What tonic?"

"Your cologne."

Excusez-moi? "What's wrong with my perfume?"

I can't believe I am even discussing my toilette with a woman wearing a flannel lumberjack shirt and corduroy trousers. There's nothing wrong with my perfume. It was made in Grasse, France and has top notes of Tahitian Vanilla and coconut. It is decadent and delicious.

"You smell like a damned birthday cake," she says. "Bears are attracted to strong scents, especially food."

She turns and walks away, leaving an unspoken "duh" hanging in the air between us.

Isn't it bad enough that I will probably have to trade my Burberry boots for remarkably hideous sheepskin footgear? Now, I am supposed to forgo wearing my signature scent to avoid having my bones picked clean by a ravenous brown bear? It might seem like a simple choice, but if some bear is going to drag me into the woods and use my femur as a toothpick, I at least want to smell good. I don't want some hot park ranger to find my flannel-and-sheepskin-clad carcass sans the luxurious scent of L'Heure Eau de Parfum. Just saying.

I am rolling my carryon in the general direction of the baggage carousels and one-hand texting Vivian, when I collide into another passenger. The collision nearly knocks me on my ass. I drop my iPhone, and it skitters across the slick tile floor.

"Easy, lass."

I look up into a pair of impossibly blue eyes, and my stomach does a crazy flip flop. The other person involved in this collision is not some potbellied salesman hurrying home to his wife and kids. He's a tall, muscular Scotsman with twinkling eyes and dimpled cheeks.

"Calder?" Calder freaking MacFarlane. Mister MacFlirty himself. The man who tried to seduce my best friend by plying her with whisky and wit. "What are you doing here? Run out of women to charm in the United Kingdom?"

A slow, seductive smile stretches across his handsome face, and my heart races like a BMW on the autobahn.

"I might ask ye the same, lass." He bends over and retrieves my iPhone. "Was your plane diverted, then? Are ye headed to Paris in the pursuit of some frivolous trinket or bauble?"

Arrogant ass. I snatch my iPhone from his hand.

"I see you haven't changed one bit."

"Aye." He grins and winks. "I am still devastatingly handsome and exceptionally charming."

Even though I have always found the Scotsman to be too flirty and too full of himself, my stomach does another flip-flop.

I am probably hungry. I've only had two glasses of wine and some aspirin. That's why my stomach feels queasy. It has nothing to do with Calder freaking MacFarlane.

"Did you hear? Vivian and Luc are getting married."

Merde! Why did I say that? Considering Calder fell hard for my best friend, would've chased her around Europe if she hadn't been madly in love with Luc, my comment was kind of a bitch move.

"Aye. Fiona told me the news." He keeps his gaze fixed on me, but his smile slips a little. "I am happy for her."

An awkward silence stretches between us, and I wish I could rewind to the moment just before I needled him about Vivian.

"Do ye have another plane to catch?"

I shake my head.

He reaches for the handle of my carryon and wrests it from my grip. "Come on, then. I'll walk with ye to baggage claim, and ye can tell me what's brought a *fantoosh* like ye to Alaska."

"*Fantoosh?*"

"Posh girl," he says, resting his hand on the small of my back and guiding me down the corridor. "Ye are the last person I expected to run into at the Anchorage Airport."

I don't know why, but it bothers me that he thinks I am too posh for Alaska.

"I am not that posh, you know."

He chuckles.

"I'm not!"

He looks down at me and my breath catches in my throat.

"*Banfhlath*, you make Kate Middleton look uncultured."

My skin flushes with heat, especially where his hand is touching my spine. I wish his compliment didn't make me feel warm all over, inside and out, but it does. Changing the subject feels like the safest course of action.

"What are you doing in Anchorage?"

"I met a friend for the weekend."

"A girl friend?"

Merde! Why did I ask him that?

He grins and his impossibly deep dimples deepen. He doesn't tell me if his friend is female or male. It annoys me that I even care. So what if the Scot spent a sexy weekend with another of his female conquests. Ain't nothing but a thang, as Vivian would say.

My beautiful, glossy Louis Vuitton leather bag slides down the ramp and onto the carousel. Calder steps in front of me, seizes the handle, and effortlessly lifts the eighty-three pound bag off the carousel. Yes, I exceeded the domestic baggage weight allowance.

"How did you know that was my bag?"

He looks down at me, a grin lifting the corners of his mouth. "Look around, *banfhlath*. Ye've left the land of Louis Vuitton and entered the realm of duffle bags and backpacks."

The passenger standing on the other side of Calder snickers. I lean to the side and groan. It's the Baptist woman, still toting her prayer book. She hoists a rolling Eddie Bauer duffle bag off the carousel, smiles at Calder, pierces me with a *Repent, Ye Heathen* stare, and walks away.

My second bag slides down the ramp. Calder lifts it off the carousel and places it beside the first bag.

"Is this all? We have yer shoes, but what about yer clothes and lacy lady things?"

"Don't you worry about my lacy lady things." I sniff. "I am well covered in that department."

"Aye," he says, winking. "I'll bet ye are."

To my eternal mortification—for I know I will look back on this moment thirty years from now and still feel humiliation — my cheeks flush with heat. I open my mouth to zing him with an ego-deflating put-down, but my mind goes blank. I got nothing. I am zinger challenged. Without a single ego-deflating verbal barb in my arsenal.

Calder chuckles, which provokes a new wave of mortifying heat to ripple down my body. It starts at my cheeks and moves with devastating speed down my neck, chest, abdomen, like a tsunami of humiliation.

"Relax, *banfhlath*." He smiles, and two dimples appear on his tanned cheeks. "It's okay if ye don't wear the lacy things. I ken some women prefer those enormous high-waisted polyester knickers."

It takes me a moment to translate the Scot's sarcasm.

"Granny panties?" I sputter. "You think I wear granny panties?"

Calder throws his head back and laughs. His unrestrained belly-deep masculine laugh drowns out the busy airport sounds and makes me feel… strangely happy.

"Come on," he says, grabbing the handles of my suitcases. "There's a Chili's in the departures terminal. Let's get a drink, and ye can tell me what brought ye to Alaska."

I shift my weight from one foot to the other. Calder lets go of my suitcases and crosses his muscular arms over his broad chest.

"Do ye have somewhere else to be, then?"

"No." I shake my head, and then remember I am supposed to meet my fellow outreacher at the hotel later. "At least, not right now."

"Let's go then, lass." He grabs my suitcases again and begins pulling them away from the baggage area. "Toting these bloody bags has given me a thirst. I'll let ye buy me a whisky."

I grab my carryon and hurry to catch up with the flirty Scot. The last time we drank whisky together, at a pub in Scotland, he drove off in his sexy sports car with my best friend. Vivian swore they only kissed, but…

I stare at the Scot's bulging arm muscles and broad back and wonder how any woman could stop at just a kiss. It's like going into a Hermès boutique and saying, "I'll just buy one little scarf." Bullshit! Before you know it, you are leaving with a new wallet, purse, and leather loafers.

Moderation has never been my forte, but if the Scot tries to run his smooth-charmer game on me, I will shut him down before the first quarter.

Chapter 13

Some Like It Wet-n-Wild

Text from Vivia Perpetua Grant:
Did you know Alaska Fashion Week is an annual four day event that takes place in Anchorage?

Text to Vivia Perpetua Grant:
Oh, goodie! It's long been my secret wish to watch a model stomp the runway wearing a pair of mukluks.

We take a seat at one of the small tables in the back of the restaurant, my suitcases piled in the corner behind my chair. A young woman with a high blond ponytail and theatrical peacock blue eyeliner arrives to take our order. She rests her hand on Calder's shoulder, bats her clumpy eyelashes, and breathlessly asks if she can take his order.

The eighties just rang. They want their Wet-n-Wild eyeliner back, Tiffani.

Calder orders an appetizer—crispy cheddar bites, battered, deep-fried, and served with an ancho-chili ranch dip—and two whiskies.

"Are ye hungry, lass?" He smiles at me over the top of the menu. "Would ye like to order something else to eat?"

I am famished, but Chili's Too only offers two salads: the buffalo chicken ranch and the quesadilla explosion. I don't need to read the descriptions to know that they are probably over a thousand calories each.

"No, thank you."

Tiffani takes my greasy menu and promises to return with our drinks without as much as a glance in my direction.

We make small talk until Miss Wet-n-Wild returns with our drinks. She places Calder's whisky on a napkin, leaning over him, her breasts brushing his arm. She's less careful with my whisky. No napkin. No breasts.

"Enjoy," she purrs. "Let me know if there's anything else I can get you." She sashays away, ponytail swinging, hips swiveling.

"*Incroyable!*"

"What?" He looks at me with wide mock-innocent eyes.

"Is there a woman alive who hasn't fallen for...for..."

"For what?"

I wave my hand in his direction. "All of that."

"I dinnea ken what ye're talking aboot," he says, his brogue as thick as his forearms. "All of what, lass?"

"You know exactly what I am talking aboot, Calder McFlirty." I cross my arms and narrow my gaze. "Your whole grinning, winking, flexing Hottie Scottie routine."

"Oh, I dinnea ken," he says, leaning forward and resting his arms on the table. "It doesn't seem to be having much of an effect on ye."

He fixes me with his intense blue-eyed stare, and my stomach does another of those queer flip-flops.

"Oh my God. Are you flirting with me?"

"Do ye want me to be flirting with ye, *banfhlath*?"

"What is bafflelass?"

"*Banfhlath*," he repeats. "It means princess."

Princess? I don't even know what to say to that, so I just laugh and roll my eyes.

"Shall we?" Calder lifts his glass. "To whisky and flirting that warms yer innards."

My face flushes with heat, and I have to force myself to keep looking into his sparkling blue eyes. Arrogant bastard!

"Sláinte."

I curl my fingers around my glass, lift it in salute, and then drain the contents in one throat-stinging swallow. Calder watches me, chuckles, and tips the whisky into his mouth. Damn him! I want to look away, but the arrogant ass might misinterpret it as me being embarrassed by his faux flirting—or worse, into him.

"Slow down, lass," he says. "Drinking whisky is verra much like having a love affair. It should be done slowly and savored until the very end."

"Stop! I know all about your whisky moves, so don't even try to run them on me."

He lifts a brow. "My whisky moves?"

"Hello," I say, holding out my hand. "My name is Stéphanie Moreau. We met last year, when you tried to seduce my best friend by plying her with whisky, remember?"

"Aye, I remember," he says, chuckling. "I promise not to try any of my whisky moves on ye, lass."

"Really? You promise?"

"I swear it." He presses one hand to his heart and raises the other in the air as if making an oath. "I, Calder James Kenrik MacFarlane, do solemnly swear that I will nae rely on whisky to seduce ye."

"*Bon*," I say, pushing my empty glass away. "No winking, no whisky, and no seducing."

"Nay." He lowers his hand. "I didn't say I wouldn't seduce you, just that I wouldn't use whisky in the doing."

"*Bon chance, mon ami*," I say, chuckling. "You can try, but you will fail."

We lock gazes.

"Challenge accepted, lassie."

Tiffani arrives with a plate of molten cheese lumps and presents it to Calder as if he were Bonnie Prince Charlie. I half expect her to drop into a deep curtsy and call him "sire." Calder takes it all in stride, demonstrating that natural, effortless self-assurance that comes from being born beautiful. Beautiful people take their beauty for granted because they never suffered the painful metamorphosis from pimply, gawky, chubby teen to attractive adult.

Calder hands me one of the appetizer plates Tiffani left on his side of the table.

"No, thank you."

"Eat something, lassie."

I shake my head. "Do you know how many calories are in one of those deep fried cheese lumps? I would have to take two Boot Camp classes just to work off the weight."

"Believe me, lassie, ye dinnea need to worry about yer weight."

I am not good at taking compliments about my appearance. Deep down, I don't believe the praise is sincere. I might have shed my Éléphanny weight, but I am still carrying the baggage of being fat and unpopular.

Calder uses his fork to maneuver three cheese balls onto my plate and pushes it across the table. The aroma of hot, bubbling, greasy cheese hits my nose like a right hook. My stomach growls at the assault. The aspirin and booze aren't cutting it.

"Was that yer stomach?"

"Yes." Heat flushes over my body. "I haven't eaten since yesterday."

"Why not?"

I shrug. "I've had a lot on my mind."

"Eat something, lassie." He forks another ball onto my plate. "Then ye can tell me what brought ye to Alaska."

I look at the artery blocking bites of cheese, and my stomach growls again. Woman cannot live by booze alone.

"Maybe one," I say, forking a ball into my mouth. "Just one, though."

"Och, ye're a long time deid."

I finish chewing and swallow the diet-killing appetizer, resisting the urge to moan with pleasure. Either my body has entered starvation mode or these damned cheese balls are addictively delicious.

"What does that mean?"

"It means"—he grins and pops a cheese ball into his mouth, chews, and swallows—"enjoy life, because once ye're dead ye're going to be that way for a verra long time."

"Force me to eat another one of these crispy crack balls, and I will definitely die."

"Go on, ye ken ye want another one."

He's right. I do want another one.

"I am onto you, Calder MacFlirty. You've exchanged your whisky moves with cheese."

He grins and pierces me with an intensely sexy stare. "Is it working?"

"Maybe."

His grin widens.

I cut a cheese ball in half, dip it in the sauce, and put it in my mouth. I rationalize eating the second half by telling myself the cheese will stop the liquor from sloshing around in my belly. The whisky has me feeling a bit light headed and—*foutre!*—horny.

I am not attracted to the arrogant, feckless Scot. It's just the booze. It's just the booze.

"So do ye mean to keep me in suspense, or will ye tell me why ye're in Alaska?"

I flag Miss Wet-n-Wild down, order us two more whiskies, take a deep breath, and tell Calder about the events leading up to this moment. I tell him everything. I mean, everything—my date with the catfish, the humiliating two a.m. call, writing the misguided mission statement, getting fired, my contract with Each One, Teach One. I even tell him about my father ditching me to take his silicone-injected sex doll to Switzerland. Calder doesn't interrupt with questions or commentary. He sits, quietly listening, his gaze never wavering.

"I am in Alaska because writing that mission statement effectively destroyed my career. I did a Miley Cyrus on my career."

Calder frowns.

"Miley Cyrus. Wrecking ball." I sigh and shake my head. "Never mind. Pop culture references really aren't my thing. I should leave them to Vivian."

Calder doesn't laugh at my reference or my self-deprecating humor. He just continues to stare at me, a sad smile on his face. His silence is a bit unnerving.

Finally, he leans across the table, his face close enough for me to see the slight reddish-blond stubble shadowing his angled jawline and the cleft in his chin.

"I'm sorry, Fanny."

It's too much. The intensity of his gaze, the tenderness in his voice, the rumbling brogue as he speaks my name.

"Everything I have worked for, everything I have dreamed about, has been smashed to pieces." *Shut up, Fanny. Stop filling the silence with pathetic confessions.* "But it's fine. I will be fine."

"Dinnea do that."

"Do what?"

"Pretend everything is fine when it's nae." He reaches across the table and grabs my hand. "Ye dinnea need to be so tough. Cry, if that's what ye feel like doing."

"Thank you," I say, pulling my hand away, "but I don't cry."

He leaves his hand on the table and continues to stare deep into my eyes. "Can I give ye a bit of advice?"

"Sure," I say, drawing a shaky breath.

"Lower yer defenses, lassie. If ye want more two a.m. friends, ye need to let people see this softer side. Let people see the real Stéphanie."

Calder's advice reaches into my chest and plucks the most vulnerable chords in my soul. I know I have erected walls too thick for the average person to penetrate, but it's taken me twenty-six years to build them. Twenty-six years of pain, loneliness, disappointment, and abandonment have stacked up like blocks, separating me from anyone who might hurt me again.

"I...don't even know who the real Stéphanie is..." I have to look away. Calder's stare is too intense, too probing. I take a deep breath and return my gaze. "I thought I knew who I was, where I was going, what I desired, but I don't know anymore."

Calder clears his throat. "Have ye considered that everything that has happened—getting terminated, coming to Alaska—has been preordained?"

"Preordained? As in arranged by God?"

"Aye."

I snort. "I am not a religious person."

"Ye dinnea have to believe in God to concede that sometimes things happen in our lives for a reason. Maybe this happened so ye could figure out exactly who ye are, lass."

"You think?"

"Aye." He nods his head. "I think life is a series of tests and lessons. Ye are being tested. It's up to ye to determine what ye're gonna learn from it."

He looks at his watch.

"Do you have somewhere you have to go?"

"Unfortunately." He stands and pulls out my chair. "I have a flight to catch."

"Where are you headed?"

"Sitka."

"Sitka?" My head feels like it's spinning. "Why are you going to Sitka? You're not going there because of me, are you?"

"No, *banfhlath*," he says, chuckling. "I'm stationed there. I am a foreign exchange officer assigned to Air Station Sitka."

My heart feels like someone tethered a bunch of helium balloons to it. I am ridiculously happy, relieved, to know I will know at least one person in Sitka.

Calder throws two twenty dollar bills on the table and stands.

"Come on then, *banfhlath*," he says, grabbing my suitcases. "I will help ye load yer shoe collection into a taxi."

We follow the signs directing us to ground transportation, and Calder hails a taxi. A yellow cab pulls to a stop. I stand on the curb as Calder loads my bags into the trunk, fighting the sudden urge to burst into tears. The whisky has made me a sloppy, sappy, weepy mess.

This is really happening. I am really in Alaska. The gravity of my new situation is hitting me hard.

Calder slams the trunk and turns to face me. He looks into my eyes. I am trying to think of something flippant and clever to say when he leans down and kisses me, a slow, tender kiss that steals my breath away. I close my eyes and savor the taste of the whisky still on his lips, the scent of his woodsy cologne. I am about to press myself against his solid body when he pulls away.

Reluctantly, I open my eyes. Calder is at least a foot taller than I am, which means I have to crane my neck to look at his face.

He is staring at me with that same blue-eyed intensity that made all the ladies in our tour group sigh.

"I have to go now," he says, grinning. "'Tis certain we will see each other in Sitka, but in the meantime, remember, it's a lang road that's no goat a turnin'."

Maybe it's the drugging effect of the whisky or Calder's kiss, but I feel disoriented. I see his lips moving, hear the words, but...

"It means, don't lose heart in dark times. Things can't keep going in the same direction forever."

I am still trying to catch my breath, when he turns and strides back into the airport. In my head, I hear myself telling Vivian, "Girl, he was worth the Dior lip gloss."

Part Two

My dream is to save women from nature.
Christian Dior

Chapter 14

Panty Pinching Pervos

Text from Vivia Perpetua Grant:
Did you know the fragrance Jicky, created by Guerlain in 1889, was named after a girl who broke Aimé Guerlain's heart? 120 years later, Jicky is still a best-selling luxury perfume. Moral of the story? Heartbreak doesn't have to stink. Bloom, Fanny!

I close my eyes until I see splinters of light and say a little prayer to the goddess of fashion. That I am praying to a higher power underscores the dire nature of my present situation.

"Please, please, please, let them be there," I whisper. "Pretty please."

I open one eye and then the other, but the Fashion Goddess hasn't answered my prayers. My suitcases are still missing.

After checking into the Klondike, an economy motel conveniently situated in the shadow of the new, sleek Marriott, I stacked my suitcases in my room and went for a brisk walk down Seventh Avenue. I had to do something to work off the booze and cheese ball calories and the tension of Calder's sweet kiss.

I returned to the motel with wind-chapped cheeks, frozen fingers, and the singular ambition to take a hot shower before meeting my new suite mate, Delaney Brooks, for dinner. I knew something was tragically amiss when I found my door ajar.

Some miscreant has pulled a Patty Hearst on my Louis Vs. Thousands of dollars' worth of chic, sleek, luxurious luggage kidnapped. All of my clothes…and shoes!

Oh, *putain de merde!*

What kind of knuckle-dragging, mouth-breathing barbarians inhabit this miserable frozen tundra? The worst kind. The kind that break into a shitty motel room and steal a woman's La Perla panties and bras. Crack whores. Tweakers. Panty-sniffing perverts.

I slam the door open and walk all of the way into the room, too fucking pissed to worry about my personal safety. Actually, I hope one of the panty-pilfering Neanderthals is still lurking about so I can take off my size six Burberry Finways and jam my stiletto heel into his sloped forehead. I haven't been sweating my ass off in Body Combat and Krav Maga classes just so I can fit into size-two skinny jeans.

The tacky western-printed curtains flutter. The window is open. That's strange. I didn't leave it open. Wait a minute! Maybe they were in the middle of pinching my panties and kidnapping my Louis Vs, heard me coming down the hall, and jumped out the window.

Hurrying to the window, I trip over something solid and fall flat on my face. What the... I push myself up on all fours, stand, and prepare to deliver a swift uppercut elbow to my assailant's throat, but there's no assailant, just my battered carry-on.

Yanking the curtains open, I stick my head out the window in time to see two teenagers dressed in Goth garb running away with my suitcases.

"You better run you freaky little motherfuckers"—I climb onto the windowsill—"because when I catch you, I am going to—"

I am just about to jump out the window onto a pile of snow when I feel a solid grip on my forearm.

"Stop! What, are you totes cray cray?"

I turn around and find a tall brunette with heavy bangs and big round black glasses standing behind me, clutching my arm.

"Let go of me." I try to pull my arm free. "They stole my luggage. I am going after them."

"Oh, no you're not."

"Yes, I am."

"It's not safe. They could be legit jerries." She sticks her head out the window and looks down the street just as the Marilyn Manson groupies are tossing my luggage into a rusted out pickup truck. "Shitballs! They're jerries, all right."

The groupies jump into the back of the flatbed and the truck speeds off, gears grinding, wheels crunching over the snow packed road. She pulls her head back into the room. I hop down off the windowsill.

"Who are you? And what in the hell is a jerry?"

"I'm Delaney Brooks," she says, using her index finger to push her ridiculously large glasses up her nose. "The other outreach worker with Each One, Teach One. We're traveling to Sitka together."

I stare at her mouth. She is speaking because her lips are moving, but my mind must be on a five-second delay. All I can hear is the sound of that shitty pickup truck speeding away with my precious luggage.

"You're Stéphanie Moreau, right?"

I nod. Too numb to speak. This isn't happening. This. Is. Not. Happening. *Non*. There's been some kind of mistake. I want to cry, to rage, to bargain—all of the typical reactions of someone in grief.

I blink several times and look back at the girl with the chunky bangs and chunkier glasses. "I'm sorry. Who are you?"

"Delaney. Delaney Brooks." She holds out her hand and smiles a big Colgate-white toothy grin. "My friends call me Laney, though."

"*Bonjour*, Laney." I shake her hand. "I am Stéphanie, but my friends call me Fanny."

"Fanny, Fanny. Bi-Banny. Fee-foe-fi-Fanny." She strums her fingers as if playing an invisible guitar. "Fanny! Fanny Price. Fanny Farmer. Fanny around with press releases."

She finishes her air guitar solo and does a little bow. You know that awkward moment when you're checking yourself out in a store window and then realize there's someone on the other side watching you? Or when you say you need to lose weight and then realize there's an obese person standing nearby? Yeah, this awkward moment is worse—much, much worse. I am not sure if I am supposed to applaud or respond with a Laney song.

"Um, thanks for the..." I don't know how to finish the sentence. Bizarre greeting? Freaky song? Mentally disturbed rambling?

"It's nothing." Laney shrugs her shoulders and laughs. "Just a little trick I use to help me remember names."

"Oooo-kay." I have to fight to stop from making a circle with my finger near my temple, because the girl is a little black dress short of a wardrobe. "I think I understand your little ditty, but what is 'fanny around with press releases?'"

"Bridget Jones."

Make that a little black dress and tailored slacks. The girl is certifiable. "I don't know Bridget Jones? Is she a singer?"

"I can't even..." Laney stares at me as if I were the crazy one, all wide eyes behind her hipster specs. "*Bridget Jones's Diary?*"

I shake my head.

"You've never heard of *Bridget Jones's Diary?*"

"*Non*."

"It is only, like, the holy grail of all chick lit novels and rom coms." She exhales. "Bridget Jones works for a pervy man who accuses her of wearing short skirts while fannying around the office with press releases."

Speechless. She has rendered me speechless. I thought Vivian was slightly eccentric with her random pop culture references and free-flowing stream of consciousness, but Laney makes Vivian look totes normal.

Laney must notice my bewilderment, because she hurries to explain.

"Bridget Jones. Short skirts. You just lost a luggage full of clothes. Some of those clothes were probably skirts." She tilts her head and fixes me with a "get it?" expression.

I still don't get it.

Laney sighs. "Bridget Jones equals short skirts. Short skirts equal clothes. Clothes equal you. You see, Fanny. It's all connected. It makes perfect sense."

"Right." I edge my way toward the door. "It's been fabulous meeting you, Laney, but right now I need to have a conversation with the head of security about filing a police report for my missing luggage."

"Listen, Fanny," she says, patting my shoulder. "I dig that you're totes devo about your luggage, but those jerries are long gone."

What just happened? Did the pilot make a wrong turn? Am I in Alaska or some alternate universe? Someone needs to Google translate Laney-speak because I am not fluent in hipster.

"I am sorry, Laney. English isn't my first language. I think I know what totes means, but what does devo mean? And who is Jerry?"

Laney laughs.

"Totes devo means totally devastated and jerries are stoners, druggies, meth heads." She reaches around me, slides the window shut, and tugs the curtains closed. "I read online that Alaska has a huge drug problem. Those jerries are probably on their way to pawn your knickers for crack cash."

"Fabulous." I bend over, pick up my carry-on, and hug it to my chest. "What am I going to do now?"

"Chillax, it's only luggage."

"Only luggage?" I cry. "Those crack-smoking jerries just stole two Louis Vuitton Pegase cases."

Now it's Laney's turn to look around the room for a translator. I don't need to peek in her hotel room closet to know she's probably toting a plastic daisy-covered roller bag. I sigh and sink to the bed, cradling my little orphaned Louis.

"I'm sorry this happened to you, Fanny." Laney takes a seat beside me and we sit quietly for a few seconds. "It sucks."

"Totes."

We laugh.

"What am I going to do now? I only have the clothes on my back." I stretch my legs out in front of me. "Something tells me 7 For All Mankind skinny jeans and six-inch heels aren't gonna cut it in Sitka."

Laney hops to her feet.

"Come on," she says, heading toward the door. "Stow your travel case and let's go talk to the front desk clerk. Maybe she can tell us where there's a Target."

"Target?" The word came out more as a strangled cry than a question.

Laney stops at the door and looks back at me. "What's wrong with Target?"

There's no way to answer her question without sounding like an insufferable prig, so I just stare at her polka-dot Peter Pan collar blouse beneath her vintage store cardigan. Target does yoga pants, Hanes tees, and Playtex bras, but I am pretty sure it doesn't do hipster.

Chapter 15

Meet-Cute

Text from Curtis Bower:
You've become a cause célèbre, darling. I had some tees made with J'Abhor L'Horreur, We Love Fanny, and Fabulous Fanny for Hire, and I've been selling them around Haight-Ashbury and The Castro. Mycastro. com interviewed me (off the record). The grassroots movement to exonerate Fanny has officially commenced.

Text to Curtis Bower:
I appreciate what you're doing & I like the slogans, but please be careful, Lady Loafers. If Nicola finds out, she'll have you sacked.

Text from Curtis Bower:
I don't care if Maleficent fires me. My fairy tale does not begin and end with L'Heure. I am working on a sexier happily ever after.

"I am so sorry, ma'am, but the Klondike is not responsible for lost or stolen items." The front desk clerk taps a laminated sign affixed to the counter with her unmanicured fingernail. "It even says so right here."

"My suitcases weren't sitting unattended in the lobby, they were locked in my room." I resist the urge to throttle Mistress Obvious and keep my tone pleasant. "Surely the hotel assumes some responsibility for failing to provide adequate security?"

The desk clerk looks around helplessly, like an Alaskan deer caught in a rusty old pickup's headlights. I have to draw in several calming breaths.

"Maybe we could talk to one of your security guards," Laney suggests in a perky tone.

"Guard."

"Excuse me?"

"Guard. We only have one security guard, and he is out today for personal reasons."

Convenient. Klondike's only security guard takes a vacation day, and meth heads break into my room—the only room filled with expensive luggage. Coincidence? I don't think so.

I shift my gaze from the clerk to the digital clock hanging on the wall behind her. It's already six o'clock, which means it's nearly time for the Yukon Jacks to close up shop so they can head back to their cabins to feast on Caribou stew. I am assuming a claptrap town like Anchorage is locked down by sunset. Actually, the sun set hours ago.

"Look," I say, giving the clerk poor-me sad eyes. "I know it's not your fault that someone waltzed into the hotel, broke into my room, and absconded with tens of thousands of dollars' worth of my belongings, but I am leaving Anchorage tomorrow, and I only have the clothes on my back. I don't even have clean undergarments. Are there any stores nearby? Somewhere I could go to purchase necessities?"

Like a gun, so I can track down your security guard, the meth heads who stole my luggage, and the person who thought it would be charming to establish an American city fifty-five miles east of Siberia?

"Oh, there are several clothing stores in SoNo."

"SoNo?"

"South of Nordstrom," the clerk says, pulling out a map and a Sharpie. "Downtown Anchorage is divided into two parts: South of Nordstrom and North of Nordstrom. SoNo and NoNo."

She bisects the city by drawing a fat red line across the map. I literally have to press my hand to my mouth to restrain the hysterical laughter bubbling up my throat. SoNo and NoNo? Are you kidding me? Anchorage's equatorial line was decided by a single department store?

The clerk pivots around and looks at the orange glowing digital clock.

"I am not sure what time Nordstrom closes, but you can try there." She uses the Sharpie to outline the route from the hotel to the all-important Nordstrom store. "You might also want to stop in at About Face. It's a lingerie and beauty boutique. And Blush has pretty clothes."

She hands me the map.

"Great," I say, clutching my purse. "Would you please ask the valet to hail a cab?"

She tilts her head and wrinkles her nose, as if trying to translate my simple request from ancient Greek to Anchorage-speak.

"I don't think they have a valet, Stéphanie," Laney leans close and whispers in my ear. "The Klondike is kinda bijou."

Never has a more true statement been uttered.

"Never mind."

I look at the map and count the blocks between the Klondike and the SoNo shopping district. One. Two. Three. Four. Four mean, hostile blocks standing between me and my retail sanctuary. I can almost hear the soothing piped-in classical music, smell the comforting waft of Chanel Number Five. Proper cosmetics counters, a designer handbag department, round tables artfully arranged with Franco Sarto boots and Jimmy Choo heels. Maybe I could apply to the manager for amnesty. Every Nordies has a café. I wouldn't even have to venture beyond her walls for food.

Laney and I are rolling my orphaned Louis across the lobby—because there was no way I was leaving him again—when the clerk calls out.

"Ms. Moreau?"

"Yes?"

"If Nordstrom doesn't have everything you need, I would be happy to run to Walmart after my shift."

I might be an über-retail snob, as Vivian would say, but the clerk's generous offer almost brings me to tears. Random acts of kindness by friendlies in a hostile zone always have that effect on me.

"Thank you," I say, and I mean it.

Laney and I roll out of the Klondike and begin our "arduous" four block walk to the no-fire zone. I have never been a big Nordies girl, but I am beginning to think of it as the only safe area in this hostile land of human-hungry bears and panty-pinching jerries.

"Thanks for coming with me, Laney."

"No probs." She tosses one end of her daffodil yellow scarf over her shoulder. "It's what any decent suite mate would do. You would have done the same for me if those jerries had stolen my suitcases."

Would I have been as compassionate if I had stumbled upon Laney crying over her lost luggage? Hmmm. I don't think so. It's not that I am cold-hearted. I care about people. I really do. It's just…compassion doesn't come easy for me. I have to work at it. Maybe I was born with a compassion gene deficiency. Maybe I was supposed to learn that skill from my parents, but my mom died when I was a baby, and my father left me to the care of nannies and boarding school matrons. Whatever the cause, I seem to be missing the ability to demonstrate softer emotions. I was supportive and gentle with Vivian after she lost her fiancé and job, but that's because she is my best friend.

"Hello, Fanny?" Laney waves her daffodil yellow gloved hand in front of my face. "Are you chasing unicorns?"

"I'm sorry," I say, smiling sheepishly at my new friend. "What did you say?"

"I asked if you were off chasing unicorns."

"I don't know what that means, Laney."

"It means you're a million miles away. What's eating you, Gilbert Grape?"

"I was just thinking about my best friend, Vivian."

"Ooo, I love hearing BFF meet-cute stories." She reaches over and takes my carry-on from me. "Tell me yours."

"Meet-cute?"

"Yeah, you know, the way you met."

"We met when we were still in college."

"You went to the same college, then?"

"No." My breath comes out in a cottony puff. "We went to different colleges."

"Roommates?"

"Nope.

"Ooo-kay, you've successfully built up the suspense, now give me the big dramatic ending."

I laugh. "It's not that cute of a meet story, really. We met in a dive bar."

"Seedy. I like it. Go on."

"Not a real dive bar. A Dive Bar is the name of a popular *taqueria* and *cerveceria* in San Francisco." I laugh again. "Actually, come to think of it, maybe it was a little seedy."

"Yes!" She fist pumps the air. "Proceed."

Laney is really funny. Bizarre, but funny. She reminds me of an airier version of Vivian.

"Vivian was on a *tragique* blind date."

"Was the guy a complete uggo?"

I assume uggo is Laney-speak for ugly. "No, not entirely."

"What made it so *tragique* then?"

"Vivian didn't want to go on the date, but her mom pressured her into going. You have to know Vivian's mom. She's…"

…an older version of you, actually. A bit random and kooky, with high-octane speech, and a take-charge personality.

"…very persuasive. Anyway, Vivian had a miserable cold. Fever. Cough. Body aches. The whole works."

"Why didn't she just cancel?"

"Vivian's a pleaser."

"Ah."

"And the guy sent her four dozen roses. Who does that before a first date?"

"Frodos."

"Translate, *s'il vous plaît*."

"Frodo. A short, hairy hobbit with a huge heart. Frodos know they're not the hottest creatures in the realm, so they amp up the affection and generosity." She shakes her head. "Sad, really."

"I've had my share of Frodos...and catfish."

"Oo, now that sounds like a story I would like to hear."

"Another time."

"Promise?"

"*Oui*."

"So, Vivian the pleaser was manipulated by her momma and handled by the hobbit. Poor girl. Then what happened?"

"Her date showed up. Maybe it was the cold. Maybe it was his super handsy, super chatty personality, but Vivian was not into him. Anyway, she had taken a few Sudafed before the date. By the time their meals arrived, Vivian was super drowsy. Her date excused himself to go to the men's room, and when he returned, he found her face down in a plate of guacamole."

"Like, asleep?"

"Like, passed out." I laugh as I remember Vivian staggering into the bathroom, guacamole smeared across her face. "Sound asleep. Hair in the salsa, drool on her chin."

"Ohmygod."

"I walked into the ladies room and found her bent over the sink, trying to wash the salsa out of her hair. She was a mess. The water was spilling out of the sink and soaking the front of her blouse, her makeup was a disaster, and her cheeks were flushed from the fever."

"What did you do?"

"What could I do? I washed the salsa out of her hair, picked the guacamole out of her ear, gave her my cardigan, and called her a cab."

"And you've been best friends ever since."

"Not exactly."

Laney makes a rolling motion with her hand as if to say, "Go on. Go on. Tell me the rest of the story."

"I thought Vivian was a sad train wreck, not best friend material. She proved me wrong. She returned my sweater with homemade cookies and tickets to go to a concert."

"You went to the concert and became soul sisters?"

"Nope."

Laney slants me a frustrated look and sighs.

"I thanked her for the cookies and declined the concert invite. Most people would just fade away, but not Vivian. She kept coming back, bringing me little gifts, and inviting me to parties. So eventually, reluctantly, I became her friend."

"That's soooo sweet."

"Vivian is the best thing that almost didn't happen in my life." I have to swallow a lump of emotion. "I say I became her friend, but really, she became mine. I think she sensed I was lonely, and that's why she kept jumping all of the hurdles I threw in front of her. She's got the biggest heart."

"It sounds like your awkward meet-cute developed into an awesome friendship."

We arrive at the entrance to Nordstrom. I am reaching for the door to hold it open for Laney when a small voice inside my head says, "Laney is kind and easy to talk to. If you knock down a barrier, she might become your next two a.m. friend."

"Laney?" I turn around and look at her, but the words get stuck in my throat. "I…I was feeling lonely and lost before you came into my room. Thanks for being kind to me. I really appreciate it."

She tilts her head and her glasses slide down her nose. "No prob, Fanny. I know losing your luggage totes sucks, but you have to admit it made for a wicked awesome meet-cute."

Chapter 16

Getting Humped

Text from Poppy Worthington:
V told me what happened at L'Heure. She said you're headed to Siberia
to live in an ostrog and teach sewing to convicts. I think she was joking,
but one can never be sure with Vivia. Beating a hasty retreat might be
quintessentially French, but it is not you. Don't give up, Frenchie. Ditch
the convicts. Apply at Chanel.

Poppy's text hits my phone as I am hopping around the fitting room
on one foot, struggling to shove my other leg into a pair of Rag & Bone
stretch skinny jeans.

Poppy Worthington is a blue-blooded socialite and the heiress of the
Worthington Hotels fortune. Vivian introduced us last year when we all
went on a vacation to a working sheep farm in the Highlands. I hated
Poppy when I first met her. I hated her clipped patois, uninspired Burberry
plaid poncho, habit of pointing out etiquette faux pas, and her blossoming
friendship with my best friend. More than anything, I hated her because
she was *très* British.

My abhorrence for Poppy and her Burberry checkered wardrobe
lessened upon further contact. We eventually bonded over Amaretto-
spiked hot chocolate and an Ashton Kutcher movie.

She sent me a few emails after our trip, but I had been too busy with
work to respond.

And that is why you don't have many two a.m. friends.

I zip up the skinnies and collapse on the padded bench. My breath is
leaving my body in sharp, shallow bursts, and it is not because the jeans
are too tight. I feel like someone just used my abdomen as a speed bag.
That I am the only one to blame for my tragically anorexic friends list
literally hurts.

When I would see a group of women my age laughing together in a restaurant, I would tell myself I was too busy to indulge in silly pajama parties—that's what I call girlfriend get-togethers. Vivian is big on pajama parties. I used to tease her about her Chick Flick Fridays and Pedi Parties.

Oh, wah! Poor me! I don't have pajama party pals. It's time I stop whining and do something.

I read Poppy's text again and type my response.

Text to Poppy Worthington:
Chanel doesn't want me. D&G, Prada, & Bautista don't want me either, but that's okay because I have come up with a new career plan. We'll pool our resources & buy a sheep farm. You can take care of the sheep & I'll knit fabulous ponchos. LOL

Poppy's response hits my phone in seconds, which is amazing since it is a little after four in the morning in London.

Text from Poppy Worthington:
What an absobloodylutely ace idea! I'm in.

I laugh. I haven't heard that ridiculous synthetic word since our trip to Scotland. It annoyed me then, but it makes me feel warm and connected now.

I slip my phone into my purse, pull the skinnies off, slip my old jeans back on, and exit the fitting room.

"Well?" Laney says, smiling hopefully. "Are you going to get those rags for your bones?"

"Yes," I say, chuckling at her pun.

Laney has been a godsend. She guarded my bag while I tried on clothes, thoughtfully recommended I purchase a pair of thermal leggings, and found a beautiful cashmere Missoni scarf and gloves set on the clearance table.

Two hours later, I am rolling a new Longchamp hard shell suitcase filled with sweaters, jeans, undergarments, flannel pajamas—Vivian would squeal with victorious glee—and two pairs of... wait for it ... Ugg boots! Two pairs of hideous, but practical, overpriced sheepskin footgear. One in versatile black suede and the other a pseudo riding look in brown leather and suede.

We are rolling my cases down Sixth Avenue, past a city park with pine trees decorated with glowing blue Christmas lights, when I suddenly realize Laney has been so busy helping me, she hasn't even had a chance to eat dinner.

"Laney, it's getting late. Aren't you hungry?"

"A little." She maneuvers around a slushy puddle. "I had some yogurt-covered lingonberries at the airport gift shop."

"That's it?"

She nods.

"You've been such a help today. I would like to buy you dinner to thank you."

"No worries."

"Please?"

She shrugs. "If you insist."

"I do."

An elderly man with a grizzled beard is coming toward us, so I stop and ask him if he could recommend a good restaurant. He narrows his eyes and then turns his head and spits a stream of tobacco-brown saliva onto the snow-packed sidewalk.

"Humpy's," he says, looking back at me.

"I...I beg your pardon?"

"Humpy's Alehouse. They make the best steamer crabs this side of Valdez."

"Ooo-kay," I say, trying not to stare at the enormous gap between his two tobacco-stained front teeth. "Could you tell me where to find Humpy's?"

There's a sentence I never expected to utter.

"I could."

I wait, but Copenhagen Charlie doesn't speak. He just reaches into his pocket, pulls out a can of chew, pinches some leaves into his mouth, and grins.

"Are we close?"

"Couldn't get much closer."

He points across the street to a stone building. The word HUMPY'S is painted in big block letters over the door with a mural of a prehistoric-looking fanged fish.

"Thanks," I say.

He spits again and continues on his way.

I look at the fanged fish and back at Laney.

"Do you want to find another place? There's got to be a few more restaurants downtown."

"Are you kidding?" Laney steps off the curb and starts crossing the street toward the fanged fish. "We can't pass up an opportunity to eat at a place called Humpy's."

I look around the square for another restaurant, but only find a pizzeria with a bright blinking closed sign in the window.

"Come on, Fanny." Laney looks over her shoulder and smiles. "Let's get our hump on!"

We enter the loud, dimly lit restaurant, shivering against the sudden blast of heated air. A hostess wearing a T-shirt with the slogan, "I got crabs at Humpy's" greets us and asks if we would prefer to sit in the dining room or on the terrace.

I look at Laney and send her a telepathic message. *Inside. Please say inside.* Laney must be proficient in telepathy, because she asks the waitress for a table in the dining room.

She leads us past the bar crowded with fleece-wearing locals cracking gigantic red king crab legs in half and picking the flaky meat out with their fingers. The hostess stops at a small table near a makeshift stage.

"Jessica will be your server tonight," the hostess says, handing us two plastic menus. "Enjoy your meal."

"This place is so indie," Laney says as soon as the hostess is out of earshot.

"Indie?"

"Yeah." Laney smiles. "Indie. As in, original. As in, the opposite of mainstream."

"Is that good?"

"Totes."

A blonde with a long side-parted fishtail braid approaches our table.

"Welcome to Humpy's," she says. "My name is Jessica and I will be serving you tonight. Why don't we start with drinks? What can I get ya?"

"Can you recommend a good local beer?" Laney asks.

"Sure," Jessica says. "How do you like your beer? Thick and stouty? Pale? Fruity?"

Fruity. If I were in Monaco, I would put one hundred down on Laney liking fruity beer.

"Definitely fruity!"

Laney tilts her head and I have to bite my lip to keep from laughing. She's so quirky and cute. I'll bet she has contact book full of two a.m. friends.

"Then I would recommend Broken Tooth Hard Apple Ale or the Woodchuck Pear and Berry."

"Oooo!" Laney coos and claps her hands. "Pear and berry, please."

"And what about you?"

Jessica the waitress is staring at me, but I have suddenly noticed the tagline on her T-shirt and find myself at a loss for words. I stare at the cartoon prehistoric fish emblazoned across her chest and read the words beneath it again: Humpy's Great Alaskan Ale—because there's nothing like a dry hump.

She notices me staring at her chest and her cheeks stain a violent crimson. Ohmygod! She probably thinks I am a lesbian—not that there is anything wrong with being a lesbian. People on our bike tour through Provence thought Vivian and I were lesbians...

"Ma'am?"

"I would love a glass of Chardonnay." I avert my gaze, pretending to study the drink menu. "Do you have any wines from the Beaujolais region? Perhaps a Domaine Béranger or a Chateau Montmelas?"

"Err, domaine what?"

"Never mind," I say. "Just bring me a glass of whatever Napa white you have in your cellar."

"Yeah." Jessica puts her hand on her hip. "We don't have a cellar. We have a storeroom, but I am pretty sure we don't have anything from Beaujangles."

"Beaujolais. It's a region in France."

Jessica rolls her eyes. "We don't sell wine, but could I interest you in a vintage bottle of beer from the Kodiak region?"

"Do you have Belgian beer?"

"Sure," she sighs. "We have King's Street Holy Water and The Monk's Mistress."

"I'll take the Monk's Mistress."

"Fine." She takes our drink menus. "I'll be back to take your dinner orders."

Laney widens her eyes and whistles. It's clear from her expression she is equally astounded by Jessica's snotty behavior.

"I know, right?"

"You sure put her through the paces."

"What? Me? What do you mean?"

"Look around." Laney laughs. "We are in a dive bar...in Alaska. There's a stuffed fish hanging over the bar, and our waitress is wearing a shirt that says she likes to dry hump. Does this look like a place that serves a 2000 Le Petit Mouton de Mouton Rothschild?"

"Did I sound snobby?"

She holds up her fingers and makes a pinching gesture. *"Un peu."*

"Sorry."

"No worries." Laney smiles softly. "You picked guacamole from a stranger's ear."

"So?"

"So, a snobby person would never pick guacamole from a stranger's ear, let alone give her their cashmere sweater."

I shift in my seat. Normally, I would change the subject, because talking about touchy-feely things makes me extremely uncomfortable, but I suddenly remember the Father True Allight article and have an epiphany. Papa Light said true joy isn't obtained through the pursuit of selfish pleasure. Being stingy with thoughts and affections is a selfish act, isn't it? I have been selfish in my relationships—listening as other's share their problems, doling out advice, but never reciprocating. Keeping my feelings buried deep inside and shutting anyone down who tries to unearth them has been another of my barriers.

"Do-do do-do," Laney sings, waving her hand in front of my face. "You've just crossed over into…bum bum bum…the Twilight Zone?"

I blink. "What?"

"Are you okay? You kinda zoned."

"Sorry. I was just thinking about something."

"Unload."

"Excuse me?"

"Unload those heavy thoughts, Frenchie." She grabs her paper napkin and folds it into a triangle. "It's obvious you are carrying one totes heavy burden."

"How?"

She stops folding the napkin and looks at me, a frown creasing her brow. "How what?"

"How is it obvious?"

"Oh." She resumes her napkin origami. "Your aura."

"My aura?"

"Yes," she says, looking at me over the top of her glasses. "An aura is simply the life-energy emanated by a person that is represented through colors. You can tell a lot about a person by reading their aura."

Mon dieu! I am too French to put much stock in spirituality—whether it be inspired by the New Testament or the New Age. But didn't Father Allight say one must live spherically, be open to new ideas and experiences, to truly experience joy?

The waitress arrives with our beers. We decide to split the Humpy's Special, two pounds of steamed Alaskan king crab served with drawn butter. I wait for Jessica to leave, and then I take a swig of my "Belgian" beer and ask Laney if she would tell me what she saw when she looked at my aura.

"Well," she says, tilting her head and fixing her gaze on me. "Your crown chakra is purplish, which means your higher consciousness is guiding you to look at your relationships. You are learning how to love and be loved in return, but it's not an easy, joyful process. It will get easier, though, as you learn to release your innate goodness."

Okay, I am a little freaked out by Laney's uncanny reading of my love situation. I take another sip of my beer.

Laney squints. "Do you want me to go on?"

"Yes, please."

"Your base chakra is totes brown, which indicates a tendency to be stubborn, competitive, and materialistic. I see some movement there, though, which is good." She nods her head, and her glasses slip down her nose again. "I see some gray around your hands, which tells me you are exhausted, drained, maybe a little depressed."

Merde! I don't know about emanating colors and reading auras, but Laney is on the mark with her assessment of my...life force. I *am* drained and depressed.

"I am sorry," she says, shoving her glasses up on her nose. "I know it can be tough to hear that your aura isn't balanced and healthy."

"Great." I will not cry. I will not cry. "I have an unbalanced, ill aura. I wonder if Each One, Teach One's insurance plan covers visits to aura healers."

Laney snorts. "Nobody can heal your aura but you."

"So I'm a hopeless case, then?"

"No way!" She holds her napkin up. She has made an origami swan. "Your aura is like this napkin. It might have started out flat, square, but look at it now...transformed. You are like this napkin, Fanny. You are transforming into something totes spec."

"Spec?"

"Spectacular."

"You think?"

Laney nods her head. "I *know*."

I take another sip of my beer—a little shot of liquid courage—and then I tell Laney about Father True Allight, my mission statement, and my real reason for volunteering with Each One, Teach One.

"That's awesome!"

"It is?"

"Shyeah!" She pumps her fist as if I just finished a marathon. "Don't you see? You felt you were imbalanced, so you did something that would knock down your precariously constructed life. You're starting over, but this time you are going to use joy and insight to rebuild. It's empowering. It's beyond spec!"

"Okay, then," I say, raising my beer bottle. "Here's to healthy chakras."

"And new friends," Laney says, clinking her bottle against mine.

"And new friends."

Jessica arrives with a heaping plate of king crab and a bowl of melted golden artery-clogging butter. I mentally calculate the calories in a pound of king crab sans butter—approximately 380—and two Belgian beers— at least 300— but I stop short of calculating the time I will need to spend pounding the frozen pavement to work off those calories. The new Fanny isn't going to stress about calories...not obsessively, anyway.

"Tell me about you, Laney," I say, cracking a crustacean leg in half. "Where are you from?"

"Boulder, Colorado."

"Colorado is beautiful."

"Have you been to Boulder?"

I shake my head and dip some crab meat into the butter. "I've been to Vail, though. I went skiing there a few years ago."

"With Vivian?"

"No." I grimace. "An ex-boyfriend."

"That sounds romantic."

"It wasn't." I pop the buttery meat into my mouth, chew, and swallow. "He was a pervert."

I don't tell her that he was a proctologist with a penchant for smutty jokes and anal sex.

"Why did you volunteer to come to Sitka, Laney?"

She shrugs. "I wanted to do something. Ya know?"

"Weren't you doing anything in Boulder?"

"No." She shakes her head, and her fringy bangs move back and forth over the rims of her glasses. "Nothing of substance, anyway."

"What did you do in Boulder? I mean, were you going to school or working?"

"I graduated from the University of Colorado Boulder with a dual degree in Arts and Music three years ago. Since then, I've shown a few pieces in local galleries, worked part-time at the Art Museum in Denver, volunteered with an artist co-op teaching handicapped kids to paint, and picked up a few gigs with my band, but I just felt..."

"What?"

"Unfulfilled."

I think about the life I led in San Francisco—working overtime, working out, always working, working, working—to get a raise, get a new purse, get some praise. If someone as spherical as Laney could feel unfulfilled with her coops and creative outlets, it's no wonder I felt unfulfilled.

"So," she says, smiling brightly. "I am headed to Sitka to teach their indigenous people art utilizing recycled materials and environmentally friendly paints."

By the time we make our way back to the Klondike, we have demolished a pound of king crab, consumed several beers, listened to the Wailin' Palins, a blues rock band with a lead singer who looks a lot like Sarah Palin, and bonded in a big, big way.

Chapter 17

Karma is Queer

Text from Vivia Perpetua Grant:
Um, yeah, I'm running out of designer failure-to-success stories. Don't Monet, though! I still have a little pep talk for you. Did you know Van Gogh only sold one painting before he lopped off his ear and killed himself? Keep trying to make the world beautiful, Fanny, and no matter how blue you get, please remember you need two ears to wear earrings.

When I return to my room, the little red message light is blinking, and my heart does a silly flip. Maybe the message is from Calder.

I grab the handset, jab the message button, and hold my breath, but the voice on the other end of the line is definitely not Calder's deep, sexy brogue.

"Hello Ms. Moreau, this is Paige, from the front desk. I contacted the Anchorage Police Department about your stolen luggage. They said you need to file a report at their station on K Street, but I explained you were flying to Sitka in the morning. If you call Sergeant Packwood at 907-786-8525, he will take a report over the phone. I also talked to our security guard. He promised to review the security footage first thing tomorrow morning. I hope you were able to purchase a few necessities. Goodnight and have a safe flight."

I hang up the phone and fall back onto the bed. There's a possibility the police will catch the tweakers who stole my luggage. I might even be reunited with my beloved Louis Vs. I should be ecstatic, but I just don't care. A tiny voice whispers in my head, *Admit it, you'd trade your luggage and Louboutins for a call from Calde*r.

* * * *

It is still dark out the next morning when Laney knocks on my door. I have already done my hotel room workout, showered, dressed, packed my new suitcases, and phoned Sergeant Packwood.

"*Bonjour,* Fanny!" Laney chirps. "*Êtes-vous prêt pour le petit déjeuner?*"

"*Tu parle français?*"

"*Oui.*"

Laney is one of the most unpredictable people I have ever met. She doesn't fit any specific stereotype. She's part breezy hipster and part wise sage. One minute she's spouting new age gibberish about auras, and the next she's standing in the hall outside my room, a furry panda hat on her head, speaking fluent French.

"*On se bouge.*"

We start our power walk from the Klondike to the Snow City Café, a popular diner reputed to serve the "best breakfast in Alaska." I am not a morning person, so I am hoping Laney doesn't want to engage in mind-numbing chitchat. The cold is numbing enough, *merci beaucoup*!

I expect Laney to be like Vivian—someone who leaps out of bed with irritating, boundless enthusiasm. Vivian even sings a song. *Merde!* Now I hear Vivian's voice in my head. Good morning, Good morning, it's great to stay up late. Good morning, good morning, to you.

Vivian says the song is from some classic Hollywood musical, but I think she made it up just to annoy me. I don't wake up with my best friend's effervescence and optimism. I just want to sip my two espressos and be left alone until at least midday.

Thankfully, Laney appears to be a reluctant riser too.

"How do you like your new boots?" Laney's breath billows from her lips, forming small mushroom clouds. "Are they comfy?"

So Laney is a talker. Fine, just please, please, don't let her start singing.

"Actually," I say, wiggling my toes against the sheepskin insole. "They are the ugliest footwear ever created, after those clunky Danskos clogs and plastic Crocs, but they are quite comfy."

"I love my Uggs."

"So does Vivian. She tried to talk me into getting a pair years ago by saying they were as 'warm and comfy as a pair of slippers.'" I laugh. "Not the most persuasive argument. Do we really need to wear our slippers in public?"

"You're Parisian, which means you take particular offense to anything that is not beautiful," Laney reasons.

"*C'est vrai!*" I think of the women who wear yoga pants to the grocery store and shudder. "Americans don't get it. You don't dress to make yourself feel good, you dress so you don't make others feel bad."

"Perhaps," Laney says, picking up the pace. "Or maybe people use clothes to express what they are afraid to say out loud."

"What do you mean?"

"Have you ever considered that you dress in expensive, trendy clothes to impress others or to keep them at arm's length because you're afraid they might not like what's underneath?"

Wow! That stings.

"So my clothes are just a way to say, 'I am worth getting to know.'"

"Or they're saying, 'I am afraid you won't think I am worth getting to know so I am going to intimidate you with my fancy labels.'"

"Wow," I gasp. "You're not afraid to go deep, are you?"

"Sorry." Laney shrugs. "I don't do superficial."

And there it is—the reason I don't let people close. Laney hasn't even known me a full twenty-four hours, and already she has decided I am as shallow as a puddle.

Laney suddenly stops walking. I stop walking too, but it takes me a few seconds to muster up the courage to look at her. When I do, there's no judgment, no condemnation, just kindness and sympathy reflected in her big bespectacled blue eyes.

"You don't need Coco Chanel and Christian Dior to impress people. All you need is Stéphanie Moreau." She grabs my hand and squeezes it. "You're enough."

A powerful wave of déjà vu washes over me. Two years ago, I gave Vivian similar advice. Be authentic. Keep it real. Now, the universe has done one of those queer Karma things, and I am the one being told to be authentic and keep it real.

* * * *

"Ladies and gentlemen, as we start our descent into beautiful Sitka, please make sure your seat backs and tray tables are in their full upright position. Make sure your seat belt is securely fastened and all carry-on luggage is stowed underneath the seat in front of you or in the overhead bins. Please turn off all electronic devices until we are safely parked at the gate. Thank you for flying Alaskan Airlines."

"This is it, Fanny!" Laney says, squeezing my hand. "The beginning of our new beginnings."

I raise the shade and we look out the window. The sky is thick with heavy purplish clouds that hang low over the snow-covered mountains and cast the city in an ethereal lavender light. Sitka is small and low-slung, clinging to the base of the mountains as if it is afraid it will slip into the sea and float away.

"*Il est très joli, non?*" I am not putting my PR spin on it. Sitka really is quite beautiful.

"It looks like an impressionist painting, doesn't it?" Laney sighs. "Like Monet got bored with his gardens and water lilies and started painting mountains and frosted trees instead."

The plane banks sharply to the right as we make the final approach into Sitka, affording us a view of the narrow, frighteningly short runway. The airport is located on an islet that appears to be connected to the mainland by a single bridge. If the pilot makes the tiniest of miscalculations, the plane will slide off the runway into the sea. Takeoffs and landings terrify me. Always have.

The plane levels off. We are flying so low over the water I feel I could reach my hand out the window and grab one of the milky-white ice floes floating in the harbor. They look like jagged pieces of a puzzle.

I am not sure which crash scenario would be worse: being doused in jet-fuel and burned alive, or being trapped in your seat while your airplane plunges into an icy ocean. I think I would prefer the fiery ball over the watery coffin. I saw *Titanic*. I do not want to pull a Rose, floating aimlessly on flotsam, slowly becoming a human Popsicle. No thanks.

I grip the armrests, close my eyes, and count—*un, deux, trois, quatre, cinq*. The rear wheels touch down and we are speeding down the runway, brakes screaming, front wheels bouncing.

When the commuter jet finally comes to a stop, I open my eyes and stare out the window at the sign affixed to the small airport. *Welcome to Sitka Rocky Gutierrez Airport.*

Four minutes later, we have deplaned and retrieved our luggage from baggage carousel number one. That the airport bothered to number the carousel fills me with no amount of sardonic glee. There is only one baggage carousel at the Sitka Airport. Perhaps designating their only carousel as number one was an act of tremendous optimism. "We better call this carousel number one. Someday, we might have two carousels and we wouldn't want folks to get confused."

The moment we step out of the heated airport, Sitka gives us the ultimate "fuck you" greeting. A bitterly cold wind slaps us in the face and leaves us gasping for breath. It is not skiing in Aspen cold. It is a brutal survival of the fittest kind of cold. The kind of deep in your bones cold that can't be cured with a brandy-spiked hot cocoa and thermal blanket.

We huddle close, stomping our feet and rubbing our hands together, as we wait for a cab. An eternity passes before a blue-and-gold taxi pulls to a stop in front of us. The driver pops the trunk but doesn't get out to help us with our bags.

"I guess it's Donner Party Rules," I say, glaring at the back of the taxi driver's head. "Every woman for herself."

Laney giggles as she hoists her luggage into the trunk, but I am less amused by our driver's refusal to assist us with our bags. *Il est impoli.*

It's just rude.

I load my bags, shut the trunk with more force than necessary, and join Laney in the backseat of the cab.

"Where to?" the driver asks, looking over his shoulder.

"Good Morning to you too," I say, smirking. "We need to go to 1102 Sockeye Circle."

He whistles and shakes his head. "No can do."

"I beg your pardon."

"I can't drive you there."

"What? Why not?" I am hanging on to the very fringes of my temper, and this man does not want me to let go. "This is a taxi, isn't it?"

"Yep."

I swivel my head in all directions, looking at the inside of the taxi with wide, bewildered eyes.

"I am new to this area, so perhaps you could enlighten me. Do taxi drivers in Sitka perform the same functions as the taxi drivers in the lower forty eight?"

"Ma'am?"

I look at the laminated vehicle for hire permit affixed to the passenger side visor. His name is Alexi Baranov.

"Ah, I see we are having a cultural misunderstanding, Mister Baranov. Allow me to explain. In the lower forty-eight, taxi drivers load a customer's luggage into the trunk and then drive them wherever they want to go for an outrageously exorbitant fee." I lean my back against the manky upholstered seat and cross my arms. "Tell me, what are the transportation customs in this strange land?"

Laney gasps. I know I am being condescending, but I can't help myself. A shroud of apprehension and melancholy settled upon me the moment we stepped out of the airport. It happens every time I move somewhere new. I usually become apprehensive, and then irritable, and then depressed. It's my process. I just need to get to my new home, claim my space, drink some wine, and cry myself to sleep…and Alexi Baranov is interrupting my process.

"I would drive you where you want to go, but the road is closed."

"What do you mean it is closed?"

"We had a pretty big snowstorm last night. Most of the major roads are clear, but some of the smaller ones haven't been plowed yet."

Laney and I exchange worried glances.

"Mister Baranov," Laney says, leaning forward. "We have come to Sitka to teach with a charitable organization. We need to get to 1102 Sockeye. What do you recommend?"

"I can take you to Halibut Point Road where it intersects with Sockeye Circle, but you will have to walk the rest of the way."

"Is it far?"

"Nope."

"How far would you say 1102 Sockeye is from Halibut Place?"

"Point," he says, putting the car into gear. "It's Halibut Point. And it's not far. Maybe half a mile."

"A half a mile? Is that all?" I turn to look at Laney. "I do a half mile just to get my afternoon frappe. We got this one."

Chapter 18

Snagging a Lumbersexual

"We so don't have this one, Fanny!"

The taxi has just pulled away. We are standing at the bottom of a steep snow-covered road, clutching the handles of our rolling suitcases, and gazing up at a big, beautiful log cabin perched at the top of the hill. Trudging up the hill would be a crazy hard cardio workout, even if we weren't dragging sixty-five pound bags and Laney's guitar case.

"What the"—I draw in a deep breath and let the last word explode from my lips in one violent exhalation—"fuck?"

An endless stream of French curses flows from my mouth as I look around for a gondola, chair lift, or any motorized conveyance capable of ferrying two women and nearly two hundred pounds of luggage up the mini-Mount Everest. But all I see is snow, snow, and more snow.

The Each One, Teach One facilities are located on the outskirts of town. This is a laughable concept in itself as Sitka is barely a town. It's more of a quasi-village. Halibut Point Road, it turns out, is the major thoroughfare, skirting along the coast from one end of town to the other.

"What are we going to do?"

This is the first time I have detected anything less than buoyant optimism in Laney's tone. I look at her face. Her lips are quivering. Tears tremble on the ends of her thick lashes. The irrepressible perky girl has left the building! Great! We've only been in Sitka for an hour and already they've beaten the bounce out of her.

"It's going to be okay," I say, grabbing her frozen hand and giving it a good squeeze. "We are strong, empowered, modern-day heroines, and this is merely a trifling inconvenience. We aren't going to let a silly old hill and some snow dampen our enthusiasm for the beginning of our new beginning, are we?"

She sniffles and shakes her head. The tears fall from her lashes and plop onto her pink cheeks. "But how are we going to get up this hill? The road is buried in snow."

Frankly, I don't know how we are going to get up a steep snowy hill. We each have a suitcase and carryon. Four pieces of luggage plus purses.

"Maybe we could hire a Sherpa."

Laney does one of those hiccup laugh-cry things, and it reminds me of Vivian. My best friend believes every person is put into your life for a reason. If that's true, maybe Laney is in my life to help me recolor my aura, and maybe I am in her life to take care of her, the same way I take care of Vivian. It's just what I do.

"I have an idea!" I open my suitcase, shove my hand inside, and pull out the belt of my new flannel robe. "We'll *be* Sherpas."

Laney frowns. "You're not suggesting we carry our luggage up the hill on our backs, are you?"

"Of course not," I chuckle. "That would be insane!"

I bend over, secure one end of the belt around the handle of Laney's suitcase, and make a loop just big enough for my hand at the other end.

"*Voila*!" I tip her suitcase over so the smooth plastic side is resting on the snow. I take a few steps, pulling Laney's suitcase behind me. Although my feet sink in the deep snow, her suitcase glides over it like a sled. I stop and turn around, grinning. "We can take turns pulling the bags up the hill. You stay here while I pull the first bag up."

"Are you sure?" Laney shields her eyes with her hand and looks up at the log cabin perched on the top of the hill. "It's a long way up."

"Bah!" I wave my free hand at her. "It's a hill, not a mountain. Besides, it probably isn't as tough as a seventy minute spin class or forty minutes max incline on the elliptical."

"If you're sure."

"I am sure."

I leave her standing on the side of the road beside an evergreen with sagging branches covered in thick, sparkling snow and begin my long, plodding trek to the cabin.

I have barely made it a quarter of the way up the hill when I realize this undertaking makes a seventy minute spin class seem like a bucolic ride in the park. The snow has spilled over the tops of my Uggs and soaked my heavy woolen socks. My calves are quivering—literally quivering—and my lungs feel as if they are about to explode. I stop, take several deep breaths of crisp, clean pine-scented air, and give myself a pep talk. You've biked Provence and Tuscany. You've run the San Francisco Marathon—three times. You can do this!

By the time I reach the top of the hill, my legs are wobbling worse than when I ran my first marathon. I drop to my knees on the circular drive and draw in ragged, wheezy breaths.

My newcomer's packet listed the names of the two other volunteers assigned to Sitka TTF. Since the facility is dark and there are no signs of life, I have to assume we are the first to arrive.

I stagger to my feet. I can do this! I carry Laney's suitcase up the stairs and set it down on the porch near the front doors. After untying my belt and shoving it into my pocket, I begin my trek back down the hill.

Laney chants my name and jumps up and down like a cheerleader encouraging her quarterback to lead their team to V-I-C-T-O-R-Y! Normally, such unbridled enthusiasm would irritate me, but I deserve to be cheered. Dragging seventy pounds a half mile up a steep incline is pararescue shit! In fact, the next time I meet a *général* in the *Armee de L'Air*, I am going to recommend he send his elite soldiers to Sitka for their training. I do, however, refrain from slamming my belt on the ground at Laney's feet and doing a celebratory dance.

I hand her the belt and collapse on the ground. My legs and lungs hurt worse than they ever did after any Body Combat class.

I am lying spread-eagle on the ground only two hundred feet from Halibut Point Road—Sitka's version of a main street—and I don't even care if my new neighbors drive by and see me lying prostrate in the snow. My pride is that obliterated. I close my eyes and concentrate on my breathing.

Laney is still tying the belt to my suitcase handle a vehicle with a monstrously loud engine turns off Halibut Point Road and pulls to a stop beside us. I should sit up, put my legs together, and try to manage a modicum of decorum, but my trembling limbs aren't listening to the signals my brain is sending them. Besides, what do I care if some random backwoods, bushy-bearded, beaver pelt-wearing fur trapper thinks about me, anyway?

A car door opens and slams. Laney lets out a low, long whistle. I hear snow crunching under heavy foot and then...

"I always ken I would have ye falling at my feet *banfhlath*, but I didn't think it would happen this fast."

Putain de merde! Cela ne se produit. I hold my breath and count to myself. *Un, deux, trois...* Maybe if I play dead, he'll go away. It works with brown bears. Or is it black bears?

"Have ye stopped breathing, lass?" He squats down beside me.

I catch a whiff of his woodsy cologne. This is really happening.

"Do I need to give ye mouth to mouth, then?"

I crack open an eye and find Calder's handsome face staring down at me, his broad shoulders blocking the sun and casting a shadow over me.

"What are you doing here?"

He stands and holds out his hand. I take it and feel a spark of electricity run up my arm.

"I came to see if ye needed help with yer bags."

I stare up into his handsome, arrogant, grinning face, and my pulse, which had returned to a normal rhythm, quickens. I suddenly realize he's still holding my hand. I pull it away, but my fingers continue to tingle as if I'd shoved them in an electrical outlet.

"*Merci beaucoup*," I say, shoving my hands in my pockets. "I can manage just fine though."

"Well, I can't!" Laney steps closer and holds her hand out to Calder. "I am Delaney Brooks, Fanny's new friend and co-worker."

"*Je suis desloée.*" I look from Calder to Laney. "It was rude of me not to introduce you. Laney, this is Calder MacFarlane. We met in Scotland last year, when he made a valiant but failed effort at seducing my best friend. Calder, this is Laney."

Calder's grin never slips, but I detect a tiny spark of something—perhaps humiliation, frustration, or excitement—in his blue eyes.

"Hello," he says, taking her hand and pressing a kiss to the back of it. "'Tis a pleasure to make yer acquaintance, lass."

Laney giggles and slides her glasses up her nose with her free hand.

"Calder, Calder, bo-balder. Banana-fana, fo-Falder. Fee fi, fo—"

I clasp my hand around Laney's forearm and give it a squeeze. She only misses a beat before resuming her ridiculous name game song.

"Calder! Calder Abbey. Calder Memorial Trophy. Alexander Calder!"

She snaps her fingers twice, like some kind of poetry reciting beatnik.

Have you ever noticed how much quieter the world becomes after someone has done something extremely embarrassing? It is so quiet I can hear Calder breathing. I am just about to explain Laney's odd name association game when he starts singing.

"Laney, Laney. Bo-baney. Banana-fana, fo-faney. Fee fi, mo maney. Laney!" Calder grins at Laney and she grins back. "I dinnea ken about that last part, though."

"Oh! That's simple," she explains. "I think of something that has the person's name in it and mentally attach it to them."

"Like Laney, Ireland?" he asks.

"Sure!" Laney looks as if she has found her kindred spirit. "Only, what about Ireland reminds you of me?"

"You're friendly. The Irish are friendly." Calder quickly answers. "But maybe I should have said Laney Amps, because ye like to sing."

"Nice."

They fist bump. Fist bump! Like two prepubescent mall rats. It's really...fucking irritating!

Don't ask me why their juvenile bonding ritual is irritating me so much. It just is. I mean, they've only just met, and already they are serenading and fist bumping each other.

You're just jealous.

I am not jealous.

Yes, you are. You envy them their easy camaraderie because being at ease around strangers is a social grace you have failed to master.

I look at Laney and Calder laughing together. My officious little conscious is right. I am envious of outgoing, charming people because I want to be a let's-hug-and-be-best-friends-forever kinda girl. I come off as snobbish around new people. Erecting an invisible barrier is a defense mechanism that protects me from the sting of rejection.

Also, I am French. French people aren't as open and welcoming as Americans. Americans are like big, loveable golden retrievers, bounding up with a ready supply of affection. The French are like suspicious cats, reluctant to approach and judicious with their attentions.

"Fanny?" Laney snaps her fingers in front of my face. "How's Rod Serling?"

"What?"

"You were in the Zone again."

"Sorry." A wave of heat washes over my body. "Hauling that suitcase up the hill must have depleted my energy. I can't seem to concentrate on anything except my aching quads."

Calder looks up the hill and then back at me, narrowing his blue eyes. "You didn't carry one of your steamer trunks up that hill. Did you?"

I nod my head and wince as a lightning-hot bolt of pain shoots down my spine, starting at my neck.

Calder chuckles and shakes his head. "You didn't need to do that, lass."

"The taxi driver refused to take us up the hill," I snap, shoving my hands on my hips and glaring up at the insufferable Scot. "What was I supposed to do?"

He shrugs. "I didn't ken, maybe set aside your bloody French pride and ask for help."

I look around. "And who was I supposed to ask?"

Calder crosses his muscular arms over his chest and grins.

"You?"

"Of course." He looks around. "That is, unless you have an army of wee Frenchmen hidden somewhere nearby capable of hauling your shoe trunks up the hill."

I roll my eyes, because I can't very well admit to the arrogant Scot that I actually considered sending him an SOS text.

"Your choice, *banfhlath*. What's it to be? A single able-bodied Scotsman or an army of wee weakly Frenchmen?"

I shift my gaze from Calder to his big, shiny blue Jeep Rubicon. My quads hurt so bad I want to cry. Hauling the rest of the luggage up the hill might kill me, but admitting I need Hottie McScottie's help will definitely kill me.

"I will take the Scotsman," Laney chimes, pushing my suitcase at Calder. "Every day of the week and twice on Sunday, thank you very much."

She marches over to the jeep, opens the back passenger door, kicks the snow off her boots, tosses her guitar case on the seat, and hops inside. She waggles her eyebrows at me before slamming the door.

"What about you? Will you take the Scotsman?"

My stomach flips, and the breath leaves my body in a quick rush. I have a slightly woozy, disoriented feeling that reminds me of rappelling, that moment right after I step off the ledge and am suspended in midair. Will I land it, or will I lose control and fall to my death? Pure adrenaline. That's what it feels like when Calder fixes his dimpled grin on me. A shot of pure white-hot adrenaline.

"A ride would be fabulous." I look him in the eye because I don't want him to know how much his flirting affects me. "Thank you."

"A ride?" His blue eyes twinkle in mock innocence beneath raised eyebrows. "Is that what you want?"

"Never mind," I say, seizing my suitcase handle. "I'll walk."

Calder grabs the handle, putting his hand over mine, lacing his fingers between my fingers. I can't move. The adrenaline, the fight, the flirt, drains out of me. Calder. Sitka. Life. Suddenly, it's all just too much. I look up at him and tears—stupid, weak, hot tears—fill my eyes.

Calder's grin fades. "I am sorry," he says, taking his hand off mine. "I didn't mean to upset you."

He is standing across from me, staring at me.

Putain! Stop crying, Fanny. Do you want him to think you are one of those silly over-wrought girls who weeps at the first sign of stress? The kind of girl who shreds a box of Kleenex watching insipid rom-coms? This is not a rom-com and you are not a sniffling fool, so stop acting like one!

"I'm fine," I say, willing the tears away. "I am just exhausted after traveling and having to get new luggage."

"New luggage?" He looks down at my new suitcase and then back at me. "What happened to your other luggage?"

"Some jerries broke into my hotel room and stole it."

"Jerries?"

"Drug addicts."

Calder says something in Gaelic that sounds rather profane and runs his hand through his close-cropped hair.

"You weren't hurt, were ye, lass?"

"I'm fine." Happiness rises inside my chest like effervescent golden champagne bubbles. It might seem ridiculous, but Calder's obvious concern makes me feel less alone in this great, wild frozen place. "I wasn't in the room when it happened."

Calder speaks again. The words rumble somewhere deep in his chest before coming out of his mouth, too thick with his brogue for me to decipher. Honestly? I don't want a translation. It's sexier to imagine what he meant to say.

He takes my suitcase from me and walks to the back of his jeep. He opens the trunk, tosses my suitcase inside, and strides back to me.

"Come on, *banfhlath*," he says, holding out his hand. "Your chariot awaits."

I put my hand in his. He leads me around the vehicle to the passenger side and opens the door. I have to climb onto the running board to get inside his jeep—a slightly humiliating reminder of my height deficit sans Louboutins. He waits until I have slid onto the seat and fastened my safety belt before closing the door.

Laney leans forward. "You are my hero, Fanny!"

"Why? Just because I carried your suitcase up a hill?"

"No," she whispers. "Because you've been in Alaska less than twenty-four hours, and already you've snagged yourself a totes bae lumbersexual."

Calder slides another suitcase into his trunk, preventing me from immediately responding. When he walks back to retrieve the last carryon, I swivel around and look at Laney. Her wide eyes are twinkling behind her massive glasses.

"What is a lumbersexual?"

"A metrosexual man, but with more brawn."

I am about to respond when I notice two bags of groceries on the seat beside her. Laney has it all wrong. Calder isn't into me. He didn't seek me out. He was probably out running errands and saw me on the side of the road.

Calder tosses the last of our luggage into the back of his jeep and slams the trunk.

"I haven't snagged anyone."

"Oh," Laney chuckles. "If you haven't snagged him yet, you're almost there. Keep reeling, girl. Keep reeling."

Chapter 19

It's Called Foreplay

"Thank you for...."

"Rescuing you?" Calder winks. "Go ahead. You can say it. You were a damsel in distress, and I rescued you."

We are standing on the front porch at the Each One, Teach One facility. Actually, I am standing and the cocky Scot is leaning against the railing, looking far too lumbersexual for his own good.

"Thank you for rescuing us."

Calder really did rescue us. He drove us up the hill, carried our bags into the facility, started a fire in the fireplace, and, you know those two bags of groceries? It turns out they were for me. A few welcome to Sitka goodies from the hottie.

Calder stands and walks down the stairs. I follow him to his jeep and awkwardly stand beside his driver's side door. I should say something else, but I just don't know what. My emotions are as fragile as the icicles hanging from the eaves over our heads. The slightest provocation and I might shatter into a thousand pieces.

It starts to snow, iridescent flakes tumbling from the sky and falling on Calder's broad shoulders, making lacy patterns on the sleeves of my black coat. I reach up to brush them from his shoulders when he wraps an arm around my waist, pulls me against him, and kisses me. It's not slow and tender like the airport kiss. This kiss is urgent and demanding.

The heat from his lips spreads down my body like a forest fire. I moan low in my throat and lean into him, oblivious to everything except the fast, furious flames of desire consuming me. He pushes his tongue inside my mouth, the flames ignite between my thighs, and I am in deep trouble.

This is crazy. I need to throw some water on Hottie McScottie before he starts thinking I am seriously into him—or worse, I start thinking he is seriously into me. Because he's not. Calder is just a big handsome grinning flirt. He flirted with Vivia. He flirted with most of the women in our tour group. Now, he's flirting with me.

I pull away and run a hand over my wet, swollen lips. Calder draws in a jagged breath and stares at me, blinking, as if he is a caveman who has stumbled out of his dark cave and discovered the first cavewoman. I am waiting for him to thump his chest and grunt, "Me, man. You, woman."

"Look," I say, taking a step back to put some space between us. "I don't know what that just was, but—"

"It's called foreplay," he says, a grin stretching across his tanned face. "Didn't ye ken what foreplay is, lass?"

And just like that, the red hot flames of passion turn into white-hot flames of anger.

"Of course I know what foreplay is, you egotistical—"

Calder throws his head back and laughs. I am less amused. He opens his door and climbs inside.

"Do you like salmon?" he asks, rolling the window down and leaning his arm on the frame. "I ken a place that serves a seafood fondue that will make you swoon."

"Seafood fondue?" I repeat, trying to follow the turn in conversation. "Swoon?"

"You ken you didn't make it easy for a man to ask you out on a date?"

Date? Am I hearing things? Is the thin air messing with my brain or did Hottie McScottie just ask if he could take me to dinner?

"I'm here to fix my life, not fall in love."

"I'm asking you to dinner. Who said anything about falling in love?"

"If I let you take me to dinner, you'll want something more, and that will only lead to heartache."

He chuckles. "You are definitely a Parisian."

"What does that mean?"

"It means you have an inflated sense of self. Just because a man asks you to dinner doesnae mean he is going to fall in love with you. Do you really believe you're that irresistible? Or are you afraid to be alone with me because you find *me* too irresistible?"

I hear Vivia's voice in my head. Damnnnn, girlfriend! You can close the books, because the man just schooled you.

"Pfft." I roll my eyes. "I am not afraid to be alone with you."

"Then what is it?"

"My life is as complicated as a ball of yarn right now. I don't need one string to tangle me up."

His grin slips, and he shakes his head. An uncomfortable silence hangs in the air between us. Finally, he turns the key in the ignition, and the jeep rumbles to life.

"This isn't San Francisco or Paris, *banfhlath*. Alaska is rugged and lonely and sometimes unexpectedly brutal. You need friends."

I look down the road and notice the smooth channel Laney's suitcase left in the snow when I pulled it up the hill. Calder is right. If I am going to survive the next year in Sitka, I am going to need a few friends. Besides, making friends was one of the reasons I agreed to come to this miserable frozen tundra, wasn't it?

"Ah!" He smiles broadly and dimples appear on either side of his lips like two enthusiastic punctuation marks. "There it is!"

"What?"

"That look that tells me you ken I'm right."

The smile that lifts the corners of my mouth is as instinctual as inhaling and exhaling. I can be a pessimistic person, inevitably seeing the glass on the verge of being half empty even as it's being refilled, but it is becoming increasingly difficult to maintain my natural negative state while in Calder's presence. He's too damned charming for my good.

"Seafood fondue, huh?"

"The best."

Why not have dinner with Calder MacFarlane? Sure, the restaurant might disappoint—I mean, it is Sitka—and we might discover we have absolutely nothing in common, but I won't know unless I step out from behind my wall.

"Okay," I say, trying not to stare at his dimples, white teeth, and sexy, kissable lips. "I would love to have dinner with you."

"I knew you would," he says, winking. "How about Saturday?"

"Umm. Let me check my social calendar." I press a finger to my temple and pretend to think before breaking into my own grin. "Saturday sounds great."

It's only Monday. I wish Calder would have suggested dinner for Tuesday or even Wednesday night. *Merde!* Maybe Laney had it all wrong. Maybe I haven't snagged Calder. Maybe he's already snagged me.

"I'll pick you up at eighteen hundred hours."

"Aye-aye, Captain," I say, giving him a salute.

"First, you fall at my feet and then you salute me? You're making this too easy, lass."

"Shut up!"

Calder only laughs and reaches around his seat, grabs the bags of groceries, and hands them to me.

"What are these?"

"Only a few necessities. I thought you might be hungry after your flight, and I wasnae sure if the facility would have food in the pantry."

The unexpectedly thoughtful gesture takes my breath away. Literally. I stand there, holding a plastic grocery bag in each hand, my mouth hanging open. Calder throws the jeep in reverse.

"Welcome to Sitka, *banfhlath.*"

Before I even have a chance to thank him for rescuing me, he backs the jeep up and drives off. The snow is falling heavier now, tumbling from the cobalt sky like a troupe of tiny dancers spinning and pirouetting. I turn my face up to the heavens and let the flakes dance across my cheeks. Tears burn behind my eyes, but it's not from the sunlight.

Chapter 20

Blue Balls

Text from Vivia Perpetua Grant:
Abso-fucking-lutely amazing news! After a skazillion rejection letters, I finally got the call! Kensington Books wants to publish my novel! Love & Horror: A Mary Shelley Romance will live! Mwuahahaha!

Text from Vivia Perpetua Grant:
P.S. Wait! Can you send a postscript text? I am going to have to google that. BRB

Text from Vivia Perpetua Grant:
I am baaack. Big Boss Lady just gave me an über-fab assignment, which means I will be incommunicado for a while. Check your mail. I sent you a little something—something so you don't go through Vivia withdrawals.

Vivia's trifecta of texts pulls me from a deep, dreamless slumber. The room is still dark even though a quick glance at the clock on my bedside table tells me it is already half past eight. The sky outside my window is a deep bruised purple. The bloated silver moon hangs low in the sky, half-hidden behind the snow-covered mountains that wrap around Sitka like an embrace. In the distance, a dog lets out a long, baleful cry as if distressed at morning's arrival.

I read Vivia's texts again and wince as a pang of jealousy stabs my heart. A book deal, an über-fab assignment, and a fabulous French lover. Some people have all of the luck.

Vivia is lucky. No matter how fast she runs or how far she falls, fortune seems to follow her wherever she goes. She bumps into celebrities, befriends heiresses who invite her to swank parties, and lands plum assignments that take her all over the world.

We've had the providence versus perseverance debate dozens of times. Vivia believes success is earned through perspiration and perseverance. She doesn't believe in luck, but people who are inherently lucky usually don't believe in luck. They are standing too close to their lucky star, blinded by the silvery light of serendipity, to notice that others aren't covered in the same stardust.

Once, we were standing in a long queue at the airport in Miami, waiting to check in for a flight, when a passenger service agent approached Vivia and offered her a courtesy bump up to first class. Even though there were hundreds of passengers standing in line, this agent made a beeline to Vivia. No explanation. Just a completely random act of kindness. And things like that happen to Vivia all of the time.

That's not to say she hasn't worked hard for her success. Vivia is a very hard worker, but she labors under one generous lucky star.

Text to Vivia Perpetua Grant:
Congratulations, *mon amie*! I always knew you would hit the big time. Just don't forget us little people when your book is made into a movie and you are rubbing elbows with stars.

Text from Vivia Perpetua Grant:
Whaddayacrazy? You'll be sitting beside me, sharing my popcorn and ogling Zac Efron (he will, of course, play the part of the young, tortured poet).

Barely a second passes before I get another text from Vivia.

Text from Vivia Perpetua Grant:
Are you okay?

I respond immediately, my fingers tapping like mad. This is my best friend's moment to shine and I don't want to steal her sunshine with my gloomy musings.

Text to Vivia Perpetua Grant:
I am fine. Tell me about your über-fab assignment.

Text from Vivia Perpetua Grant:
Can't. It's top secret. I could tell you, but then I would have to kill you. Gotta go. *Bisous*.

I am still in bed, staring at the ceiling, and trying to unravel the mystery of Vivia's top secret mission, when Laney knocks on the door connecting our rooms.

"*Entrez.*"

The door slides open and Laney walks into my room, clad in fuzzy pajamas with feet and carrying two steaming mugs. The scent of coffee tickles my nose before she puts the mugs on my nightstand and plops down at the end of my bed. I scoot to a seated position.

"Yikes!" She waves her hands in front of her as if conducting an invisible orchestra. "What is all of that about?"

"What?"

I quickly run my fingers through my hair, but I don't feel any snarls or nests.

"Your aura," she says. "It's, like, all gray and green."

I grab one of the mugs from the nightstand and act nonchalant even though her uncanny ability to read my moods kinda freaks me out. "Am I to decipher from your tone that my aura is bad."

"Bad." She tilts her head and her thick fringy bangs part to one side. "You must be dwelling in the negative space this morning—the place where bitterness, jealousy, self-defeat, and depression reside. What's up with that?"

"So gray and green are bad colors?" I ask, purposely ignoring her question.

"Oh, no! Green can be a good aura, symbolizing peace and healing, but when in combination with other colors, like brown and gray, it indicates a totes neg energy." She narrows her gaze. "So what's up with that?"

I sigh. "It's nothing, really."

"I disagree. It's definitely something."

I take a sip of the scalding coffee, curse when the liquid burns my lip, and put the mug back down on my nightstand. Then, I grab my iPhone, open the texting screen, and hand it to Laney.

Laney's eyes dart back and forth as she reads the text exchange. I hold my breath and wait for her to finish reading.

"Ah," she says, handing the phone back to me. "I see."

"You do?"

Laney nods. "Gray is sadness, green is jealousy, and that teeny bit of pink I see around your chest is friendship. You're jealous of Vivia and that makes you sad."

"*Incroyable!*" I gasp. "How do you do that?"

Laney shrugs. "It's a gift."

We sit in my room, the purplish light of a winking sunrise streaming in through my window, and say nothing. Laney must think I am the worst kind of person, a jealous, petty, and shrouded-in-gray-aura kind of friend. I want to grab her hand and pledge my burgeoning loyalty to her. I want to tell her that I am not always jealous and swathed in ugly auras. Because, even though we have only known each other a few days, I really like Laney.

"You can go if you want," I say, dropping my chin to my chest. "I'll be fine."

"Let's both go," she says, hopping up.

"Where?"

"Let's get dressed and walk into town. Change your scene, change your aura, that's what I always say."

An hour later, we are walking down Halibut Point Road when Laney grabs my hand and gives it a quick squeeze.

"What was that for?"

"It's okay, you know?"

"What's okay?"

She stops walking and looks at me over the tops of her thick plastic glasses. "It's okay that you feel jealous of Vivia. It doesn't mean you are a bad person, Fanny."

I stop walking too, and turn to look at her. "It doesn't?"

She shakes her head. "Nope, it doesn't."

"So you aren't horrified by my hideous gray-green aura?"

Laney laughs. "Don't be ridiculous! Your aura was muddled gray, green, pink, and some white."

"So."

"So?" Her glasses slide down her nose and she shoves them back up with her gloved finger. "Don't you see? Muddled auras indicate growth and change and conflict."

"Great, so I am a muddled, conflicted mess."

"We're all muddled, conflicted messes, Fanny. That's what makes us human." She takes a deep breath, holds it in her lungs, and then exhales slowly. Her warm breath creates a wispy ghost of a cloud that hangs in the air between us. "You are jealous of Vivia, but you feel horrible about it. That tells me this is a transient feeling, something you are working hard to conquer. Everyone feels jealous; it's what is done after that spark of jealousy that really matters. So what are you going to do?"

She starts walking again before I've answered. I fall in step beside her, turning her question over and over in my mind. What am I going to do? What am I going to do?

"Oo!" Laney stops walking and points at a store window. Behind the glass, arranged appealingly, stand large apothecary jars filled with candy. "Look at all of those yummies!"

We open the door and a mélange of sugary, chocolatey, fruity aromas assails us.

"Welcome to Moose Balls!" A jolly apple-shaped woman carrying a silver platter laden with tiny pouches filled, presumably, with candy ambles up to us. "Would you like to try Sitka's world famous Nut Sacks?"

I practically choke on my own saliva. Did she just say what I think she said?

"Here," she says, thrusting the tray at us. "Once you put one of our nut sacks in your mouth, you will be ruined for life. I'm Betty, by the way."

Laney snatches one of the bags off the platter, opens it, pulls out an oval shaped piece of chocolate, and pops it into her mouth, closing her eyes and groaning as if in ecstasy. She pops two more candies into her mouth.

"These are really good," she mumbles, her cheeks as fat as a chipmunk's. "Is it hazelnut?"

Apple-Bottomed Betty grins. "Our nut sacks are made using several different nuts. We grind them fine, gently fold them into a ganache, roll them into balls, and cover them in dark chocolate."

I tentatively open a sack and put one of the nut balls in my mouth. The dark chocolate quickly melts away, leaving a nutty, crunchy soft ball on my tongue.

"Here," Betty says, lifting the lid off an apothecary jar filled with more chocolate balls. "You have to try our Moose Balls. They're lingonberry-flavored malted milk covered in dark chocolate."

Laney plunges her hand in the jar and pulls out two quarter-sized chocolate balls. She hands me one and pops the other into her mouth.

"And why do you call them Moose Balls?" I ask.

"Moose eat lingonberries," Betty says, as if the answer were obvious. "They're considered a super-fruit. High in antioxidants."

"Sweet!" Laney nudges me in the ribs with her elbow. "You know what that means, don't cha, Fanny? We can reduce our risk of getting major diseases just by eating these chocolatey balls of goodness."

"A moose ball a day keeps Alzheimer's away." Betty grins and pats her rotund belly. "That's my theory, anyway."

I look at Betty's quivery turkey wattle and jiggly pink jowls. If I am ever her size, I hope I have Alzheimer's. I would hate to be obese and still have all of my mental faculties. Who wants to wake up every day remembering they were once thin and fit? A skinny person trapped in a fat suit. *Non, merci.*

Betty's smile slips a little, and my cheeks flush with guilty heat. I pop the moose ball in my mouth and pray the jiggly, jocular candy pusher didn't read my thoughts. I am not proud of it, but sometimes I can be superficial and severely critical. All of this time, I thought I was discerning, urbane, and witty. Maybe I was wrong. Maybe I am just a *salope*. Who am I to judge Betty so harshly? Just because she has a higher BMI than I do?

"These are very good," I say, swallowing the last bit of crunchy, creamy chocolate. "The tartness of the berries contrasts nicely with the sweet chocolate."

"I agree!" Laney chimes in. "Lingonberries taste like cranberries, don't they?"

"They're called the low-bush cranberry," Betty says. "A wide variety of wild berries grow on the hills and in the fields around Sitka. Salmonberries, crowberries, cloudberries, blueberries. If you're ever in town in August, you should go berry picking."

"We'll be here in August!" Laney declares. "We are working at a teaching facility up the road."

"You're teachers? How wonderful!" Betty says. "What do you teach?"

"I teach art, and Fanny teaches fashion merchandising and design."

"Fashion?" Betty cries. "Have you been to my sister's store yet? Make Knit Work?"

"No."

"Oo, you must go. All of her garments are made by local craftsmen." Betty ambles behind the counter, opens a drawer, pulls out a business card, and hands it to me. "Make Knit Work has been mentioned in the Best of Alaska guide for five years running."

I envision a shop full of hideous Christmas sweaters, misshapen hats, and ridiculous tea cozies. Nonetheless, I thank Betty and slip the card into my pocket.

Laney buys a pound of moose balls and a cellophane bag filled with salmonberry licorice nibs. I wait for Betty to count out Laney's change before making a move for the door.

"Whoa, sister!" Laney cries, dropping her coins into a plastic frog-shaped coin purse. "Where do you think you're going?"

"I'm sorry," I say, turning around. "I thought you were done."

"I'm done, but you're not." She adjusts her panda hat. "You can't leave here without buying some candy. It would be, like, sacrilegious."

I am about to tell Laney that I don't need the hollow calories when she accurately reads my thoughts. Her mind-reading, aura-analyzing abilities are beginning to creep me out.

"And don't you even think about rattling off the caloric value of a malted milk ball. Seriously? A single ball can't be more than forty, fifty calories."

"Twenty-five," Betty interjects.

"Thank you, Betty!" Laney grins. "Twenty-five calories? That ain't nothing, Fanny! Now get your French fry-thin ass over here and buy some candy before we body slam you to the ground and force feed you moose balls until you reach your healthy body weight."

"I'll take two nut sacks," I say, handing Betty a ten dollar bill. "Thank you."

Could you tell me where to find Humpy's? I'll take two nut sacks. What in the hell? I've been in Alaska less than a week, and already I've uttered two sentences I never thought I would utter.

Nuts and balls in hand, we head out of the store and up Halibut Point Road toward Sitka's answer to all that is fashion, Make Knit Work.

We are walking by a wooden pole covered with advertisements when I notice one that might interest Laney.

"Laney, look." I point to the colorful advert. "Ernie D's Old Time Saloon is hosting an open mic night next month."

"So?"

"So? You should go."

Laney grimaces.

"What? Why the grimace?"

She shrugs and keeps walking. I hurry to catch up.

"What's going on?"

"What do you mean?"

"Your aura." I wave my hands in front of me, mimicking what she did in my bedroom earlier. "It's all beige."

Laney snorts. "Beige?"

"Yeah," I say, doubling my step to keep up with her. "Beige is boring, conservative, and just…blah. Why are you being so blah?"

"I am not blah."

"So you'll perform at the open mic night?"

"I don't see why I would."

"Because you have a degree in music, performed in a band, and most certainly possess wicked rhyming skills."

Laney chuckles, but it is one of those humorless, wry chuckles. "My parents would disagree."

"What do you mean?"

"My parents hated my band. They thought it was a 'prepubescent diversion' that kept me from 'pursuing fiscally responsible employment.'"

"Harsh."

"Tell me about it." She slows her pace and looks over at me. "You know what really sucks?"

I shake my head.

"They never even came to hear us play."

"Wait a minute." I grab her arm and force her to stop walking. "Are you telling me you have given up something you love because your parents didn't feel it was worthwhile? And they made that decision without ever finding out if you had any real talent?"

"Yep."

"Wow. That's just…"

"Just what?"

"Sad."

"My parents mean well. They're afraid I will end up on a street corner, playing songs for tourists who toss change into my guitar case."

We start walking again. What Laney just told me reminds me of someone else I know, someone I love, who tried so hard to please others she lost herself in the process.

"You remind me of Vivian."

"That's a good thing, isn't it?"

"Not entirely."

I tell Laney about Vivia pre-Luc. The Vivia who wanted to please others so desperately that she compromised her wishes, denied her desires, and altered herself to conform to other's standards. Laney listens without interrupting.

"Nathan, Vivian's fiancé, didn't like for her to read romance novels, so she read them in secret. He didn't like the music she listened to, the clothes she wore, the movies she watched, so she changed her attire, started drinking wine instead of margaritas, and started listening to Michael Bublé instead of the rock bands she preferred." I take a deep breath. "Vivian has always had a big, bold, beautiful personality, but she didn't believe in herself. She didn't see the value in her uniqueness. She let less original people tell her who to be, how to act, what to think."

"Was she happy?"

"She thought she was, but she wasn't. Not really."

Laney takes a deep, jagged breath, and I realize she is on the verge of tears. My words have made an impact.

"Your personality is as bold and beautiful as Vivian's. Don't let others force you into some boring beige mold. Be you, bold and colorful Laney."

"Thank you, Fanny." She reaches out and squeezes my hand. "Truly."

"Does that mean you'll perform at Ernie D's?"

"I'll think about it."

We continue our stroll down Halibut Point Road, stopping to read a wooden sign posted beside a small lake.

"Swan Lake, also known as Sitka's Central Park, was created by Russian immigrants in 1851," I read aloud, trying not to scoff at the idea of comparing a pond and a few metal benches to a grand urban park designed by a world-famous landscape architect. "Originally, Swan Lake was designed as a commercial venture. Ice harvested from the lake was sent to California. Today, the lake is a habitat for waterfowl and a destination for recreational enthusiasts."

We each drop a dollar in the Swan Lake Restoration Project charity box and continue down the road, meandering our way through a Russian Cemetery, until we come to a large gray building with a domed copper roof.

"What an interesting building."

"I think it is Saint Michael's Cathedral, an old Orthodox church," Laney says. "I read about it on *Accidental Adventures*."

"What's *Accidental Adventures*?"

"This cool travel blog," Laney explains. "It's actually called *On Life, Love and Accidental Adventures*. The writer has the most amazing, serendipitous encounters—she crashed Colin Farrell's movie set in Ireland and took part in a séance in Marie Antoinette's private apartment at Versailles."

"Interesting."

"Right?" Laney grins. "Anyway, she came to Alaska to stay in some abandoned Cold War bunker town not too far from Sitka. She wrote a whole piece about the cathedral. Apparently, it was founded two hundred years ago by some Siberian monk."

I step back and crane my neck to look up at the Greek cross atop the bell tower. "It doesn't look that old."

"Well," Laney says, tipping her head back and squinting up at the copper dome. "There was a hellacious fire in the sixties, and the cathedral had to be entirely rebuilt."

"Ah."

We keep walking.

"This all must be so…pedestrian for you."

"Pedestrian?" I step over a patch of ice. "What do you mean?"

"What do I mean? What do I mean?" she cries. "Paris, France, baby! Anyone raised in the shadow of Notre Dame and Sacré-Cœur surely must find a church covered in vinyl siding hopelessly pedestrian. Sitka is so not exotic."

"I don't know," I say, looking at the twinkling icicle lights dangling from the store fronts. "Sitka is exotic-ish. After all, we do have Alexi the taxi driver and—"

"—and Calder MacFabuleux, the Scottish lumbersexual."

"Ha-ha!" I laugh. "Very funny."

"Who's joking?" Laney says. "Have you looked at the man? Calder is one tall, gorgeous glass of sex juice. You better pay the bartender before someone else orders him."

I snort.

"What does he do for a living?"

"He's a search and rescue helicopter pilot for the Coast Guard."

"Mayday!" Laney presses her hand to her forehead and pretends to swoon. "Quick! Put in an S.O.S. call. I think I am going down!"

I laugh and swat her on the shoulder. "You're such a dork!"

"You laugh, but I would literally rent a leaky old fishing trawler, sail twenty miles out to sea, and scuttle it, if I thought it would net me a catch as sexilicious as Calder."

"Shut up!"

"I'm serious," she says, sticking her hand in her bag. She pulls out a moose ball and pops it into her mouth. "Coast Guard guys are totes hot."

"Are they?" I play it cool.

"Are they?" Laney tilts her head, opens her eyes wide, and stares blankly. "Gee, Laney. You mean the tall, ripped Scotsman who maneuvers a helicopter over a violent sea to rescue souls in distress is hot? I never noticed."

"Okay, okay!" I laugh and hold up my hands in defeat. "So Calder is a little hot. Can we move on now?"

"Calder is more than a little hot. On the Scoville Scale for rating hot guys, Calder is the ghost pepper. He's, like, Adam Levine hot. Orlando Bloom hot. Aidan Turner hot."

"Who's Aidan Turner?"

Laney stops walking and stares at me with her mouth hanging open. She closes her mouth for a second before letting it hang back open. It's clear I have made a faux pas in showing my ignorance of hipster hotties. I am assuming Aidan Turner is a hipster—or some obscure indie singer—because I haven't ever heard of him.

"Who is Aidan Turner?" Laney gulps. "Kíli, of the House of Durin?"

I shrug.

Laney slaps her hands on her cheeks and shakes her head back and forth like an aghast bobble head dog. "For the love of Thorin!"

We start walking again.

"Is it a band?"

"No, the House of Durin is not a band! Seriously? The House of Durin is a line of dwarves descended from Durin the Deathless from Tolkien's *The Hobbit*."

Now, it's my turn to stare aghast.

"Anyway," she says, flushing, "Aidan Turner is the Scoville-hot Irish actor who plays Kíli in the Hobbit movies."

"What is it with you and short hairy mythical creatures?"

"Aidan is not short, hairy, or mythical!"

We arrive at Make Knit Work, and I am so happy to have an excuse to end our conversation about Calder MacFarlane and Aidan the Hairy Hobbit that I open the door with more strength than necessary, causing a cascade of tiny bells affixed to the doorknob to tinkle madly.

I am not ready to think about Hottie McScottie, our fondue non-date, and what the future holds for us. Thankfully, there are plenty of things inside Make Knit Work to divert us. I am stunned, and immensely relieved, to discover Apple-Bottom Betty's sister's store doesn't contain a single cheesy tea cozy or Christmas sweater. In fact, the store is kinda... swank. There are artfully-battered armoires filled with delicate cashmere cardigans and patterned fisherman sweaters, cool slouchy berets, on-trend infinity scarves, and cowls in chunky, nubby yarn.

"This place is pretty fab," I whisper, grabbing a pair of fuchsia fingerless gloves that would make my pink-obsessed BFF lose her mind.

"Thank you."

I spin around and find Apple-Bottomed Betty's clone, minus the ruffled apron and silver tray laden with moose balls, standing behind me.

"You're welcome. Did you make all of these garments?"

"Good heavens, no!" She clasps her hands and rests her arms on her ample belly. "I employ several freelance knitters."

"You must be Betty's sister?"

"Yes, I am." She smiles and her blue eyes twinkle. "Did my sister send you this way, then?"

"She did."

"I am Netty, by the way."

"Pleased to meet you, Netty. I am Stéphanie and this is my friend Laney."

"It's a pleasure to meet you, both. I see you come bearing bags with the Moose Balls logo on them," Netty says. "I hope Betty gave you Blue Balls."

"I beg your pardon?" I sputter.

"Betty's Blue Balls, white chocolate blueberry cheesecake balls. They're my favorite." She pats her stomach. "Obviously."

I never know what to say when an obese person makes a self-deprecating joke about her fat, so I hold the fingerless gloves up and compliment the knit work. "These are such a pretty shade of pink. Do you dye the yarn yourself?"

"Heavens, no."

"Huh." I rub the yarn between my fingers. "Betty said the hills around Sitka are covered with different types of berries. Have you ever thought of picking them and making your own dye?"

"Why, no," Netty murmurs, narrowing her eyes. "No, I haven't."

"Fanny is a designer," Laney says.

"Is that so?"

"Well, not—"

"She worked for L'Heure," Laney interrupts.

"That's impressive."

"Hey!" Laney cries. "I have a fantastic idea! Why don't you and Fanny work together to create unique dyes made from local berries? You could call it Dyed in the Woods…or something like that."

"Oh, I don't know—"

"My heavens! That is a fantastic idea." Netty reaches in to her pocket and pulls out a business card. "Here's my card with my personal contact information. When you get back to the lower forty-eight, send me an email and we can talk about it a little more."

I take the card and slip it into my pocket.

"Oh, we won't be going back to the lower forty-eight for at least a year," Laney interjects. "We're teachers with an international charity committed to offering post-secondary study to people living in remote locations."

"You're with Each One, Teach One, then?"

"Yes!"

"How lovely," Netty says. "What do you teach?"

"I am an artist." Laney's voice wavers, as if she's not yet convinced of her own value. "I will offer mixed-media art lessons with an emphasis on utilizing recycled, reclaimed, and environmentally friendly materials."

"I would be happy to donate yarn clippings, buttons, and spools to your cause."

"Seriously?"

Netty nods.

"That would be totes fab! Thanks!"

"Of course." Netty turns her gaze on me. "And what about you? Will you be teaching Sitka's budding Christian Sirianos how to make it work?"

The door bells tinkle, and a brown-clad UPS guy carrying half a dozen boxes walks into the store.

"Excuse me." Netty hurries over to the delivery man, taking two of his boxes and leading him to a storeroom.

"Saved by the bell," I say, smiling at Laney.

"Saved from what?" Laney asks. "You are going to share your mad skills with young Sitkians who might grow up to be the next big name in fashion."

I can only snort. I grab the pink gloves, walk over to the counter, and hand them to a bubble-gum chomping teen with a blue fishtail braid and terminally bored expression.

"Pink?" she asks, one side of her mouth pulled up in a semi-sneer.

"Yeah, so?"

"Never mind." She taps the cash register keys with her black-to-blue ombré painted fingernails. "It's cool. I mean, if you like being one of, like, a billion mindless minions dancing to a misogynistic tune meant to brainwash women into believing they must remain girlishly ridiculous."

Wait! What the...

"I am sorry." I frown and look around the store as if I am lost. "I thought I was in a knit shop in Sitka. I didn't realize I had stumbled into a NOW rally. Have I missed *The Feminine Mystique* readings? Am I too late to shave my head and stick pins in tiny man dolls?"

I can't believe I am getting into a disagreement with someone over the color pink. I respect Christian's mantra—"The tones of gray, pale pink, and turquoise will always prevail"—even if I personally loathe the color. Vivian likes pink, so I feel I must represent.

She snorts and rolls her eyes. "Whatever."

Ohnoshedidn't! Did she really just "whatever" me? In France, we say "pffft" when we are dismissing someone from a conversation. I should know. I am the Queen of Pffft. I have given my share of pfffts, but getting one really pisses me off...especially by some immature, self-impressed, affected teen in a tattered flannel shirt and Timberland boots. Timberland! Seriously? Only crap rappers like Kanye West and overweight construction workers wear Tims.

"Every woman should have something pink in her wardrobe. It is color of happiness."

"Who said that, Clueless Barbie?"

"Clueless Barbie!" I laugh. "That's funny. It's actually a Christian quote...Christian Dior. World famous couturier. Perhaps you've heard of him?" I flick my gaze from her muddy boots to her frizzy fishtail. "No, I don't suppose you have."

"Fanny!" Laney gasps.

"You're such a bitch."

"And you're such a c—"

"Oh, good!" Netty ambles up to the counter. "I see you've met Nolee. She's one of those Sirianos I was talking about."

"I beg your pardon?"

"Nolee wants to be a fashion designer," Netty says, smiling and nodding her head at the fishtail feminist. "She applied to Parsons, but—"

—but her application was rejected because the market for acid-washed jeans died along with Loverboy albums and hair scrunchies?

"But I decided to pursue a more worthwhile vocation," Nolee says, flushing a little.

I want to ask her if making minimum wage selling knit infinity scarves and insulting customers was her more worthwhile vocation, but Laney is shooting me a death glare, so I settle on a patronizing simper.

Nolee hands me my receipt and a gift bag with Vivian's gloves. I take it and spin around, marching toward the door without so much as a *merci beaucoup*. Laney says goodbye to Netty and the less funny Sandra Bernhard and follows close on my heels.

I am reaching for the doorknob when I notice a life-sized cardboard cutout of Tim Gunn standing just inside the door, a thought bubble taped above his head with the words "Make Knit Work, People," and a scarf tied around his neck.

Am I wrong to feel the Universe is mocking me?

Chapter 21

Vivian's Box

By the time we trudge up the hill—our bellies filled with chocolate, our cheeks slapped pink by the cruel Alaskan air—I feel better. I am pretty sure my aura has changed. I wouldn't say I am rocking a Pucci pantsuit riot of bold, happy colors, but I am fairly positive I am working a mellow Tiffany blue aura. I might have been able to project a Pucci kaleidoscope of joyful colors if I hadn't encountered Nolee, the bra-burning, pink-hating buzz killer. I just left Make Knit Work irritated.

I don't know why I let Sitka's own Gloria Steinem-wannabe get under my skin, but she did. Maybe because she brought out my ugly. It's true, her snotty attitude irked me so much I pulled my most hideous self out of the closet and slipped it on. What right did I have to imply the girl wasn't good enough for Parsons or that she was too uncouth, too ignorant to be familiar with Christian Dior? It was haughty. *You owe her an apology. She might have fired the first shot in the battle of the bitches, but you are the adult.* I make a mental note to apologize to Nolee the next time I am near Make Knit Work.

"What's that?" Laney hands me her bag and takes the stairs two at a time. She squats down near the door and lifts a large brown box covered in foreign postal stamps. "It's for you, Fanny!"

I know it is from Vivian without looking at the return address. Who else would send me a package plastered with headlines clipped from magazines? I take the box from Laney, laughing as I notice a few of the titles: *Sex Again? What Are You An Alley Cat?* and *Brady Says, My Balls Are Perfect.* There's a picture of a fat toddler sticking her tongue out and the headline, *21 Reasons to Hate Kids.*

"It's from Vivian," I say, following Laney into the cabin.

"Oo, more goodies." Laney claps her hands. "Quick, open it and see what's inside."

We hurry to my room and hop onto my bed like two slumber party pals, kicking off our boots and shedding our coats and mittens. Laney pops a few moose balls in her mouth and munches on them while I unwrap the box. Once I have carefully removed Vivian's handiwork, I hand the paper to Laney and she reads the headlines aloud, giggling.

"*Untamed Va-jay-jays*," Laney chortles. "*Bush is back!*"

She thrusts the paper at me. Vivian has taped a photograph of ex-President George W. Bush beneath the headline. I groan and continue to pull strips of tape from the box.

"*His Butt Uncovered: What the Size and Shape Reveals about His Character*," Laney continues reading. "*New Ways to Use Your Loofah…*"

I remove the last strip of tape and open the box. In typical Vivian fashion, she wrapped every item in pink tissue paper and tossed the lot with a liberal dose of glitter. I lift the first wrapped item out of the box and glitter floats in the air, finally settling like shimmering metallic snowflakes on my bed, lap, and floor. I remove the tissue paper and laugh out loud when I see what had been wrapped inside.

"What is it?"

I hand the nightshirt to Laney. She shakes it out and holds it up, chuckling as she stares at a cartoon version of Marie Antoinette standing on the scaffold, a shocked expression on her face, a smudge of frosting on her cheek, and the tagline, "What? All I said was, 'Let's have cake.'"

"Vivian has a massive pajama collection," I say, trying to explain the emotional significance of the gift without going into detail about my preference to sleep sans clothes. "This is her favorite nightshirt."

"Ah."

I finish unwrapping the gifts until they form a pyramid of goodies on my bed. There are bars of Savon de Marseilles, my favorite soap, and tubes of Email Diamant, a clove-based French toothpaste. There is a box of chocolates from my favorite chocolate shop in Bruges, a bottle of wine from Castillo del Trebbio, a vineyard we visited during our bike tour of Tuscany, and fashion magazines from several European countries. There is also an envelope with something lumpy inside. I open the envelope and remove a neatly folded letter written on pink paper embossed with my best friend's initials. A silver chain falls out of the envelope onto my lap. I lift the chain and stare at the sunflower pendant dangling from it.

"That's pretty!" Laney coos.

It is pretty, but the delicate sunflower pendant doesn't look like anything I would ever purchase or wear.

I open the letter and begin reading Vivian's large, loopy handwriting. I don't get too far before tears fill my eyes and a thick lump clogs my throat.

My dear Fanny,

I'll bet you are thinking, "I wonder why Vivian sent me a necklace with a sunflower pendant?" I'll bet you are also thinking it doesn't look like the type of necklace you would ever wear. "Where's the Tiffany tag? Where's the Cartier stamp?"

Relax, *ma puce*, there is a method behind my madness—for to send a Platinum Princess a sterling silver necklace does indeed border on unbridled madness. (Insert maniacal laughter here.)

I am certain you already know that the sunflower is the symbol for the South of France, perhaps because of Van Gogh's paintings, but I'll bet you didn't know that the sunflower originated in North America. Like you, it was taken from its native home and forced to endure in a foreign land. More than endure, the sunflower now brings joy to millions of tourists who flock to Provence to gaze at vast fields of the blossoms. I know you have it in you, sister of my soul, to do more than endure in your new foreign land. I know you have it in you to bring joy to everyone you encounter.

There is one more reason I have chosen the sunflower as your spirit flower. Did I really just write spirit flower? Somewhere Mum is saying an Our Father for my New Age transgression. Anyway, I chose this sunflower pendant because the sunflower bends in the breeze, never breaks, and it always, always turns its face to the light.

I know this is a difficult time for you, Fanny, but you will bend with this breeze You will not break. You will find the light.

Love,

Vivia

Laney gets up, walks to the bathroom connecting our rooms, and returns with a fistful of toilet paper. She hands me the wad and returns to sitting cross-legged on my bed.

I dab my eyes and blow my nose before handing her the letter.

"You don't mind?" she asks, taking the letter.

I shake my head.

Laney's eyes move back and forth, like the eyes on those vintage cat clocks, until she comes to the last line. She folds the letter, slips it back into the envelope, and tucks it beneath my pile of goodies.

"Was she right?"

"Excuse me?"

"Vivia said you would look at the necklace and wonder why she would send you something that wasn't from Cartier or Tiffany. Was she right?"

I chuckle and nod my head. "It was my first thought."

"And now?"

I look at the hand-carved sunflower pendant resting on my palm, and my smile fades.

"Now"—I unclasp the necklace and hook it around my neck—"there is only one thing I treasure more than this necklace."

I think of my mother's Dior diamond-and-ruby brooch, the one my father gave on my fifth birthday, and a new lump forms in my throat. It suddenly occurs to me that my two most treasured possessions came to via great loss. The loss of my mother and my job.

Text to Vivia Perpetua Grant:

I don't know where you are or if you are getting texts, but I want you to know that you are the best friend a girl could ever hope to have.

Text from Vivia Perpetua Grant:

Yes I am!

Chapter 22

Love & Other Drugs

Text from Curtis Bower:
Don't lock yourself in the tower just yet, Sleeping Beauty. Powers higher than Maleficent aren't happy with the way she's running this jacked up fairy tale world we call L'Heure North America. A rotund little fairy—whose real identity must be protected to keep this from looking like pure, unadulterated gossip—told me the end of her cruel reign might be near.

Text from Vivia Perpetua Grant:
OMG! I just saw Austin Carlile in the Duty Free at Charles de Gaulle. I am dying.

Text to Vivia Perpetua Grant:
Who is Austin Carlile?

Text from Vivia Perpetua Grant:
WHO IS AUSTIN CARLILE? The lightly bearded, heavily tatted hottie who visits me each night (in my dreams). Voice of a saint, body meant for sinners. Lead singer of my favorite band, Of Mice & Men.

Text to Vivia Perpetua Grant:
I thought Ronnie Radke was your favorite singer?

Text from Vivia Perpetua Grant:
Who? Oh, you man that boy from Falling in Reverse? *insert chuckle* Oh, Fanny, that was a mere idling crush of my misguided youth. This is for reals.

Text to Vivia Perpetua Grant:

Why are you in Paris?

We are just finishing our dinner, onion soup and crusty French bread we bought at a bakery in town, when the other volunteers arrive.

Keith Wisdom is a tall, handsome African American from Minneapolis. He has a bright, beaming smile and a laugh that makes you feel warm inside.

I pour four mugs of coffee, and we go into the common room to become better acquainted. Laney assumes a cross-legged position on the ground beside the fireplace, while the rest of us sit on the artfully battered vegan leather furniture.

"What will you be teaching, Keith?" Laney asks.

"Carpentry."

"Cool! Did you build furniture before volunteering to come to Sitka?"

"Naw." He shakes his head. "I flipped houses."

"Like Jeff Lewis?" I ask.

"Yeah, man," Keith says, smiling broadly. "Only I don't have a nympho Mexican maid, make mad cash, or lose my mind."

I nod because I am familiar with Jeff Lewis and his hyper-sexual maid. Laney frowns. I am guessing she doesn't watch Bravo.

"So you're teaching how to flip houses?"

"What? Ain't enough time or Prozac to teach all the crazy that goes into flipping." He crosses his arms and the muscles in his biceps bulge. "I'm teaching people how to make smokehouses."

"Smokehouses?" Laney tilts her head and wrinkles her nose. "Like a place to smoke hookahs?"

Keith throws his head back and laughs.

"It's cool," Laney says, flushing a little. "I'm from Colorado."

"No, girl! Smokehouses for smoking herring and salmon." Keith smiles so broadly, his teeth look like keys on a piano. "But I would be happy to fire up the hookah with you."

Laney only laughs, which leaves me wondering if she smokes flavored tobacco—or something even stronger. It might explain a few things.

Merde! There I go again, getting all judge-y. What does it matter if Laney likes to spend her time in dimly lit dens, sucking on genie lamps? Who am I to judge? It's not like it's crack, meth, or opium, right?

I hope she doesn't smoke a hookah, though. I used to think people smoked marijuana out of hookahs, until Lady Loafers set me straight. He even offered to help me lose my "hookah cherry" by throwing an

Arabian Nights party with bare-chested harem boys bearing trays of spice-scented tobacco.

I declined. I've never been about that life, and I just don't know if I could be super close to someone who makes killing brain cells a regular recreational sport.

I study the other volunteer, an extremely handsome, slender man who introduced himself as Hector Montoya from Coos Bay, Oregon.

"What about you?" I say, smiling at Hector. "What will you teach?"

"Massage therapy for healing and herb growing for holistic medicinal purposes."

"Hector? Hector, bo-bector. Banana-fana, fo-fector Montoya!" Laney rocks back and forth to her own melody as if she's hopped up on caffeine. "You're not the Hector Montoya, are you?"

Hector's cheeks redden. "I am Hector Montoya."

"Any relation to Inigo Montoya?" Keith asks.

Hector opens his mouth, but Keith doesn't wait for him to answer.

"'Ello. My name ees Inigo Montoya," Keith says in a thick Spanish accent. "You killed my father. Prepare to die."

Whoa! What is up with Bob Vila going all racist with the bad accent and the strange threat? I am waiting for Hector to freak out, but the freak out never comes. Instead, he laughs.

"Yo, man," Keith says, his thousand-watt smile dims just a watt or two. "That was wrong. You probably get that shit a lot, don't you?"

I must look confused, or outraged, because Hector smiles at me and says, "Inigo Montoya is a character in the movie *The Princess Bride*, and that is one of his famous lines."

"Ah!" I nod. "I see."

But I don't see. In fact, I feel as if I am the Helen Keller of movie trivia. I don't watch a lot of movies, so I am pathetically handicapped when it comes to movie references.

Laney, who has been tapping away on her iPhone, cries out, "Yes! I knew it! You are Hector Montoya!"

"I believe we have already established that he is Hector Montoya."

"Yes, but he is *the* Hector Montoya."

Keith and I exchange bemused looks.

"Hector Montoya?" Laney prompts. "The man who created Balanced."

"Balanced?"

Hector blushes and looks down at his feet.

"What is Balanced?" Keith asks, looking from me to Hector to Laney.

"Balanced is a line of alternative medicine and wellness products," Laney explains.

"Wait a minute!" My voice comes out one octave below fangirl screech. "I know your products. I use your products."

"Get out," Laney says.

"I do!" I am staring at Hector through wide, adoring eyes. The kind of eyes I have seen on the faces of countless teens scoring their first Lady Dior bag. The kind of eyes I have seen on Vivian when she has mentioned Luc—or one of those tatted-up rock stars she lusts over. "I use Balanced's You're Off Your Rocker, post-exercise vitamin pack."

"Thank you," Hector says.

"I don't know what you put in those packs, my man," Keith says, slapping Hector on the back. "But it's working. Girl has got it going on."

"Thank you." I keep my gaze fixed on Hector. "This is incredible! I can't believe I am going to be sharing a cabin with Hector Montoya, the man who transformed a few acres of herbs into an international multi-million dollar health and lifestyle brand. Hector Montoya! The man who brought healthy back into health care!"

"Did my director of marketing and public relations pay you to say that?" Hector laughs softly.

"Last year, my best friend lost her job and her man. She was depressed. So you know what I did?"

Hector shakes his head.

"I slipped a little of your Get Out of Your Head into her water bottle."

Hector looks at me through wide—more shocked and frightened than adoring—eyes. "You didn't."

"What?" I cry, defensive. "It was for her own good."

Hector doesn't blink.

Keith whistles.

"Do I sound like I've joined the cult?"

"A little," Laney says.

"A little?" Keith repeats. "Girl, you've been drinking the Kool Aid."

"Well it worked!" I argue. "Vivian got a new job and a new man before the bottle was empty!"

"For reals?" Keith looks at Hector. "Well then hook a brother up, will ya? I could use some of that magic genie shit."

"Unlucky in love, Keith?" Hector asks, without a hint of condescension.

"What?" Keith puffs up his chest. "Shit, no! The ladies love me."

"Then why do you want magic genie shit?" I tease.

"Man, you ladies are like iPhones—"

"—because we like to be held?" Laney blurts.

"—because we keep you organized?" I chime in.

"No," Keith says, clucking his tongue "—because you're expensive, require too many damned updates to keep working, and there's always a newer, more enticing model on the horizon."

Hector chuckles. Laney laughs out loud.

"I think we just figured out why you're single," I say, smiling.

"Because I am a male chauvinist pig?" He crosses his arms in front of his chest, but his grin widens. "I've been called that a few times."

"Well if the snout fits"—I slap him on the shoulder—"wear it."

We all laugh. This is the first time in ages—maybe forever—I've been relaxed enough to banter with strangers, especially ones as eclectic as this bunch. I've never been one for idle chitchat because it can be so banal, so insipid. At work, I firmly adhered to a self-imposed "no fraternizing" rule. After work and on the weekends, I always had Vivian around to break the awkward ice.

Maybe Vivian is right. Maybe there is such a thing as serendipity, because the woman who couldn't break the ice has landed in Alaska.

Chapter 23

Pushing Buttons

Text from Calder MacFarlane:
How are you settling in, *banfhlath*?

Text to Calder MacFarlane:
Surprisingly well, actually.

Text from Calder MacFarlane:
It doesn't surprise me. I always knew there was a tough girl under those designer clothes.

Text to Calder MacFarlane:
How? You barely know me.

Text from Calder MacFarlane:
You forget I saw you wrestle an army of luggage, shear sheep, drink Scotch like a Scotsman, and organize a search party when Vivia was missing.

Text to Calder MacFarlane:
Thanks. What do you have planned today?

Text from Calder MacFarlane:
You know, same old, same old. Play the hero, rescue the world. Are we still on for dinner tomorrow night?

Text to Calder MacFarlane:
Yes. What should I wear?

Text from Calder MacFarlane:
Those lacy lady things would be nice. See you at six, *banfhlath*.

Apparently, it takes more than three days in Alaska to become proficient at breaking ice, because I am standing in my classroom, staring at fourteen strangers, and I got nothing.

Nuh-thing.

I've gone through my whole speech, outlining Each One, Teach One's mission statement, my education and experience, and what I hope we will accomplish. I took a few questions, and now they are just staring at me, expectantly, unspoken accusations written all over their faces. *Is that all you got? No wonder you were fired from L'Heure.*

To make matters worse, loud and uncontrolled laughter is coming from Laney's classroom next door. It's like an ironic laugh-track for the flat sitcom going on here.

Share, a tall, slender, and strikingly beautiful young woman with hair and skin the color of *café au lait*, raises her hand. "I have an idea."

"*Oui*," I say, audibly exhaling. "What is it?"

"Since we will be spending so much time together, why don't we all take turns introducing ourselves?" She smiles easily. "Maybe we could tell a little bit about ourselves and say why we are taking this class?"

I am mentally smacking myself in the forehead. Why didn't I think of that?

"*Bon*! That's a very good idea." I return Share's smile. "Why don't you start?"

"Okay!" She swivels around in her chair so she can face the rest of the classroom. "My name is Share. I am obsessed with designer handbags and would like to start my own line. That's why I am here. In my free time, I like to sketch bags and read the dictionary. I love coffee, and I hate chocolate."

The girl next to her gasps. "You're kidding?"

"No, I am not!" Share closes her eyes and shudders, as if she just downed NyQuil. "Hate it. I had a date bring me an enormous Hershey kiss for Valentine's Day once. Nice to meet you. Date over."

A few people snicker. It's not exactly Laney's laugh track, but it's a start.

The girl seated next to Share stands up and waves at her classmates. She's plump, with long, glossy brown hair and sparkling green eyes.

"My name is Isabell," she says in a cheerful tone. "I have a passion for fashion design. My dream is to work for a major designer in New York

City. When I am not going to school, I like to take photographs and listen to rock music. I love rock music."

She sits back down.

"My best friend loves rock music and is obsessed with Ronnie Radke—or she used to be. Now she is crazy about Austin Someone-or-other from some metalcore band."

"Austin Carlile? The lead singer of Of Mice & Men?"

"*Oui!*" I smile and send my best friend a telepathic thanks for helping me make small talk. "She texted me yesterday to tell me she ran into him at the airport in Paris."

"Shut up!" Isabell falls back into her chair. "Dying."

Several people laugh out loud.

Maddy is the next to introduce herself. Although she is wearing bright red leather ankle boots and socks with tiny bells sewn along the hem—definitely a Notice-Me ensemble—she seems shy, smiling with her mouth closed and looking around nervously.

"I am a poet and artist," she says, her cheeks flushing. "I am taking this class to nourish my inner Van Gogh. Gotta feed the soul, right?"

The other students nod their heads and smile.

"Are you from Sitka, Maddy?" I ask.

"Me? From Sitka? No." She keeps her gaze averted. "I was born, raised, married and divorced three times, in Toledo, Ohio. Worked as a hairdresser for forty years before deciding I needed to make some life changes."

"I think I heard someone once describe it as shaking your life up like a snow globe."

For the first time, she looks me in the eye. She has kind eyes. "You get it, girlfriend. Like a damned snow globe. That's what I did all right."

"*Bon!*"

The class applauds.

Thank God for Share and her meet-and-greet suggestion. I am loving this group. Teaching them is going to be the easiest, most relaxing thing I have ever done.

The last person, a teenage boy with flaming red hair and an overly energetic personality, is introducing himself when the door suddenly opens and a girl with a blue fishtail braid walks into the classroom. She is wearing combat boots and a leather miniskirt. *Foutre!* It's that little snot from Make Knit Work. What was her name?

"Hey, Nolee!" Share chirps, scootching her chair to the side to make room at the table. "I was hoping you would make it."

Nolee!

"Hey," she says, clomping over to a chair and dragging it across the floor to sit beside Share. "Sorry I'm late. Had to work."

I want to lecture her about being late, tell her that she will never make it at Parsons School of Design if she can't master something as simple as punctuality. I want to squat down in front of her, lower my voice to a soothing level, and say, "Do those little hands confuse you? Should we get you a watch with a digital display or maybe even one that talks?"

But I don't.

Instead, I force a smile and ask her to introduce herself.

"I am Nolee Alooni."

"Okay?"

"Okay, what?"

I grit my teeth. She's only been in my class for two minutes, and already I want to wrap that fishtail around her neck and yank it until her face is as blue as her hair.

"Perhaps you could share a little about yourself?"

She shrugs her shoulders. "What d'ya wanna know?"

Oh, I don't know. Maybe you could tell us what happened to make you such a Château de Versailles-sized royal pain in the ass?

"What do you do in your free time?"

Sacrifice male infants on the altar of Hera, goddess of Feminists everywhere?

"Work."

I cross my arms and lean back in my chair. "Where are you from?"

She snorts. "Alaska."

"Nolee lives in Angoon, which is a Tlingit island village," Share says, obviously accustomed to being the buffer between sharp-edged Nolee and the rest of the polite world.

Nolee focuses her gaze on me and narrows her heavily lined eyes. "Do you even know what Tlingit is?"

There is no way in hell I am going to tell her that I don't have the faintest, foggiest idea what a Klinkit village is, so I cross my arms and return her stare. Our silent battle—because it *is* a battle—continues for several minutes.

I don't care if you are a bra-burning, card carrying member of NOW, I am the damned Alpha, so shut up and present.

"I didn't think so." She smirks, rolling her eyes. "The Tlingit is one of the oldest American Indian tribes in Alaska. We call ourselves Lingit, which means People of the Tides."

Well, light the peace pipe and let's carve a totem.

Who the fuck cares if she is from some ancient tribe? I sure don't. Being part of a tribe doesn't excuse bad behavior. I smile and try to channel Papa Allight, Laney, Vivian, and all the sunshine and unicorns people I know.

Deep Breath. Look Within. Project Peace.

"That's fascinating," I lie. "Okay then, if that's everyone we can—"

"That's not everyone," Share says. "You haven't told us anything about yourself."

"I would but"—I look at my watch—"it looks like we've run out of time."

"No worries." Share smiles and looks around the room. "I don't think any of us are in a hurry."

I take another deep breath. "I was born in Paris, but I attended boarding school in Switzerland."

Nolee mumbles something under her breath that sounds like, "Of course you did." Share elbows her.

"I attended Parsons for a year"—I shift my gaze to Nolee and smile a big, broad, patronizing smile—"before transferring to the Academy of Art in San Francisco. I was recruited by L'Heure before graduation, and I worked there until I came here."

"Are you effing kidding me?" Nolee cries.

"*Excusez-moi?*"

"You left the best design school in the world to attend some inferior college in San Francisco?"

Maddy gasps. Share drops her chin to her chest and exhales. The others stare at me, waiting for my reaction.

Deep Breath. Look Within. Oh, fuck this!

"The Academy has an outstanding merchandising program, and they are the only fashion school to show at New York Fashion Week." I take another deep breath. I don't need the air. It's a stalling technique, to stop myself from asking her why a blue-haired Parsons reject who sells knitwear thinks she has the right to judge an Academy grad. "Besides, Parsons is not the best fashion design school. It's second best. Central Saint Martins in London is the best."

Maddy winks at me and mouths, "Go, girl."

Share lifts her head and grins.

The rest of the class have shifted their gaze back to Nolee.

"And then you quit a job at L'Heure to teach cutting and sewing to a bunch of rejects in Sitka, Alaska?"

"Now see here, young lady," Maddy says. "There is nothing wrong with throwing off the shackles of greed and engaging in philanthropic pursuits."

To my surprise, Nolee apologizes to the class.

"And we are not rejects," Share hisses.

"Now, if there are no more questions—"

"Wait!" Share raises her hand. "I have a question, Miss Moreau."

"Please, call me Fanny," I say, sitting back down. "What is your question?"

"You told us about your professional life, but you still haven't told us who you are? Like, what do you do in your free time? What will you do when you finish volunteering here?" She grins and waggles her eyebrows. "Do you have a boyfriend?"

I can't very well tell them the truth: that I don't know who I am, that I rarely have "free time," and I have no idea what I am going to do after my year in Sitka—so I put my a little PR spin on it. Highlight the positive and ignore the negative.

"I enjoy rock climbing and cycling. I like wine and Belgian chocolate. Sorry, Share," I say, smiling at the beautiful girl still grinning at me. "*Je deteste* slackers, pajamas, Kitty Kat's perfume, Wonder Bread, my father's silicone-injected girlfriend, and tardiness."

I try not to look at Nolee.

"I am pleased to have the opportunity to share my knowledge with you and to be living in a place that is *trés jolie*."

It isn't until the last person leaves the classroom and I am sitting in the kitchen, my hands wrapped around a steaming cup of coffee, staring out the window at the snow frosted mountains that I realize I really am pleased to be in Sitka.

Part Three

Make me a perfume that smells like Love.
Christian Dior

Chapter 24

Cheesy Love

"So where's Hottie McScottie taking you on your date?"

Laney is sitting cross-legged on my bed, strumming a ukulele she purchased at a pawn shop earlier. Her chatter and string-plucking have distracted me from thinking about Calder and our non-date.

"A fondue restaurant."

"Oh, the handsome Scot is verra smart," she sings, strumming along. "For cheese is the way to a French girl's heart."

I stop applying the Dior gloss and look at her over the top of my compact. "Very funny."

Laney grins and keeps strumming her instrument.

"And it's not a date," I say, closing the gloss and tossing it into my purse. "He doesn't like me that way."

Laney snorts.

"What? We are just friends."

"Poor Fanny has traveled many miles, but she still resides in a place called denial," Laney sings.

"Miles and denial don't even rhyme."

"Sure they do!" She stops strumming. "What's going on with you? Why are you afraid to call this a date? It's obvious you're attracted to Calder. So why not release the brakes and let it roll where it's meant to roll?"

"I am not attracted to Calder."

"Puh-leez," she scoffs. "You would have to be deaf, dumb, blind, and in a coma not to be attracted to that man. He's totes gorgeous!"

I suddenly see an image in my mind of Calder in a flight suit, the green fabric straining to contain his broad shoulders, and my stomach does a frightening lurch. Calder was in command of the helicopter that conducted the search and rescue mission to find Vivian when she got lost in the Highlands. I saw a different side of him that day. The charming, flirty, winking-at-the-ladies Calder had been replaced by a serious, commanding, steely-eyed airman. Thinking back, he was pretty damned hot.

Fantastique! Now I am more nervous.

"He is pretty cute, isn't he?"

Laney nods her head. "So what's the prob?"

"I don't know," I say, pressing my hand to my queasy stomach. "I didn't come to Alaska to fall in love."

"Okay then, don't."

I chuckle.

"I am serious. Don't fall in love." She strums the strings softly. "Only…"

"Only?"

"The heart has its reasons which reason knows nothing of."

"Who said that?"

Laney shrugs. "Beats me. I saw it on a Snapple bottle."

And so now I am taking advice from high caloric beverage manufacturers. *Fantastique*!

I walk to my closet and pull out my Burberry boots.

"Nothing that has happened in the last month has been reasonable." I zip up my boots. "Falling in love with Calder MacFarlane would be the most illogical, unreasonable thing of all!"

"Some things can't be scheduled and organized, Fanny," Laney says, putting down her ukulele. "But you know what? Those are usually the best things of all."

I don't bother reminding Laney that Calder was once in love with my best friend. Sure, Vivia and Calder never dated. They flirted, maybe kissed, but that's all. Still, I can't help feeling I am violating the girl code—the unwritten rules prohibiting a girl from dating a friend's brother, father, ex-boyfriend, or any man she was really into.

My phone suddenly chimes and vibrates, announcing the arrival of a new message. I grab it off my nightstand and take a deep breath. It's probably Calder saying he can't make dinner after all.

I open the text screen and let my breath out in one long exhalation. The message isn't Calder cancelling dinner. It's much worse.

Text from Vivia Perpetua Grant:
What do people do for fun in Sitka on Friday nights? Got any plans?

I consider lying to Vivia, but I have never lied to my best friend and I don't want to start now, over something as unimportant as a boy.

I consider telling her the truth. I even mentally compose a text: *Vivian, I am going to have dinner with Calder.* I don't send it because I know what will happen. Vivia will blow up my phone with probing texts—*Are you kidding me? I thought you didn't like Calder? I thought you said he was a cocky cowboy? How serious is it? Are you gonna have crazy hot monkey sex with him?*—and then she will tease me relentlessly.

Or she will be hurt and angry because I violated the girl code. I imagine those texts—*So all of that talk about Calder being arrogant and too flirty, was that just bullshit? Were you lying to me the entire time we were in Scotland? Did you like him back then? Is that why you steered me away from him? How could you do this to me?*

I turn the ringer off, toss my phone into my purse, and promise myself to keep things strictly platonic with Calder until I have a chance to speak to Vivia.

Chapter 25

Just Blow It

I am sitting in Calder's jeep, watching him casually talk with a friend in the parking lot of Ernie D's. Why was I ever worried about him wanting anything more from me than a platonic relationship?

All of my stressing about falling in love and upsetting the chronology of my life plan. My worries about violating the girl code. Agonizing over this being a date or non-date. My nervous stomach. It was all for nothing.

Calder picked me up at six o'clock, looking devastatingly handsome in dark jeans, a button-down plaid shirt, a charcoal wool sweater, and a navy pea coat with the collar turned up. The slouchy gray beanie on his head and expensive leather boots on his feet gave him a hip, hot young actor look. If Zac Efron were starring in a movie set in Sitka, he would work this look, and he would work it just as hard as the sexy Scot is working it now.

I introduced him to Hector and Keith, and the three of them talked about guy stuff, like the Scottish football leagues, ice fishing around Alaska, and where to find sexiest cavewomen in, grunt grunt, Sitka. Then, Laney arrived.

Laney and Calder did their little name-game thing, Laney beaming like a supermodel who has just been told she can eat a grape when Calder remembered to call her Laney Amps.

When Laney said she was headed to Ernie D's to check out the venue's acoustics in case she decided to play at the next open mic night, Calder offered her a ride.

"You don't mind?" Laney asked.

"Of course not," Calder answered.

After dropping Laney off in front of Ernie D's, Calder pulled into the crowded parking lot behind the bar.

"I need to talk to a friend," Calder said, shifting into neutral and pulling the parking brake. "Be right back."

And now I am sitting in the jeep, holding my hands up the heat vent, and listening to the muffled music coming from a place that proudly proclaims they have "slow service, dirty glasses, great tunes, loose women, and liver-punishing liquor."

This is not the way dates go down. It's too laid back. Too casual. He didn't bring me flowers or a big Hershey kiss. He didn't compliment my ensemble or kiss my cheek.

Maybe Calder was serious when he said we could just be friends. Maybe he's not that into me.

Putain! I should have skipped the Dior!

I wiggle on the seat, trying to reposition my lacy thong.

I should have skipped the La Perla!

Calder's friend, a squat, muscular man with dark stubble on his jaw and head, suddenly reaches into his pocket, pulls out a small package, and hands it to the Scot.

If I didn't know Calder better—if I hadn't seen him pluck my best friend off the side of a cliff and fly her to safety—I would think he was up to shady business. Helicopter pilot, sheep wrangler, and drug dealer?

Ridicule!

Totes Ridiculous!

Calder takes the package and slaps his friend on the back. The other man laughs, shakes his head, and waves at me before disappearing through the back door of Ernie D's.

The driver's side door opens, and Calder hops in. I get a whiff of his dark, woodsy cologne, and it reminds me of that day at the airport in Anchorage when he pulled me to him and kissed me until my knees trembled.

A tendril of cold snakes its way down the back of my jacket and I begin to shiver.

"Are ye cold, *banfhlath*?" Calder turns a dial to the right and a blast of heat pours from the vents. "Ye'll be warmer in a minute."

He turns, bracing himself on my seat, and reaches into the back of the jeep to grab a wool blanket. He tosses the blanket over my legs, tucking it around my waist as if I were a child.

"*Merci*," I mumble, trying to keep it cool and casual, trying not to let him see how much he is affecting me. "But I am not a child."

"Aye, ye're definitely not a child," he says, chuckling. "Ye are as light as a wee bairn, though. 'Tis no wonder yer teeth are clacking together like castanets. Ye need to eat more, woman."

He is only teasing, but my cheeks flush with heat.

"I believe that was the plan"—I give him a sickeningly sweet smile—"yet we are sitting beneath a neon sign, outside a bar that promises to provide its patrons with the opportunity to acquire STDs and cirrhosis of the liver."

Calder glances out the windshield at the sign and laughs.

"Sorry about the detour"—he reaches into his pocket, pulls out the package his friend gave him, and hands it to me—"but I had to pick up a wee gift for ye."

"For me?"

I stare at the package as if it could give me one of Ernie D's promised STDs. I don't do presents. Presents are thoughtful. Presents are Belgian chocolates-sweet. Presents imply emotional bonds, commitment, and a need for reciprocation.

"Aye." He grins and winks. "Take it."

Putain de merde!

Ohmygod! So this is what it feels like to suffer with chronic RBD? I have talked Vivian through her most manic bouts of Romantic Bipolar Disorder. I have plied her with expensive French wine, spoken to her in soothing tones, and stood in mute horror/wonder as her feelings for a man swung like a pendulum in a Tiffany tall case clock. I can almost hear her teary voice in my head, "I love him…I hate him! I want him soooo bad! I want him to just go away!"

I take the package from Calder, carefully remove the simple brown wrapping paper, and open the box. Inside the box, resting on a mound of cotton, is a flat silver whistle on a keyring. A small silver charm is also connected to the ring.

I look at Calder, frowning.

"Take it out of the box," he says.

I lift the whistle out of the box and hold it close enough to see that the little silver charm is a high-heeled shoe. The underside of the whistle has been engraved with one unrecognizable word.

"What does it say?"

"*Banfhlath*."

I hold the whistle in my hand, rubbing my thumb over the cold, smooth metallic surface. I don't know what to think or how to feel about this unusual gift.

"It's a rape whistle," Calder says.

I close my hand around the whistle and stare at the large, brawny Scot through wide, incredulous eyes.

"Whhh…whhhy? Do you intend to rape me?"

He laughs—a deep, rumbling, happy laughter that makes me feel hot from my aubergine-painted toenails to my flat ironed hair.

"No, *banfhlath*," he says, leaning close enough for me to see the tiny specks of light blue sparkling in his dark blue eyes, like shards of sea glass. "When I take ye to my bed, ye'll not protest."

He leans even closer and presses his lips to mine tenderly, slowly, confidently, as if he had done this a thousand times. My stomach lurches, and I am afraid I am going to have to reach down and pull it up from inside my boots.

Calder pulls away and stares at me. His lips pull back in a cocky teeth-baring "yeah, you know you want me" grin. Normally, I would make some ego-deflating, semi-humorous comment that would knock a man back down to my size, but the cocky Scot is right. I do want him. I want him bad.

He slams the jeep into gear, pushes the accelerator, and maneuvers out of the parking lot. We are speeding down Halibut Point Road, away from town, when he finally speaks again.

"The whistle is in case ye encounter any other meth-head shoe bandits, and I'm not there to protect ye." He shifts into a higher gear. "I ordered it from a shop in Vancouver and Mangler picked it up?"

"Mangler?"

"Mangler, my friend back there. He's a fixed-wing pilot. That's his call sign."

"Ah," I say. "What does it stand for?"

Calder chuckles. "I dinnea think ye wanna know, *banfhlath*. 'Tis not a story fit for ladies."

"What?" I slug him in the arm. "Well, now I have to know. Come on. Tell me."

He shakes his head.

"Please?" I bat my eyelashes at him. "I promise not to let it wound my delicate sensibilities."

He rolls his eyes and groans.

But the eyelash batting works, and he tells me the whole sordid, painful story.

"Mangler got pissed one night, picked up a woman at a bar, took her to a hotel, and discovered she was actually a he. Mangler jumped out of bed, grabbed his pants, and zipped them up so fast that he got his…" Calder takes a deep breath and exhales slowly before finishing the story.

"He went to the ER and they called it 'testicular mangling.' Henceforth, he has been called Mangler."

"C'est horrible!"

"Oui!" Calder laughs. *"C'est trés horrible."*

I forgot he speaks fluent French. Hearing his deep, rumbling voice speaking my native tongue does a little something to my heart.

"What's your call sign?"

Calder laughs again, but this time it is flat, forced. "Ye dinnea want to ken my name."

"Yes, I do."

"'Tis not important, really."

"It is important to me," I say. "Please?"

"Verra well." He sighs. "But 'tis stupid."

"Stop stalling, Calder MacFarlane."

"Aye, ma'am!" He shifts gears and exhales again. "Flatline."

"Excusez-moi?"

"Flatline."

Calder tells me the story of how he earned his call sign. One of his first missions was to respond to a distress call from a point hundreds of miles west of Sitka, in the frozen unforgiving Bering Sea. The crewmember of a fishing vessel took a nasty fall and was having difficulty breathing. The ship's physician believed the fisherman had a punctured lung and internal bleeding. Besides Calder, his co-pilot, the rescue swimmer, and mechanic, a young bright-eyed public affairs officer tagged along to observe and photograph the rescue for a new article.

"'Twas a challenging rescue," Calder says solemnly, his gaze fixed on the dark, twisty road. "We took off around zero five hundred and it was still dark. The winds were twenty-five knots out of the north, and the sea was churning like the water in a washing machine. Monstrous swells. Anyway, we located the trawler and lifted the patient off the ship. We were securing the patient when a wave knocked one of the trawler's crewman off his feet and carried him overboard."

"Merde!"

"Oui!" Calder makes a sharp right turn, and we are climbing up a steep road. "The rescue swimmer made his way down the line and dropped into the sea. Several minutes passed, with wave after wave lifting him high in the air and plunging him back into the sea. He finally got a lock on the victim. We lifted them into the helicopter and raced back to the base."

"With two patients, not one."

"Aye."

"How does the rescue swimmer survive in such cold water?"

"They wear Nomex drysuits, seven-millimeter neoprene gloves, neoprene hoods, helmets…"

"*Incroyable!*"

"Aye. 'Tis an incredible sight to behold."

"So did one of your patients perish?" I ask in a soft, reverent voice. "Is that how you got the call sign Flatline?"

"What?" Calder turns into a small apartment complex parking lot. "Nay, lass. I didn't lose a patient. They both recovered."

He pulls to a stop and puts the jeep in park, then turns to look at me, a big Calder-esque grin on his handsome face.

"Remember the public affairs officer?"

I nod.

"He stepped off the helicopter and passed out, collapsed right there on the pad." Calder shakes his head. "Poor lad had a heart attack."

"Are you kidding me?"

Calder shakes his head.

"Did he have a preexisting heart condition?"

"Nay."

"Are you telling me that your hotshot flying caused an otherwise healthy young man to have a heart attack?"

The grin widens. "Aye."

"What kind of man are you, Calder MacFarlane?"

"The best kind."

I snort and roll my eyes.

He reaches for his door.

"Wait a minute!" I peer out the window at the glowing windows of the apartment building. "Did you bring me to your place?"

"Aye."

"I thought you said you were taking me to the best fondue restaurant in Sitka?"

"Aye," he says, smiling. "I make the best fondue in Sitka."

I frown.

"Didn't ye believe me, then?"

"Nay!"

He chuckles.

"Your apartment?" I look around nervously. We are perched high on a hill, overlooking the cruel, black sea. It's a fairly isolated spot. "Isn't that a bit intimate for a first non-date?"

"Didn't fash yerself, *banfhlath*," he says, pressing one hand to his heart and raising the other. "I promise to be a perfect gentleman."

I look at him through narrowed eyes, my lip lifting in skepticism.

"If it makes ye feel any better, lass, ye're surrounded by several men who have been trained to risk their lives to aid others."

"What do you mean?"

He nods his head at the building. "Half a dozen rescue pilots live in this building. That should make you feel a wee bit better."

"It does."

He grins before opening his door and climbing out of the Jeep. A few seconds later, he opens my door and helps me down from the vehicle. We stand close together, breathing the same air, but not touching.

"Besides"—he leans close and his warm lips brush against my ear—"you have your whistle."

I lift my chin and look directly into his twinkling eyes, a tiny challenging smile curling my lips. "I thought you said when you took me to your bed I wouldn't protest?"

He puts his hand on the small of my back and laughs. It is one of those smooth, belly-deep laughs that makes my knees go weak.

Chapter 26

Wrapped Around You

Hottie McScottie was right: When he finally decided to take me to his bed—swooping me up in his massive arms and carrying me into his room—I didn't protest. Not even a wee outraged peep.

After helping me out of the Jeep, Calder held my hand and led me to his apartment. He gave me a brief tour of his home, which turned out to be surprisingly classy, with a James Bond meets Man from Uncle feel. Modern, masculine, and stylish. Sleek leather furniture, am impressive collection of cut-crystal decanters and whisky glasses, and framed black-and-white photographs printed on slick metallic paper. The high quality photographs weren't of sports cars, airplanes, or scantily clad supermodels—images you would expect to see cluttering the walls of a bachelor's home—but of his family and their homestead in the Highlands. Calder's apartment reflects his appreciation for the finer things in life and his deep, abiding love for his family and homeland.

He opened a bottle of Chenin Blanc, and we sat on his porch, warming ourselves in front of an outdoor fireplace, sipping our wine, and sharing our histories and hopes. I never would have believed it, but the cocky cowboy and I have a lot in common. We love fine wines, luxurious living, adventure sports, and hard work. And we both miss living in Europe.

We talked, laughed, drank wine, and exchanged enough sexual banter to make foreplay totally unnecessary. When he finally took my hand and led me into the kitchen, I thought we were going to strip naked, slather each other in chocolate sauce, and have kinky kitchen sex.

No stripping. No chocolate sauce. No kinky kitchen sex.

Instead, Calder served me a delicious meal. Fresh bread from the bakery in town, grilled sockeye salmon, filet mignon, and gooey fondue made of Emmentaler and Gruyere. If a meal could be compared to sex, Calder's dinner was slow, delicious foreplay that progressed to a multiorgasmic climax, and ended leaving me feeling blissfully satiated. I took everything he gave me without thinking about the repercussions.

After our meal, Calder poured us each a snifter of Drambuie and we sat in his living room beside the fireplace, savoring the liqueur's nutmeg and honey flavor.

Calder reminded me that the last time we drank together was at a pub in Strathpeffer, Scotland, near his family's sheep farm. What he didn't mention was that he left me sitting in the pub with one of his mates so he could make out with one of mine.

"Connor liked you verra much, lass."

His husky voice moved through me with all of the heat and potency of the whisky.

"I didn't like him, though."

"Why not?"

I took another swallow of Drambuie for courage.

"Because I liked...."

He reached out and tucked a strand of my hair behind my ear, his knuckles brushing my cheek, a shiver of pleasure working its way down my spine.

"Who, lass?"

My stomach roiled—and it had nothing to do with the liquor. Somehow, though, I dug down deep and found the bravery to say what was in my heart.

"You."

And that was it.

Calder picked me up and carried to me to his bed.

I don't remember taking my clothes off. One minute we were bantering over whisky, and the next minute we were making frantic, crazy-hot love. His chiseled body pushing me into the mattress. My legs wrapped around his waist. His mouth claiming mine. My fingernails scratching his back. His solid cock....

Usually, I like to be on top. I want to be in control. I don't like the feeling of being pinned, smothered, but it was different with Calder. He stripped my gossamer-thin veil of control away as easily as he stripped my La Perla thong from my thighs.

I waited an appropriate amount of time after his climax before trying to make my getaway. My plan was to retrieve my clothes, call a cab, and leave while he was still lost in the post-coital masculine slumber world, but Calder trapped me with his arm and pulled me back against him.

I prayed he wouldn't want to spoon, because it's such a cloying, needy, predictably romantic position for lovers to assume.

Calder didn't want to spoon though. Instead, he kept an arm under my neck and turned me so I was forced to drape an arm over his chest, a leg over his long, powerful legs.

He fell asleep fast, his muscular chest rising and falling with each breath, his solid body warm against mine.

I stared out the window at the full moon and sang the lyrics to Zella Day's song "Sweet Ophelia" in my head. Day's song is about Shakespeare's Ophelia, how she lost her innocence, fell in love, and became careless.

When I woke a few minutes ago and squinted at the clock on the nightstand, I was stunned to discover I had spent the entire night in Calder's arms.

I rarely spend the night with a lover. Not the entire night. I am not afraid for a lover to see me with my hair tousled and my face sans makeup—nothing that nauseatingly girly. I just don't want to endure that awkward feigned intimate morning-after chitchat.

Spending the night breeds unwanted intimacy and expectations. Inevitably, the man uses a term of endearment, which always makes me want to vomit bile.

"*Bonjour, banfhlath,*" Calder whispers, pressing a kiss to my forehead.

I should be cringing, vomiting bile over his the term of endearment, but Calder's linguistic mashup makes me smile.

"*Bonjour.*"

My voice comes out throaty, unwittingly sultry. Calder groans and pulls me on top of him. His massive erection pulses against me, and I gasp against his lips.

He rolls me over, keeping one arm around my waist and the other under my neck. Murmuring something in Gaelic, he eases into me with painfully sweet slowness and starts a measured, unhurried rhythm that soon has me moaning low in my throat.

In....

One, two, three, four...

Out....

One, two, three...

In....

Calder is making love to me as no man has—with restrained passion and profound, almost terrifying intensity. He's making love to my soul, not my body. He's making me feel things I can't fathom, can't describe.

And I am...

I am...

Putain!

I am crying!

"Are you crying?" Calder pushes up on one arm and looks down at me. "Did I hurt ye, *banfhlath*?"

I stare at his handsome face, avoiding his probing gaze. I don't know how to answer him without sounding like a clingy psycho.

He swears and pulls out of me.

"I'm sorry, Stéphanie. I didn't mean to hurt—"

"You didn't hurt me," I say, sniffling.

"Then what is it?" he whispers. "Please tell me."

"I...I..." My voice comes out as one of those pathetic, weak girly whines, high-pitched and faltering. "I really like yooou!"

Calder gets it. He knows how much it took for me to make such a raw confession, pulled from my independent, aching soul. He pushes himself back inside me, kisses my tears away, and whispers in my ear.

"I really like you, too, *banfhlath*. More than I ever thought possible."

This time when he climaxes, I don't try to make a getaway. I lie there, his throbbing cock still deep inside me, his ragged breath fanning over my bare shoulder, and my heart aching for a need I never knew I had.

A need to be protected.

A need to be possessed.

A need to be loved.

With the same blinding clarity of a summer dawn, I realize am just like Hamlet's Ophelia. I have been careless. I have fallen in love.

Chapter 27

Enter the Perpetual Virgin

"Thank you for a most amazing morning," Calder says, brushing a lock of hair from my cheek.

It is mid-morning, and we are standing on the porch at the TTTF cabin. Calder has a flight in a few hours and I have to mentally flagellate myself for telling him I really like him and for crying.

"It beat a cappuccino and cardio class."

He laughs and then bends down to kiss me. He snakes his arm around my waist and pulls me close. I press my hands to his chest and am just about to push my tongue between his lips when the front door opens.

"Well, this is freaking awkward."

My heart stops beating and I freeze in place. Even through the fog of desire, I recognize the voice.

"Vivian!" I pull out of Calder's arms and run to my best friend, hugging her until there are tears in my eyes. "What are you doing here?"

"I had a feeling you might benefit from my fabulous company, and that uncharacteristically spontaneous hug tells me I was right!" She squeezes me before breaking our hug. "You sounded so defeated when we talked, and the tone of your texts kinda freaked me out. I had to make sure you were okay. So whassup with my Hype Girl?"

I laugh and then groan. "I see Urban Vivia is still in the house."

"Word."

She throws down her ridiculous version of a gang sign and we both laugh.

"I can't believe you flew all the way from France."

"Why not?" She puts her hands on her hips. "We made a pinky pact, didn't we?"

I frown.

"Scotland?" Vivian says, prodding my memory. "We were standing in the cottage, and I was thanking you for picking up the pieces of my life. I promised you that if you ever made a mess of your life, I would be there to pick up your pieces. So here I am."

"Your timing could not be more perfect!"

"It looks like it," she says, glancing over my shoulder at Calder. "From the looks of that kiss, you'll need me to play Annie to your Lillian soon."

I stare at her blankly until Vivian sighs, rolls her eyes, and says, "Hello? *Bridesmaids*?"

I shake my head.

"Puh-leez tell me you downloaded that movie?"

I grimace.

"Fanny!" She stomps her foot. "It's only my new favorite movie."

"*Desolée*."

"Whatever! We'll watch it while I am here." She smiles one of her big, toothy smiles that usually precedes a ridiculous statement. "You might pick up a few wedding pointers."

I turn around to look at Calder. His face is as red as the Coast Guard patch on his flight suit. I know his pain intimately. Vivian is fabulously funny, but her missing filter means she often speaks before she thinks.

"Don't be absurd, Vivian. That kiss was not what it seemed." I adopt a blasé tone and expression, stopping short of covering my mouth with my hand and feigning a yawn. "In fact, it was nothing, really. Nothing at all. You read way too much into things, *mon amie*."

Calder clears his throat and fixes Vivian with a tight smile.

"It was nice to see you again, Vivia," he says, taking a step off the porch.

"You're not leaving?" she asks.

"I have a flight."

"Still saving the world?"

"One lost American tourist at a time," he says, his smile softening.

"Thanks again for that, by the way," she says, referring to the time he airlifted her off the side of a mountain. "I owe you one."

"It was nothing." He stabs me with an icicle cold stare before smiling at Vivian again. "Nothing at all."

"Luc would disagree." Vivian flushes. "I disagree. You saved my life and I will never, ever forget it, Calder."

Calder grins and winks at Vivian, slipping the charming, flirty mask back on, before walking to his jeep, climbing in, and driving off without looking back.

"Well that was harsh."

"I know, right? He left without even saying goodbye."

"I was talking about you, Fanny."

"*Moi?*"

"*Oui!*" She crosses her arms and stares at me through accusing, narrowed eyes. "I arrived last night. I stayed up all night worrying about you, imagining you in the pokey for having stabbed the 'cocky cowboy' with the heel of your Louboutin! Trust me, you wouldn't survive in the pokey, Frenchie. I know. I did hard time."

I have tears in my eyes, but I can't suppress my smile. I've missed my best friend's outrageous imagination and unfiltered slang-peppered conversation.

"You were only in the pokey for three hours, Vivian."

She rubs her nose with her thumb and sniffs gangster style. "Just enough to earn some serious street cred."

The idea that my pink-wearing, exercise-hating, rock music-listening best friend could ever have serious street cred is laughable. Hold your sides, wet your panties laughable.

"As you can see"—I gesture at Calder's jeep turning on to Halibut Point Road—"I did not stab the cocky cowboy."

"Oh, I don't know," she says, pressing her hand to her forehead and staring down the road. "You might not have lodged your Louboutin heel in his heart, but I think your words did just as much damage."

"Pfft." I wave my hand in the air. "You're so dramatic."

"Don't pfft me, Stéphanie Elise! I live in France now. I know what you French mean when you pfft."

"Fine," I say. "I apologize for the pfft, but I won't apologize for calling you dramatic."

"Ooo," she says, holding up her hands and wiggling her fingers. "Hurt me."

We laugh again.

"Seriously, Vivian," I say. "What you saw—it's no big deal. It was just a kiss. There's nothing real there."

"I don't know. It looked pretty real to me. In fact, Hottie McScottie looked really hurt."

I can't even process the guilt I feel over hurting Calder, so I switch subjects. "I am sorry I didn't tell you I was having dinner with Calder."

"Why didn't you tell me?" She wraps her arm around my shoulders and squeezes me to her side, before letting me go and stepping away. "I thought we told each other everything? *Pas de secrets.*"

I am silent for a long time, and surprisingly so is Vivian. She is never silent for long, which tells me her question is serious—or for reals, as she would say—and she expects a serious answer.

"I didn't tell you because I violated the girl code."

"Girl code?" She rubs her hands together and stomps her feet. "You mean the one that says, 'don't poach your friend's hairdresser or manicurist?'"

"No," I whisper. "The one that says don't date someone your friend once dated or—"

"I never dated Calder!"

"—or anyone they were into," I say.

"But I wasn't into Calder...like ever."

"Yes, you were."

"No, I wasn't!"

I hold up my thumb and forefinger, leaving a tiny space between them. "*Un peu?*"

"*Non*! Not even *un peu*," she says, mimicking me with her fingers. "Sure, he's cute, and it was flattering to get male attention when I was in the throes of break-up agony, but nothing was ever going to come of it. Ever."

"Why not?"

Vivian crosses her arms over her chest and purses her lips. It is the petulant, you-won't-budge-me Vivian pose I have seen so many times before—like the time I tried to convince her to go on a juice diet with me, or when her mother begged her to work it out with her douchebag ex-fiancé.

"I won't answer that until you answer something for me."

"Okay, what?"

"Are you in love with Calder MacFarlane?"

"*T'es folle!*"

"You're crazy if you think I didn't see the look on your face when he walked off without saying goodbye."

"I can't be in love with Calder."

"Why not?"

"I hardly know him."

"I hardly knew Jean-Luc when we had crazy-hot monkey sex in Cannes, but that didn't stop me from falling in love with him."

"Who says we had sex?"

"Puh-leez." She snorts. "He picks you up for dinner and brings you home the next morning with stubble burn on your jaw and a rat's nest in your hair."

I comb my fingers through my hair.

"Are you mad at me?

"What?" She frowns. "Of course I am not mad at you. I am glad you and Calder are hooking up."

"You are?"

She nods. "Ever since you told me about your *un peu l'engougement* I secretly hoped you two would hook up."

"What *un peu l'engougement*? What are you talking about?"

"Remember when we were in Scotland and we went to that pub and ran into Calder and his mates?"

"I remember."

"Do you remember returning to the cottage chatty drunk?"

"I was not chatty drunk. I am never chatty."

"Ha!" Vivian laughs. "You kept hugging me and telling me all of the things you loved."

"What? I did not!"

"Vivian, *ma cher Vivi*," she says, affecting a horrendous French accent and slurring her words. "I love you sho much. I love you and my Louboutins. I love wine for breakfast and the Luxembourg Gardens at twilight. I love Shcotland and the sheep."

"Now I know you are lying. I did not say I loved the sheep."

"I love you, Vivian," she continues. "And I think I am a little in love with that stupid grinning, winking sheep cowboy."

I am about to protest, but the words colliding in my head become a twisted, tangled mess. I stand there with my mouth hanging open. Did I really say I was in love with Calder a year ago? How is that even possible?

"Stop trying to talk yourself out of it, Fanny." Vivian wraps her arm around my shoulder again. "If I hadn't been head over heels, sappy rom-com, can't-think-of-anything-else in love with Jean-Luc, I would have hit that."

"Vivian!"

"Sorry, but he rides a horse like a rodeo champion, shears sheep the old-fashioned way, pilots freaking helicopters, and rescues people for a living. Who wouldn't hit that?"

"Shut up!"

"What?" She laughs like a cheesy sixties movie villain. "Is the pricey heel on the other foot, Frenchie? Remember how you teased me about Jean-Luc? You were merciless."

"And now payback is a *salope*?"

"Damn skippy!"

She opens the door to the cabin, and I follow her inside. I consider apologizing for teasing her about her budding feelings for Jean-Luc— if only to stop her from singing the song I sang to her back then—but resistance is futile. Vivian is an unstoppable force.

We go to my bedroom, flop on my bed, and she grins at me.

"Go ahead, Vivian. Get it out of your system."

"Fanny and Calder sitting in a tree. K-i-s-s-i-n-g. First comes love, then comes—"

Chapter 28

Mommy Issues

Text to Calder MacFarlane:
I am sorry.

Text from Calder MacFarlane:
Does that mean you still like me?

Text to Calder MacFarlane:
Yes.

Text from Calder MacFarlane:
Enough to let me take you ice fishing tomorrow?

Vivian didn't exaggerate when she said she traveled to Sitka to help me pick up the pieces of my pathetic life. In only three days, she has managed to bring Hector out of his shy shell, convinced Laney to sing at Ernie D's open mic night, brokered a deal on my behalf to work with Netty to design an exclusive line of sweaters for Make Knit Work, and located my stolen luggage by telling the Anchorage Police Department she was researching a story on the crime wave against tourists.

She's even unraveled the complex, angry ball of yarn that is Nolee Alooni.

"Did you know Nolee's mother took off when she was just a baby?"

"No."

"Yep," Vivia says, popping a moose ball into her mouth. "Her father is an alcoholic, and her mother is totally MIA. Might explain her rough edges, huh?"

"I guess."

"Did you know she has had a job at Make Knit Work since she was old enough to see above the counter?"

"No." I close my eyes and rub my temples. I feel a Vivian-induced headache coming on. She is going to probe and prod me to ponder deeper meanings and feelings. "How did you find all of this out?"

She drops her chin and looks at me through her eyelashes. "How did I find all this out? I'm a reporter, Fanny."

"Thanks for sharing."

"Did you know Nolee was set to attend Parsons, but someone stole the money she saved to buy the ticket to New York?" Vivian pops another ball into her mouth. "Some people think her father took it."

I sigh.

Vivian narrows her gaze.

"What, Vivian? What are you getting at?"

"Well, your mother left you when you were a baby."

"My mother died, Vivian. It's not the same."

"Same exit wounds, though."

"So what is your point?"

"My point?" She pushes the candy bag away and rests her forearms on the kitchen table. "My point is that every person who comes into our lives enters for a specific and divine purpose."

For the love of Papa Allight. Not divine purpose talk.

"I doubt my Higher Power—if I even have one—sent a bitter, snotty feminist Inuit into my life for any reason except to torment me."

"Or maybe He sent Nolee to you to force you to delve into your shuttered psyche and bring your mother issues into the light."

"What does that even mean?"

"It means, the loss of a parent—whether through death or cruel and conscious abandonment—leaves deep and permanent scars on a child's psyche."

"Drama."

"I am not being dramatic." She reaches across the table and grabs my hand. "Fanny, you know I love you, but you have serious intimacy issues."

I pull my hand away. "No, I don't."

"Is it difficult to walk in heels along the river Denial?"

"Ha-ha."

"I am serious." Her smile fades. "Your mother's death affected you profoundly. If you can't admit, you can't commit."

I roll my eyes. "Thank you, Johnny Cochran."

Vivian sits back in her chair and crosses her arms over her chest. She is silent for several long beats, but she never breaks eye-contact. I think she is wrestling with herself over what to say, how far to push me.

"Have you ever considered that the roots of your blind devotion to all things Dior were planted by your mother?"

"What?" I shake my head and scoff. "What are you even talking about, Vivian?"

"That brooch your father gave you on your fifth birthday?"

"What about it?"

"It belonged to your mother, didn't it?"

"So?"

"Okay, Appaloosa, I've led you to the water, but I can't force you to drink."

The conversation ends there, but I play it over and over in my mind, throughout my class, during dinner, and now, as I am lying in bed beside Vivian.

I finally, grudgingly come to the realization that my frequently dramatic, always intelligent best friend is right: I have mother issues.

My desire to please my dead mother—even if it was only her unseen spirit—propelled me into a career in fashion. Her love of couture, especially Dior, is one of the few details my father ever shared with me about her.

My grandmother rarely spoke of her either. I asked her once why she never spoke of my mother. Her gray eyes grew misty, and she stared at a place far in the distance, perhaps a place where she was still the young, gay mother of a beautiful, vibrant daughter.

"It was easier to bury her body than it is to resurrect her memory, *mon enfant*. How can I speak of her when just saying her name inflicts lacerations on my heart?"

Then, she patted my cheek, took me to Angelina for *chocolat chaud*, and to La Samaritaine for a new dress.

Two years later, when my grandmother collapsed on Dior's runway during Paris Fashion Week, I took it as a sign. People will abandon you, but fashion is forever.

I pursued a career at Dior with a determination that bordered on obsession because I believed working there would somehow keep me connected to my mother and grandmother.

What if I finally got hired at Dior and didn't like working there? What if I don't even want to work in high fashion?

The thought makes my breath freeze in my chest.

You know how we do that word association thing when we look at ourselves in the mirror? Brown hair. Brown eyes. Nice smile. Likes chocolate. Hates pepperoni. Dreams of being a world famous designer. I am afraid the next time I look at myself in the mirror my mind will go blank. I will stare at person in the mirror and see only a strange shell person.

What if Vivian's Dead Mother-Dior Theory is more than a theory? What if, deep down, I don't even like fashion?

Chapter 29

Embracing My Inner Bush Woman

I have just finished my shower and am slathering tinted moisturizer on my face in preparation for a day of fishing with Hottie McScottie, when I have an epiphany. The only way to prove or disprove a theory is through rigorous testing. Before I can repudiate Vivian's Dead Mother-Dior Theory, I will have to embark on a scientific exploration of my psyche.

I have been operating under the premise that fashion is my god and Dior is my temple. Like any religious fanatic, I have been moving through life as if on automatic pilot. Fashion is good. With couture, all things are possible. Praise be to Dior. I have been showing up for the services, my prayer book of Vogue tucked neatly under my arm, listening to the rhetoric, but not really hearing, not analyzing what the word meant to me.

I have never considered the alternative. What if fashion doesn't exist? What if couture isn't the only answer? What if Dior is merely a building, a place for the lost and searching to gather so they might feel less alone?

I stop rubbing the moisturizer into my cheeks and stare at my fuzzy reflection in the steamy mirror.

A bold, brave, and frightening idea is taking shape in my brain. What if I go on a fashion fast? What if I purge myself of all things fabulous, all things refined, for a specific period of time? Maybe I will be cleansed of my dependency on worldly goods. Maybe I will gain clarity and wisdom and a greater sense of purpose.

Having a plan, even if it is a nebulous plan, makes me feel empowered. I will not allow myself to wander aimlessly through the world with no purpose, no clarity, no depth. Maybe I will discover my passion for fashion is as phony as the Prado bag Vivian purchased from some random shady street vendor, but that doesn't mean I have to spend the rest of my life in Passion Purgatory. If I discover fashion is no longer my passion, I will find a new one.

I grab my cosmetics bag, pull out a tube of Dior Rouge lipstick, wipe the mirror with a dry washcloth, and begin drafting the rules for my fashion fast.

1.   Delete all fashion apps from iPhone & unsubscribe from all newsletters, alerts, & fashion blogs.

2.   Throw out copies of *Vogue*.

3.   Drastically reduce time spent on morning toilette. 30 minutes for showering, whitening teeth, waxing brows, exfoliating skin, shaving legs, applying anti-aging products, styling hair, and applying cosmetics.

4.   When in Sitka, do as the Sitkians. Pack away designer clothes and wear only chain store garments.

5.   Refrain from referring to items by brand.

I slide the bathroom door open and hurry to Vivian's pink Louis Vuitton Astralis 50 leather weekend satchel—the one I gave her for her birthday last year—and grab…

Merde! I am only sixty seconds into my fast and I have already violated one of the rules: refrain from referring to items by brand name. Vivian's bag is not a Louis Vuitton Astralis 50, it is merely a weekend satchel.

I grab the first shirt I can get my fingers on and pull it out of the satchel.

Putain!

Obviously, I am being tested.

Of all of the garments I could have pulled out of my best friend's bag, I have managed to seize the most offensive, most ridiculous garment. Vivian's tattered "I Like It Raw" tee from her days of working at Raw, a sushi place in the Marina district. It is faded, a bit tattered, and features a screen print of a grinning cartoon sushi roll. I have begged, pleaded, and bribed Vivian to purge her wardrobe of the tee, but she refuses. It is her comfort piece. Some of us have cashmere Burberry cardigans… *Merde!* I did it again. My name brand dropping appears to be a bigger problem than I realized…some of us have soft sweaters or robes, Vivian has a juvenile tee. She even wore it on our cycling tour of Provence and Tuscany.

Well, Paul the Apostle slept in a lion's den to test his faith. Maybe this is my test. Or was it Daniel who slept in the lion's den? The extent of my religious schooling includes running the stairs of Sacré Cœur, listening to summer classical concerts in Sainte-Chapelle, and attending one Christmas mass with Vivian and her parents.

I grab a bra out of my dresser, slip it on, and pull the Raw tee over my head. Next, I pull a pair of black leggings out of Vivian's bag and put them on. Vivian towers over me. Her leggings are too long by several inches, so I scrunch them around my ankles like leg warmers.

I walk through the bathroom and knock on Laney's door. When she doesn't answer, I knock again.

"You cannot not pass!"

"Um, Laney? I am sorry to bother you, but may I come in for a minute?"

The door slides open and Laney is standing there in fuzzy, footed pajamas, a paint brush in her hand, a smudge of radiant orchid paint on her cheek.

"Of course you can come into my room."

"Are you sure?"

"Of course I am sure." She pivots on her heel and goes back to an easel she has set up in front of her window. "Why?"

"Why?"

"Why would you think I wouldn't let you into my room?"

"Oh." I walk over to the easel and stare at the beginnings of a spectacular landscape of purple-gray mountains and a lavender streaked sky. "Because you said I couldn't pass."

"Oh, that!" Laney laughs. "I was quoting Gandalf in the book *Fellowship of the Ring*. In the movie, he says, 'You shall not pass.' I think cannot sounds more badass, though."

I compliment Laney's painting to keep from making a sarcastic comment about her fangirling over mythical characters again.

"This is fantastic, Laney."

"Thanks." She shrugs her shoulders. "Painting landscapes relaxes me. I get jazzed looking at Renoir's paintings, especially *Auvers sur Oise*, and Paul Huet's *Chateau des Pierrefonds*, with its shadowy, slightly ominous foreground. Oo! And Jules Breton's golden, gauzy light." She turns to look at me. "Speaking of golden light, your aura is really strong this morning. Were you visited by a spiritual being last night?"

"What?"

"Maybe the ghost of an ancestor?"

"No."

"Did you dream about a spiritual leader? Maybe the Dalai Lama or the Pope?"

"Nope." I chuckle. "Although I did have an epiphany about some of my life choices this morning."

"Ha!" Laney's declaration echoes in the room. "I knew it. We like to believe we are the author of our epiphanies, but really, our spirit guardians whisper the words to us. You must have been visited by one of your spirit guardians this morning."

"While I was in the shower?"

"Sure, why not?"

"Sounds a little pervy if you ask me."

Laney laughs. "What was your epiphany?"

"Oh, just a connection between my mother and my obsession with fashion. It's too complicated to explain right now, but I promise to tell you about it later."

"Cool." She dabs her brush into a glob of paint and dots it on the canvas. "So why are you here?"

"I was hoping you might lend me some of your clothes."

"Sure"—she waves the brush at her closet—"take whatever you need."

"*Merci.*"

I grab a plaid flannel shirt and green field jacket. They're Urban Outfitters meets Patagonia. Utilitarian chic.

"Vivia said Calder is taking you fishing. Was she serious?"

"*Oui.*"

Laney peeks around the canvas, crinkling her nose and clucking her tongue. "You might want to consider wearing your thermal leggings and a warm hat that covers your ears."

"Will my slouch beanie be warm enough?"

"I don't think so."

"But I don't have any other hats."

"Take mine."

"You don't mean your panda hat?"

"Why not?"

I look around the room as if I will find a plausible explanation as to why I couldn't possibly wear her panda hat, like ever, when I catch my reflection in the mirror hanging over her dresser.

Why not? Because I would look stupid. Because the black-and-white fur will clash with my plaid. Because I don't even like pandas. They destroy beautiful bamboo forests, and their hairless babies make creepy screaming noises when they are first born.

On the other hand, wearing Laney's panda hat would be the ultimate test of my commitment to the fashion fast.

I snatch the panda hat off the top of Laney's dresser, thank her for the use of her clothes, and go back to my bedroom before my resolve weakens.

I grab another pair of wool socks from my dresser, put them over my first pair, and stick my feet into my Uggs. I slip my arms into Laney's flannel shirt and pull the Panda hat low over my ears.

Vivian is tapping away on her MacBook when I walk into the kitchen.

"Good Morning. Good Morning," she sings, her gaze focused on her screen, her fingers flying over the keyboard. "It's great to stay up late. Good Morning. Good Morning…"

"…to you," I say automatically.

I finished the song because if I hadn't, she would have sung it over and over again, like an iPod set on repeat. Vivian is an irrepressibly, nauseatingly cheerful morning person. She wakes up smiling, with tiny cartoon birds and woodland creatures fluttering around her and a rainbow arching over her bed.

I pour myself a cup of coffee and grab a protein bar.

Vivian stops typing and fixes her gaze on me. Her eyes widen, and she lets out a whistle.

"Wow…okay," she says, her lips pressing together as if she is trying to contain her laughter. "That's an interesting choice in attire for your second date with Scotland's hottest heli-hunk."

She waits a beat.

"See what I did there?" She asks. "Instead of hella I said heli, as in helicopter."

"You're a wit, Vivia Perpetua Grant."

She punches the air over her head. "Yes, I am!"

She's wearing a pair of joggers and a tee with cartoon trolls and the slogan, "Chillin' with my Nomies."

"New shirt?"

She glances down at her shirt and her lips curl up in a big grin. "Pretty cool, huh? Nomies, as in Nome, Alaska."

"Yeah, I got it." I pull the chair across from her out and take a seat. "But you are in Sitka, not Nome."

"The Sitka T-shirts weren't as cool."

I raise an eyebrow.

"What are you drinking? Coffee or Haterade?"

"Ha-ha." I tear the protein bar package and break a piece off. "Just promise me you won't wear that T-shirt in France."

"This coming from the girl wearing a dead animal on her head." She peers over the top of her MacBook. "Wait a minute! Is that my Raw tee?"

"*Oui.*"

"You're wearing my Raw tee?"

"*Oui!*"

"Jesus, Mary and Juicy Couture! What is happening here?" She presses two fingers together to make the sign of the cross. "Be gone, evil spirit. Leave Fanny's body in peace and return from whence you came!"

I stick my tongue out at her, and she holds her crossed fingers higher.

"Don't be so dramatic." I swat her fingers away. "It's no big deal. I started a fashion fast this morning. That's all."

"By the power of Jesus and the holy spirit of Christian Dior, I command you to be silent." She holds her crossed fingers up again. "Be silent, demon!"

She drops her hands into her lap and shifts her gaze from me to a glass of water beside her laptop.

"Don't even think about it, Vivian!"

She looks at me with wide eyes. "What?"

"Don't even think about sticking your fingers in that glass and flicking water in my face. You aren't John, and I don't need to be baptized."

She leans back in her chair, closes her eyes, and laughs like a little girl, feet flailing wildly under the table, arms wrapped around her waist. I should be annoyed, but I have missed her unfiltered off-beat sense of humor and rampant *joie de vivre*. Vivian is the only person capable of teasing me without pissing me off, because she is almost completely without guile. There's never a passive aggressive barb concealed within her jokes.

I suddenly see myself through her eyes—the elephant ankle leggings, lumberjack shirt, and juvenile panda hat—and a bubble of laughter bursts from my lips. Soon, I am doing one of those psychotic laugh-cry things I have seen Vivian do in the past.

"I've m-m-missed you so m-m-much, Vivian!"

She wipes her eyes with the backs of her hands and then fixes me with a gentle smile. "I've missed you, too, Fanny."

I break off a piece of my protein bar and offer it to her. She wrinkles her nose and shakes her head.

"So what's this about a fashion fast?"

I tell her about Papa Allight and Laney's aura readings and my middle of the night epiphany. She listens carefully, nodding.

"Tell me the truth, Vivian. Do you think this is the most ridiculous thing you have ever heard?"

"Hello, Fanny," she says, holding out her hand. "My name is Vivia Grant. I wore a Wonder Woman bathing suit to my Nativity Play, told three different men they were my first lover, let an action star talk me into getting a tattoo of a cartoon sushi roll on my ass, and got arrested by

Buckingham Palace Guards for stalking Prince Harry. Do ya really think I am the best judge of the ridiculous?"

"Maybe you're right."

"Maybe."

She laughs. I laugh too, but prickly tears gather at the corners of my eyes.

"Seriously, Fanny?"

I sniffle and nod.

"I am proud of you."

"You are?"

"Crazy proud." She reaches around, grabs a napkin off the counter, and hands it to me. "It takes a lot of courage to question your path and seek a new one."

"*Merci*," I say, taking the napkin and dabbing around my eyes.

"*Je t'aime de* Givenchy *ou de* Goodwill."

Her accent is surprisingly impressive. Last year, Vivian's command of my native tongue was limited to a single key phrase, "*Je voudrais commander un café au lait, s'il vous plait.*" She would order a coffee with milk in a flawless accent—even though she detests coffee—and then just nod her head as the waiter responded in rapid French.

"I said I was on a fashion fast, but that doesn't mean I am ready for Goodwill."

"Come on, homegirl," she says, grinning. "Let's pop some tags."

"What?"

"Yo, they had a broken keyboard," she says, making devil horns with her fingers. "I bought a broken keyboard."

"Is this a reference I should get?"

"Poppin' tags." She tucks her hands in her armpits and makes a ridiculous duck face. "Twenty dollahs and we could get a velour jumpsuit and some house slippers."

"I think I'll pass."

"Come on, Fanny, Ima gonna take you grandpa-syle. It'll be hella-tight."

I frown.

"Thrift Shop?"

I shrug.

"It's a Macklemore song, muthafucka."

"Yeah, don't call me that."

"Don't harsh my mellow, yo?" She grins. "I'm inviting you to go on a thrift store spree with me."

The doorbell rings. I push my chair back and jump up.

"*Merde!* Calder's here!"

"Chill, girl."

"I can't chill, Vivian. A gorgeous Scot is waiting on my doorstep and I look like a mentally disturbed drifter!"

"No you don't!" She stands and pulls me into her arms. "You look hella dough."

"*En anglais, s'il vous plait!*"

She pulls away. "Calder just wants to be with you. He doesn't care what you are wearing. You could stomp out there in combat boots and your birthday suit, and he wouldn't care."

"I didn't ken about that, Vivian."

I spin around and find Calder standing in the doorway, his blue eyes twinkling, and his lips curved in a suggestive smile.

"But maybe we can test that theory? What do ye say, *banfhlath*? I'll supply the combat boots."

He winks.

Putain!

Oh, I am gonna pop some tags all right—and shove them in my best friend's hella big mouth.

Chapter 30

Reel Him In

Text from Curtis Bower:
Fuckme! You won't believe who I just spoke to and what she
wanted to know.

"Are you afraid of flying, then?"

"Don't be ridiculous." I look from Calder to the sleek black helicopter
parked on the pad behind him. "I love flying."

"Then what's the matter?"

What's the matter? When he said we were going fishing, I thought he
meant in a local stream. Instead, we are traveling to an island in a private
chartered helicopter. A helicopter piloted by one of his handsome Coast
Guard friends. And I am wearing a panda hat.

"I just wasn't expecting to"—I look over his shoulder at the tall,
tanned, grinning helicopter pilot in aviator sunglasses staring through the
windscreen at us—"meet your friends."

"What?" Calder glances over his shoulder and back at me.
"You mean Stiffy?"

"Stiffy?"

"It's his call sign."

"Of course it is," I say, smiling politely at the other man. "Just don't
tell me how he earned that name. I don't want to know."

Calder chuckles. "Come on," he says, grabbing my hand. "Keep
your head low."

"I'm barely five feet tall. That shouldn't be a problem."

Calder grabs a large steel-framed backpack and leads me over to the
helicopter. He has to duck way down to keep from getting decapitated by
the spinning blades. He tosses the pack into the helicopter, helps me into

the passenger compartment, climbs in after me, and slams the door behind him. He hands me a green headset.

While Calder is adjusting his headset mouthpiece, I whip off the panda hat and run my fingers through my hair, tucking one side behind my ear and artfully arranging the other side to frame my face. Then, I put the headset on, lick my lips, and give Calder a thumbs-up.

He plugs the cable hanging from my headset into a jack in the armrest between us, and I hear an unfamiliar voice in my ears.

"Welcome aboard Stéphanie. My name is John, and I will be your pilot this morning. Flight time to Biorka Island is only five minutes, so sit back and enjoy the scenery."

The helicopter suddenly lifts straight off the ground and my stomach does a loop de loop. Calder grabs my hand, lifts it to his lips, and kisses my fingers.

It's cute that he thinks fear is motivating my reluctance and not vanity. There was a time not too long ago when I would have preferred him to believe me to be vain and not cowardly. I would have gone out of my way to prove I was every bit as tough as any ball-scratching, spit-hocking man, that I was not a weak, easily intimidated, frightened, and beaten female.

We are flying over the water, headed toward a distant island on the horizon. It is a clear, sunny day, and fishing vessels of all shapes and sizes are bobbing gently in the sea below.

Calder squeezes my hand. I look at him, and he points out his window. I lean across him, my arm on his thighs. A whale fluke is sticking up out of the water. It's the most awesome thing I have ever seen.

"You're lucky." Calder's voice comes through my headset. "It's a little early in the season for whale watching. The gray whales usually don't start migrating to these waters for another few weeks."

The island, a large, rocky outcrop with towering spruce and scrubby pines, appears in front of us.

"Biorka Island is famous for its sea lion population," Calder says, nodding at my window.

I look out my window. Big bloated sea lions lounge on the shore, their silky black bellies pointed toward the sky.

We continue flying inland. John lands the helicopter in a small clearing beside a pond.

"See you back here at seventeen hundred?" Calder asks.

"Roger that," John responds, his voice crackling in my headset. "Seventeen hundred."

Calder removes his headset and hangs it on the armrest. He grabs his pack, opens the door, and hops out. He holds his hand out to help me down.

A minute later, we are standing in a frozen field as the helicopter disappears over the tops of the trees.

Calder bends down and kisses my forehead.

"Did you enjoy the ride?"

"*Oui.*" I turn my face up to him and we kiss. "It was amazing. Thank you."

"You're welcome," he says, kissing me again. He lifts his pack onto his back. "Now, are you ready for a hike?"

"*Absolument!*"

Calder leads me across the clearing and into a thick pine forest. The air smells clean, crisp, with just the hint of something woodsy, like Calder's cologne. We walk until we come to a cement structure streaked with rust and covered in patches of lichen.

"Do you ken what this is?" Calder asks.

"It looks like a bunker."

"Verra good, *banfhlath*." He grins. "The United States Army built this bunker during World War II as part of its harbor defense of Sitka. It would have had two long-firing guns."

We keep walking through the forest, passing a small log cabin, until we come to a twenty-foot-high rocky outcropping jutting over the sea.

Calder shrugs out of his pack and stands it up on the ground. He removes a silver thermal blanket and spreads it on the ground. We sit on the thermal blanket, our legs dangling over the side of the cliff, while Calder assembles two portable fishing rods. When he finishes, he hands me a rod and we cast our lines.

"What kinds of fish are we likely to catch?"

"Catch or keep?"

"Is there a difference?"

"Well," he says, letting out his line, "there are some restrictions on fishing halibut and ling cod out of season, but we might catch yelloweye rockfish, Pacific cod, Chinook salmon, or maybe even a salmon shark."

"Shark?" I pull feet up. "You're kidding."

Calder laughs. I'm not kidding, but it's unlikely we would catch a salmon shark this close to the shore."

I let my feet dangle again.

"You seem to know a lot about fishing. Is it something you have done for a long time?"

"Since I was a wee lad." There's a slight tug on his line, so he reels it in a little and lets it go. "Do you remember the stream on MacFarlane Farm?"

"*Oui.*"

"My *athair*—"

"*Athair?*"

"Father."

"Ah."

"My athair taught me how to ride, hunt, fish, drink, and, of course, raise sheep. When he wasn't around, I had half a dozen uncles."

"And Angus,"

Calder smiles at the mention of his brother. "Aye."

"He sounds like a good man."

"He was." Calder keeps working his line. "What about your father?"

"What about him?" My tone comes out sharper than I intended.

"Is he a good man?"

Nobody has ever asked me if my father was a good man. "Honestly? I don't know how to answer that. He's not a bad man."

"High praise, indeed."

"If you want a different answer, ask a different girl."

Calder whistles.

"I am sorry." I touch his arm. "Sometimes I can really be a bitch."

"Didn't say that," he says, his voice a rumble in his chest. "That is not a way a lady should describe herself, and you, *banfhlath*, you are a definitely a lady."

His unexpected praise and sensitivity take my breath away.

"Thank you." I swallow back a lump of emotion. "After my mother died, my father sent me to boarding school in Switzerland. I only saw him on random holidays, when he wasn't off to Brussels or paying to have silicone injected into his latest girlfriend. Butt jobs in Bangkok. Facelifts in Frankfurt. Sun, sand, and silicone in Sicily."

"How old were you when your mother died?"

"Five."

"Five?" Calder turns to look at me. "Your father sent you away when you were only five years old?"

I nod.

"But ye were still a wee bairn."

His brogue becomes thicker when he is emotional. It is very sexy.

"Explains my daddy issues, doesn't it?"

Calder doesn't laugh. He just stares at me with his big heart-melting blue eyes until I feel I will melt and drip off this ledge into the ocean, to be carried far, far from him.

"I am sorry, *banfhlath*." His husky voice wraps around me like a security blanket. "You deserved to be protected and adored. All girls deserve to be protected and adored by their fathers. I will protect my daughter with my body and adore her with my whole heart."

I imagine Calder as the father of my child, holding her in his arms, drying her tears with his big hands, and my heart aches. I can't breathe. I worry he can read my thoughts, so I look out to sea, staring blankly at a hazy spot on the horizon.

Something tugs on Calder's line and he curses under his breath. Out of the corner of my eye, I watch him reel the line in, let it go, reel it some more, and finally hoist a big orange fish out of the water.

"You got one!" I tuck my rod into my armpit and clap my hands. "Bravo! I am impressed."

Calder winks at me and then gets busy removing the hook from the mouth of the fish. He reaches into his pack and pulls out a hand shovel and a large silver cellophane bag.

"Be right back," he says, standing.

He walks into the forest and returns a minute later with carrying the cellophane bag filled with snow. He puts the fish into the bag and sits back down. He begins to dismantle his fishing rod.

"That's it? We're done fishing?"

"Never catch more than you can eat," he says, smiling. "I've caught my lunch, now you need to catch yours."

"Are you serious?"

"Aye."

"What if I don't catch a fish?"

He shrugs.

"I always knew you Scots were a bunch of brutes, but I never imagined you made your women catch their own dinner."

Calder laughs.

"You're barbaric!" I playfully punch his arm. "You'd really let me starve?"

He stops laughing and looks deep into my eyes. "Never."

A bolt of desire shoots through my body like white-hot lightning. I want to reach out, slip my hand inside his jacket, and feel the hard contours of his muscular chest, run my fingers along his ribs, over his flat abdomen, follow the trail of hair from his bellybutton until I feel his hard cock brush against my knuckles.

I don't care about catching a fish or eating lunch. I just want to strip him naked, press my mouth against his warm skin, and taste all of the sweet secret spots on his body.

"I suppose we might be able to work out some kind of a bargain," he says, leaning close enough for me to feel his breath on my cheek. "If I share my lunch with you, what will you give me?"

"Not so fast, cowboy." I lean away. "You didn't really think I would surrender that quick, did you?"

"Well, you are French."

"Oh," I say, letting a little of my line out. "So that's the way it is. Well, get comfortable, cowboy, because we are not leaving here until there's a fish flopping on the end of my line."

Calder chuckles.

"I'll tell you what," he says, lying back on the rock and pulling his wool cap over his eyes. "I am going to take a little nap. Wake me when that finally happens."

He pretends to snore and I poke him in the ribs. He laughs and sits back up.

"There's something I'd like to ken."

"*Oui?*"

"When did Dior start selling panda hats?"

"What?" I look up at my eyebrows and see the black fur of Laney's panda cap. "Oh, this? It's a long story."

"No worries." He leans back. "It doesn't look as if we will be going anywhere for a while."

"Ha-ha!"

To my surprise, I find myself telling Calder about my mother's death, her Dior brooch, and my midnight epiphany. I tell him everything—things I've never told anyone before, not even Vivian. I tell him about the times I had panic attacks at work and how I had to lock myself in the bathroom and breathe in a paper bag to keep from passing out. I tell him about the dark moments, late at night, when sleep remained elusive, and I would drag myself into my bathroom, stare in the mirror, and think, "You are a fake, a phony, an imposter pretending to be something you will never be. You are not chic. You are not talented. You are nothing special."

I tell him how much I envy women like Laney and Vivian, women who know their passions and pursue them without fear. More than that, I envy their innate kindness.

"You are kind," he says, resting his hand on my shoulder.

"No, I am not." I move my shoulder so his hand falls away because I suddenly don't feel worthy of his touch. "I am competitive, organized, materialistic, and judgmental. I am not kind, which is why I don't have friends. Vivian has friends. Loads of friends. She collects friendships the way I collect designer handbags."

"'Tis not the quantity of friends one has that matters, *banfhlath*, but the quality." He speaks in a gentle, chiding tone, as if I were a child, but, to my surprise, it doesn't piss me off. "Laney, Poppy, Vivian, Fee. Those are some quality women."

"Fee?"

"Fiona, my sister-in-law."

"I know who she is," I say, looking at him. "But she's not my friend."

"She will be sad to hear that," he says, smiling sadly. "She considers you a friend."

"Me?"

"Aye."

"Why?"

"She values loyalty above all other traits. You spent your holiday working on a sheep farm because you wanted to support your best friend. When Vivia went missing, you raised the alarm and led the search party. And when she was in the hospital, you slept on the floor to be near her." He puts his hand on my shoulder again, but this time I don't shake it off. "You are verra loyal."

"Fiona said that?"

"Aye."

"Thank you." I lean against him. "I needed to hear that."

He kisses my forehead. Nobody has ever kissed my forehead before, and it feels good. Comforting and good.

"I suspect you know your passion, have known it for a long time, but you let other things distract you."

"What things?"

Calder inhales and lets his breath out slowly.

"The desire to please others, to appear successful, in control, perfect." He kisses my forehead again, as if to prepare me for his next words. "You didn't need to please anyone but yourself. Not your puir, dead mother or your neglectful father."

I am about to argue with him when his words hit the mark somewhere deep in my conscience.

Putain!

Last year, I told Vivian to stop trying to be the woman she thought others wanted her to be and to start being the woman she was inside. I told her to get real, be authentic.

Who knew a year later, a cocky, sexy, flirty cowboy would give me the same advice?

A fish tugs on my line and I almost drop the rod.

"I have a bite!"

"Reel it in, a *ghràidh*," he commands, wrapping his hand around mine. "Nice and steady."

With Calder's help, I reel the flopping, writhing fish in. Calder removes the hook and slides the fish in the cellophane bag beside the other.

"Yes!" I jump up and pump my fists in the air. "I did it! I did it! I really, really did it! Ha! And you thought I wouldn't catch a fish. Score one for France, baby."

Chapter 31

Hands on the Stick

One minute, I am jumping up and down, punching the air, and doing my little fishing victory dance, and the next minute I am wailing like a baby. I am not shedding a pretty, silent tear. I am standing still, mouth wide open, tears flowing down my cheeks.

Calder comes over to me immediately, wrapping his arms around me, and pressing my head to his heart.

"What is it?"

I don't think. I just open my mouth and say the first thing that comes out. "I was afraid I wasn't going to catch a fish, and then you would think I was a big, fat l-l-loser."

"Are you kidding me?"

I'm not. OhMyEffingG! I am not kidding.

I shake my head.

Calder pushes me away from him so I am forced to look up into his handsome face. He looks into my eyes, recognizes my sincerity, and presses his mouth against mine, kissing me with a tenderness that provokes fresh tears.

I want to tell him that I love him. I want to stand on my tip toes, press my lips to his ear, and whisper, "*Je t'aime. Je t'aime de tout mon cœur.*"

But I don't.

I pull away, bend down, pick up a rock, and throw it into the sea. "You must think I am one of those weak females who weeps at greeting card commercials and hangnails."

"No." He shakes his head and sighs. "I didn't think you are weak. I ken you are strong, but…."

I turn to look at him. "But what?"

"'Tis nice to see you this way."

"What way? Whiny? Pathetic?"

"Real. Thoughtful. Needy."

"Needy?" I take a step back. "I am not needy!"

"Really?" He steps closer and pulls me back into his arms. "There's nothing wrong with being needy, sometimes, a *ghràidh*. It means you need someone...and I like to be needed by you."

We don't speak again. We stand with our arms wrapped around each other as the sea crashes into the rocks below, sending a mist as gentle as Calder's kisses to fall on our faces.

We pack the backpack and walk into the forest, hand in hand. Calder leads me the log cabin we passed earlier.

"Is this your cabin?" I ask, as he reaches up and removes a key from a hiding place over the door frame.

"Nay," he says, sticking the key in the lock. "This is Stiffy's cabin. He said we could use it."

"That was nice of him."

"Aye." Calder takes the key out of the lock and pushes the door open. "After you, my lady."

I step inside the cottage. It's sparsely decorated, but clean and cozy. There is a pull-out couch in front of a stone fireplace, a thick rug on the flagstone floor, and a small but serviceable kitchen. A large picture window offers a panoramic view of the woods and ocean beyond.

I excuse myself and head to the bathroom to clean up. I wash my hands with the sliver of soap someone left on the sink, pinch my cheeks, rub the tinted lip balm I stuck in my jacket pocket into my lips, and comb my hair with my fingers. I do a quick pit check, sniffing for any offensive odors and catch a whiff of the L'Heure I spritzed on my bath towel before drying off this morning.

I finish my toilette and walk out of the bathroom. A fire is crackling in the fireplace, creating a welcoming warmth in the small cabin, and Calder is standing at the stove, frying the fish in a heavy cast iron pan.

"That smells delicious." I look at the crusty golden fish frying in the pan. "Are you frying them in butter?"

"Coconut oil."

"Are those diced potatoes?"

"Aye."

"You brought potatoes and coconut oil?"

"Aye." He grins at me. "A highlander is always prepared."

"What else is in that pack of yours, Mary Poppins?"

Calder reaches into his pack, pulls out a bottle of white wine, and hands it to me.

"Did you pack a corkscrew?"

He lifts his shirt, giving me a glimpse of his taut abs, and unfastens a Leatherman from his belt.

"Here you go," he says, handing me the tool.

I find the corkscrew tool and twist it into the cork. "Did you bring wine glasses, too?"

His mouth drops open and I laugh.

"Relax," I say, opening one of the cabinets. "Maybe Stiffy has wine glasses."

I search the cabinets, but I don't find wine glasses. In fact, I don't find a single drinking vessel. Something tells me old Stiffy consumes his beverages from aluminum cans. This is a beer-swilling, Cheetos-eating man cabin if I ever saw one.

"We could always share the bottle," Calder says, wiggling his eyebrows at me. "That is, if it won't insult your refined French sensibilities."

"*Mon cher*, I am French," I say, putting the bottle to my lips and taking a sip. "I would drink wine out of your navel if I had to."

Calder turns the dial until the gas flame barely flickers and looks at me with a raised brow. "Oh, really?" He reaches around and grabs the back of his shirt, pulling it over his head and tossing it aside. "Well, here's your chance."

We are on each other in seconds, yanking off clothes, falling onto the rug in front of the fire, running hands over naked flesh. It is hot and urgent. It is the manic, sweaty, slightly rough kind of sex people have when they're super horny.

After, Calder grabs a wool blanket from his backpack, and we snuggle together. We lay there, staring at the flames, drinking wine from the bottle, and sharing dreams of things we want to do together.

Usually, I don't like to make long-term plans with a lover. Love affairs have short shelf-lives, and unrealized plans can be painful. It's different with Calder. I find myself daydreaming about a life that, frankly, terrifies me. I see us being together for years, spending holidays diving in Fiji or skiing in Saint Moritz, buying a pied-à-terre in Paris, settling into a work-hard play-hard life.

And it makes me want him again.

I push the wool blanket down, exposing our naked bodies, and pour wine onto his abdomen.

"You are a woman of your word, *banfhlath*."

I follow the glistening, sweet paths the wine traveled down his sides with my tongue, licking and lapping his skin until he groans and pulls me on top of him.

It's only been minutes since we climaxed, but Calder is hard again, his rigid cock pressing into me, possessing me. I ease onto him and begin riding him, moving up and down in a slow circular motion that has us both shuddering and collapsing into each other.

Spent and satiated, we lie side by side, our feet warmed by the fire. I want to stay here forever, floating on cloud nine, far above the petty problems of life.

I am high on love. Higher than I have ever been before.

And I am scared. Scared that once we leave this cabin I will come crashing down from cloud nine. Something will happen, a misunderstanding, a fight, a shift in affections, and this shimmering illusion of happiness will vanish.

Calder raises his arm and looks at the big Breitling wrapped around his wrist.

"We have to go soon," he says, pressing a kiss to my forehead. "We better eat and clean up."

The fish and potatoes are more than a little crispy on one side, but it is still the best meal I have ever eaten.

Calder extinguishes the fire. I scrub the cast iron skillet. We lock up and make our way through the forest. The light is dying, the sky a sad gray watercolor version of the earlier sky, the air bitter and wet.

We hear the dull thunk-thunk-thunk-thunk of the approaching helicopter and pick up our pace, emerging from the forest as Stiffy is landing.

Stiffy climbs out of the cockpit, opens the passenger door, and grins at Calder. I climb into the helicopter. Stiffy climbs in beside me. Calder winks at me and closes the passenger door. He climbs into the cockpit, straps himself in, and begins running some kind of checklist, flipping switches, checking dials.

Stiffy hands me a headset and I put it on.

"Is he really going to fly us back to Sitka?"

Stiffy nods. "You have to give it to the Scot, he knows how to plan a PD date."

"PD?"

"Panties dropping."

Stiffy can't know what Calder and I did in his cabin, but my cheeks flush with a guilty heat.

Calder looks over his shoulder at me and grins one of those heart-stopping, sigh-inducing smiles.

"Ready, *banfhlath*?"

"I think so."

He laughs.

The helicopter lifts off the ground smoothly. I might be biased, but I am pretty sure Calder's takeoff was smoother than Stiffy's. I find myself staring at his hands on the controls.

Those strong, sure hands touched my lips, my breasts, my...

Watching Calder piloting a helicopter is exhilarating. It is the purest, most potent aphrodisiac I have ever experienced. Listening to him talk to the control tower over the radio is the sexiest thing I have ever heard. Way, way sexier than the sexiest, slowest Michael Bublé ballad.

By the time he lands at the airport, I am so horny I worry I am putting out signals that Stiffy might pick up. As soon as the passenger door swings open, I mumble a thanks to Stiffy, jump out, and race across the tarmac to the parking lot and Calder's jeep.

Calder follows me a minute later, concern etched across his handsome face. He searches my face.

"Are you okay, *banfhlath*?"

I nod.

He opens the door, and I climb in without saying a word. When Calder climbs into the driver's seat, I grab the edges of his jacket and pull him closer, planting a kiss on him.

"I am so hot right now," I say against his lips. "I will die if you don't get inside me."

"Do you want to go to my place?"

"No!"

"Here?"

"Here, Calder."

"What if someone sees us?"

"*Je m'en fou!*"

He laughs low in his throat and slides his seat back as far as it will go. I fumble with his fly, releasing his thick, throbbing cock and stroking it slowly, torturously, until he slides his hands inside my leggings and yanks them down to my ankles.

I kick out of the leggings and climb on top of him, resting my head on his shoulder, inhaling the familiar woodsy scent of his skin.

He keeps his hands on my bum, lifting me up and down in a satisfying g-spot pleasing rhythm. I turn my face into his neck, pressing my lips against his warm skin, kissing, licking, desperate to have the taste of him on my tongue.

It feels so good to be loved by a man like Calder, a man who makes me forget about my need to be independent, a man who tames and possesses me.

I am spiraling into a familiar place. My vision fades. My ears buzz. My breath comes in jagged bursts. I am on the edge of an orgasmic chasm, about to plunge into the velvety darkness of climax, when I murmur, "*Je t'aime. Je t'aime*, Calder."

I hear myself saying the words, but it's as if I am merely an observer and not a participant. I close my eyes tight and wait for him to say something, anything.

But he doesn't.

A car pulls into the parking lot and its head beams momentarily fill the car with bright, unwelcome light. Calder stops moving me. He kisses my lips and pulls out, his big cock slick with the proof of our shared desire.

I climb back into my seat, pull my leggings on, and stick my feet into my boots.

"Sorry about that," I mumble, not looking at Calder.

"Sorry?" He zips his fly. "If ye ken anything about me, Stéphanie, ye should ken that I am never sorry about making love."

His words feel like a bucket of ice water poured on the tinder of my smoldering desire. I have always known that Calder is a flirtatious charmer, but being reminded of his numerous amorous conquests so soon after having him inside me stings.

Chapter 32

Popping My Love Cherry

"Fuck yeah!" Vivian bounces on my bed. "You really told him you loved him?"

I nod.

"That is fucking awesome! What did he say? Of course he said he loved you, too, but how did he say it? Did he look deep into your eyes and speak the words in Gaelic? Did he cry?" Vivian snorts and slaps her forehead. "What am I saying? Big, brawny, badass Highlanders don't cry. He probably grabbed you around the waist with one of his big, brawny, badass arms, pulled you against his big, brawny, badass chest, and said, 'Ye ken ye belong to me now, woman.'"

I roll my eyes. "You have the imagination of a romance novelist. Seriously? How do you come up with this stuff?"

"It's a gift," she says, blowing on her fingernails and rubbing them against her shirt. "A wonderful, burdensome gift."

"How does Jean-Luc compete with your overworked fantasies?"

"Luc doesn't have to compete with my fantasies." She closes her eyes and lets out a heavy sigh. "Luc is that magical, shimmering fantasy that makes all other dreams look sad and shabby."

She sighs again.

"Blech!" I pretend to stick a finger down my throat. "That is about the most nauseating thing I have ever heard."

"Step out of the jealous. It looks hideous on you."

We laugh.

"I'll bet you are going to be glad to get back to the South of France and that sexy fantasy man of yours."

"I am."

"What else do you have to do to get ready for the big day?"

Vivian rattles off a mind-numbing list of pre-wedding to-dos, as I knew she would. Asking her about the wedding is the *diversion parfait*. Vivian is like a toddler with ADD. It is easy to divert her. All you need are shiny things or snacks. She talks for an hour, telling me about the flowers and champagne and guest lists and seating arrangements.

"So," she says, taking a deep breath, "did Calder tell you he loved you back?"

I blink several times.

We have been best friends for several years now, but Vivian's habit of changing topics with vertiginous speed still leaves me feeling disoriented.

"Shut up!" She leans closer and forces me to look at her. "Are you really telling me that Calder 'Lucky to have someone as hot as you' freaking MacFarlane listened to you profess your feelings for him and he said nothing in return? Nada. Zip. Zilch?"

"He might not have heard me," I lie, breaking eye contact. "I mean, I whispered it, and we were at an airport, with helicopters and planes taking off."

"Oh," she sighs. "That's it, then. He just didn't hear you. Why don't you text him now and tell him you love him?"

"No! I am not texting him."

"Why not?"

"Texting is impersonal and perfunctory. It's not the way I want to tell someone I love him for the first time."

"True that, but…"

"But?"

"Technically, you've already told him you love him."

"But he doesn't know that."

"Yeah." She grabs me and pulls me into her arms in a spontaneous over-eager hug. "I am just so proud of you for telling him you love him. This is a big milestone, my little one."

She lets go of me.

"What do you mean?"

"This is the first time you have told a man you loved him."

"No, it isn't."

"Yes, it is."

"I think I told Sean the Midget I loved him."

"Nope."

"What about William?"

"The proctologist that wanted you to have anal? Yeah, I'm pretty sure you didn't tell him you loved him."

I flip through my mental address book of previous lovers and realize she is right; I have never told a man that I loved him.

"You're right."

"Yes, I am!" She fist pumps the air. "You know what this means, right?"

I shake my head.

"Calder popped your I Love You cherry."

"Eww! That's such a gross saying."

"Puh-leez! Spare me the innocent act, sistah!" She forms a circle with her fingers and holds them over her head like a halo. "You just had crazy monkey sex in a jeep that was parked in a public parking lot. I think your dirty, nasty little ears can handle hearing about cherry popping."

I don't want to laugh, because cherry popping is a disgusting saying, but I can't help myself.

"I've missed you, Vivian!"

"Aw!" She opens her arms. "Bring it here. Come on. Bring me one of those reluctant, slightly-stiff, but deep down you really want it, hugs."

I hug her extra tight and even do one of those back rub/pat things.

"Okay," I say, pulling back. "That's enough."

Vivian laughs and pulls away.

"I am going to miss you when I leave tomorrow," she says, her voice catching and her eyes filling with tears. "I wish we still lived in the same time zone."

"Me too."

"You too? Which part? The missing me or the time zone thing?"

"All of it, you big dork." I grab her hand and give it a little squeeze. "I can't tell you how much it means to me that you flew all of this way to cheer me up. You really are the best friend in the world."

"Yes, I am!"

Chapter 33

Getting My Boney On

Text from Curtis Bower:
Oh my god! I am so sorry you were mauled by a bear. How long will you be in the hospital?

Text to Curtis Bower:
WTF? I wasn't mauled by a bear.

Text from Curtis Bower:
Oh, my bad. When you didn't respond to my insanely good news, I just naturally assumed it was because some wild animal was using your skinny bones as toothpicks. What other reason could you possibly have for not responding to my text about Véronique Laroque?

Text to Curtis Bower:
I was having hot sex.

Text from Curtis Bower:
Forgiven.

The next few weeks pass in a blur.

My days are spent teaching pattern making, color theory, designing for different proportions, and building a portfolio. I assigned the students a project. Each student is responsible for producing a garment or accessory to be sold at an auction to be held at the end of the term. Several of the students show great promise. Share's handbag designs are truly innovative. Maddy's hand-painted textiles could be framed and hung in the Musée d'Art Moderne. But the student with the most promise, the

Leah Marie Brown

most vexing promise, is Nolee. As Vivian would say, the girl has mad skills. Her designs are couture meets street. Totally Parsons-worthy.

My evenings are spent with Calder. We go for walks around the lake, catch Laney's performances at Ernie D's, prepare dinner for his flying mates, sip wine on his deck, and make love, lots and lots of crazy, sweaty love.

So when the email from Véronique Laroche, Vice President of Marketing for Chanel Paris, hit my in-box early this morning, I didn't know what to feel.

I open the email and read it again.

To: Stéphanie Moreau
From: Véronique Laroche
Subj: Employment

Dear Mademoiselle Moreau:

In the words of the inimitable Coco Chanel, "In order to be irreplaceable, one must always be different." As Vice President of Marketing for Chanel, Paris Fashion Division, I have let Coco's words guide me these last two years, as I assembled an irreplaceable team.

I would like you to be a part of our team. I perused your Curriculum Vitae and was impressed by your academic achievements: top of your class at Parsons and the Academy of Art. Bravo! I was also impressed to learn you were one of fifteen candidates chosen to attend the summer programs at the School of Material, Royal College of Art.

However, the achievement I found most laudable wasn't listed on your CV. Your mission statement urging designers to include philanthropy in the management and operation of their houses was brilliant. It is that kind of out-of-the-box thinking I would like you to bring to our team.

Your supervisor at L'Heure, Monsieur Bower, assured me...

The words blur as tears fill my eyes. I can't believe I have been offered a job at Chanel! Not a boutique manager in Nowhere, North America, but in Paris at the historic headquarters on Rue Cambon! Paris, the epicenter of the universe, the fount from which everything truly luxurious and fashionable flows, eventually trickling to the rest of the world. Paris, the place of my birth.

I am finally going home!

I will return to my hometown not as an embarrassing failure, but as a victorious warrior in the world of fashion. I feel as triumphant as Julius Caesar and his Romans, as triumphant as King Philippe-Auguste and his crusaders. I feel as triumphant as Napoleon and his Grand Armée.

I have never been prone to grandiose thinking before today, but scoring a gig as fabulous as Director of Event Marketing for Chanel in Paris is pretty damned grand.

I have to call Vivian!

I open my contacts, find her name, and choose her mobile number. It is seven o'clock in the evening in the South of France. Vivian and Luc will probably be opening a bottle of wine to let it breathe before dinner.

The line rings three times before Vivian answers.

"Yes, I would be happy to."

"Vivian?"

"*Oui, c'est moi!*"

I shouldn't be startled by Vivian's *outré* greeting, but I am. It takes me a second to gather my thoughts.

"You would be happy to do what?"

"Serve as your matron of honor."

"What are you talking about?"

"I had a powerful vision earlier today of you in a vintage Dior gown, standing in an ancient stone church somewhere in the Highlands. Calder was there, too. He was wearing a kilt and his wicked grin."

"That is an awfully detailed daydream," I say, chuckling.

"That's because it wasn't a daydream. It was a vision."

"Remind me to limit your time with Laney," I say, lowering my voice so Laney doesn't hear me. "Next you will be reading my aura and asking if I want to channel a dead aunt."

"Boo! Spoilsport. Vision crusher." She blows a raspberry into the phone. "Okay, so if you aren't calling to tell me Hottie McScottie asked you to marry him in a stone church in the Highlands, what are you calling about?"

"Guess what?"

"I don't know what. That's why I asked you."

"I got an email today."

"That is very nice, Fanny, but electronic mail technology has been around for two decades." I hear her tap the keys on a keyboard. "Don't get excited, but I just sent you another newfangled digital message."

"Very funny."

Vivian, clearly humored by her own sarcasm, laughs.

"Let me know when you are finished," I say, sighing.

She stops laughing.

"I am sorry, Fan. Tell me who sent you the email."

"Véronique Laroque."

"Nothing," Vivian says. "I got nothing. The name doesn't even ring a tiny bell. Should I know Véronique Laroque?"

"She is only the Vice President of Marketing for Chanel in Paris. Paris, France!"

"I know where Paris is, Fanny." Vivian laughs. "Okay, so what did Madame Vice President want?"

"She offered me a job!" My voice is unnaturally high. "At Chanel headquarters on rue Cambon. In Paris!"

"Are you serious?"

"*Oui!*"

"Get out!"

"I know, right? I am dying here. I have a million things to do: put my apartment on the market, ship all of my stuff to Paris, find a place to live, supplement my wardrobe with a few Chanel pieces—"

"So you're definitely going to accept the job?"

"Of course! Why wouldn't I?"

"I don't know," she says, hesitating. "I thought you were on a fashion fast."

"I was, but fasts are temporary. I never said I was going to swear off fashion forever. Besides—" A knot of anxiety is twisting inside my stomach. I need my best friend to cheer my victorious return to the world of fashion, not poke holes in my battle plan. "This is an amazing opportunity, too amazing to pass up."

"What about Calder?"

"What about him?"

"I thought you loved him?"

"I do."

"But you're going to leave him there by himself?"

"It's Alaska, Vivian, not outer Siberia," I snap. "Besides, he is a big, strong military man. I think he can fend for himself for a few months."

"So you are going to do the long distance thing?"

"I don't know."

"You mean you haven't told him yet?"

"I got the email, read it a dozen times, and called you."

Vivian makes a noise that sounds a lot like a grunt of disapproval. "What about your assignment with Each One, Teach One? I thought you enjoyed working with your students."

"I do."

"And you're still going to leave them?"

"The class ends in two weeks," I say, ignoring the prickly sensation of guilt I am feeling. "I'll stay until then, but they will just have to find someone else to teach the second class."

Vivian doesn't say anything. The line crackles.

"I thought you would be happy for me."

"I am happy for you, Fanny. If this is really what you want, if it is truly the passion you feel you are meant to pursue, I am happy for you."

"You don't sound happy."

"Don't project your feelings on to me, Frenchie," she says, her tone more gentle than her words. "I said I am happy, and I meant it."

"You're happy for me, but disappointed by my decision."

"I didn't say that."

"What then?"

"Honestly?"

"*Bien sûr.*" I exhale sharply. "I wouldn't want you to lie to me."

"Okay," she says, the word coming out as a breathy exhalation. "Do you remember what you said to me a year ago, when I was considering choosing my career over Jean-Luc?"

"No. What?"

"You said you had never seen me as happy as I was when I was with Luc. You told me I would be a fool to choose a job over a man like Luc, a man who was loyal and truly loved me. You told me to choose love and let the rest work itself out."

I snort. "I said that?"

"Yes, my dear, wise friend. You said that."

"And?"

"And now I am saying it to you. I have never heard you as happy as you have been since you started seeing Calder. I have never seen you as content as you were teaching your students. You looked like a woman who had finally found her groove." She lowers her voice. "I love you like a sister, Fanny. I want to support you as you chase your dreams, but I just want to make sure you are chasing the right ones, the ones that leave you feeling truly happy and content."

"Fashion makes me happy."

"Fashion made you miserable. You were wound up tighter than a Cartier tank watch, stressed and borderline postal."

I think back to my days at L'Heure, but can only recall the titillation I felt when I walked into the store or when a new shipment of gowns arrived. If there were bad days, I have forgotten them.

I know Vivian means well—she always means well—but she doesn't understand my true feelings, not really. I am the only one who understands my feelings, and I am feeling a need to redeem myself, to prove that I am couture-worthy. I will never prove I am couture-worthy if I open a little boutique in Strathpeffer, Scotland—as appealing as that dream may be.

"I love you, Vivian. I know you want me to be happy, and I really, really think taking this job and moving back to Paris will make me happy." Calder's face appears in my mind and the adrenaline surging through my veins dissipates. "If Calder and I are meant to be together, we will be together."

Chapter 34

Au revoir or Adieu?

Later that afternoon, I am helping Nolee with a pattern when I look up and find Calder standing in the doorway, still wearing his flight suit, and my heart skips a symphony of beats. He dropped in on my class once before, to bring me a bouquet of flowers, but this time his lips are pressed together in a grim line and his blue eyes have lost their twinkle.

"I'll be right back," I say to Nolee.

When I look up again, Calder isn't standing in the doorway. I find him on the porch, leaning against a railing, arms crossed over his chest, Aviators hiding his eyes.

"Is something wrong?"

"Aye," he says, his brogue thick with emotion. "Angus had a heart attack."

"*Mon dieu!*" I put my hand over my mouth. Angus is Calder's older brother, but only by a few years. "Is he going to be okay?"

"I didn't ken." His voice sounds gravely and I know he is struggling to contain his emotions. "He is scheduled for a bypass tomorrow. We will ken more after that."

"What would you like me to do?" I move closer, wrapping my arms around his waist and resting my head on his chest. "I am here for you and will do whatever I can to support you."

"Will ye go to Scotland with me?"

"When?"

"The detachment is cutting my orders and working a ticket on the next flight to Edinburgh."

"Of course I will go with you. I will call Finn Thompson, the president of the charity, and tell him I need some time off. When do you think we would be back?"

"I am not coming back."

I stop hugging him and look up at his face.

"Ever?"

He shakes his head. "My tour is almost up anyway, and I didn't plan on signing on for another one. Fiona is going to need my help running the farm. She can't manage it alone, and I will not let her."

His brogue is so thick—with his shorter words running together and the ending consonants dropping away completely—I have a difficult time understanding him.

"You mean to stay in Scotland."

"Aye," he says, the word rumbling in his chest. "And I mean for you to stay with me."

My heart skips another beat. Is he asking me to marry him?

"I want you to live with me. We can stay in one of the cottages until Angus is back on his feet."

"You want me to quit my job?"

"'Tis only a volunteer position."

"It's my career."

"I didn't mean it that way," he says, pulling me closer. "Some things are more important than a career."

I pull out of his embrace. "Maybe to you!"

He inhales sharply and steps back.

"You don't understand," I say, trying to ease his pain and my conscience. "I received an email this morning, from the Vice President of Chanel offering me a position in Paris. It's an amazing opportunity, especially after what happened at L'Heure, and I won't let anything ruin it."

"Anything or anyone."

"It's not like that—"

"I thought you didn't want to work in fashion?"

"I thought that, too, but then I got that email, and…."

"And everything has changed."

"Nothing has changed between us." I grab his hand and lacing my fingers with his. "I still want to see you."

"How will that happen?" He opens his fingers and lets my hand drop away. "If you are in Paris and I am in the Highlands, how will we see each other?"

"It's a short flight." I smile and push my hair behind my ear. "Direct from Charles de Gaulle to Edinburgh."

"Weekend hook-ups?" He shakes his head. "I didna want that. I am looking for something more."

His words hit me like a stiletto to the heart. Something more. More than me, he means.

"I am sorry, but I can't give you any more right now."

He smiles and shakes his head.

"This is goodbye then, *banfhlath*." He bends down and presses a kiss to my forehead. "Take care of yourself."

I can't move. My feet feel as if they are frozen to the porch, and my arms hang heavy at my sides. I am standing in the same spot when he gets in his jeep, starts the engine, and drives away.

He never took off his sunglasses. I never even got to see his eyes.

My knees buckle, and I literally have to hold onto the porch railing to keep from falling on my face.

Chapter 35

Chanel-ing my Inner-Coco

Text to Vivia Perpetua Grant:
I know I have made the right choice, but my heart hurts so much.

Text from Vivia Perpetua Grant:
"I only drink champagne when I am in love and when I am not," Coco Chanel. Drink champagne.

"I can't believe this is goodbye."

"It is not goodbye," I say, giving Laney a quick hug. "You will come to Paris and live out your Starving Artist in Paris Fantasy. You will stay with me, so you won't really starve."

When we stop hugging, I see Laney's big glasses are steamy and tears are dripping down her cheeks. I give her another hug.

"Here," she says, handing me her panda hat. "I want you to have this."

"Are you kidding?" I put my hand up. "I can't take your panda hat. It's your favorite."

"Take it." She sniffles, shoving the furry hat at me. "I think the panda is your spirit animal."

I can't help but laugh. "Why do you think that?" I say, taking the hat.

"The panda is a powerful spirit animal, known for its strength and determination." She takes her glasses off and cleans them on her shirt, puts them back on, and looks me in the eye. "People who have the panda as their spirit animal are usually uncomfortable with feelings and intimate relationships, so they put up strong defenses and seek material comfort."

"Yikes!" I say, frowning at the hat. "Panda people sound cold and hedonistic."

Laney shakes her head. "Pandas are very sensitive."

"So we're not all bad?"

Laney shakes her head again.

I have already said my goodbyes to Keith and Hector, so I grab my carry-on and pull it over to where Alexi the cab driver is parked. I open the door and climb into the back seat.

"Wait!" Laney comes running over.

"What's wrong?"

"I didn't want you to leave until I told you one more thing about the panda," she says. "The panda's struggle is to find balance, but when it does, it nurtures and receives great nurturing in return. I hope you find your balance, Fanny."

"*Merci, mon amie.*"

I hug Laney again and climb into the taxi. We wave to each other and blow kisses until the taxi turns onto Halibut Point Road and we can no longer see each other.

"Excuse me," I say, swallowing a thick lump in my throat. "I need you to stop at Make Knit Work before driving me to the airport."

"No."

"Excuse me?"

"Nowhere to park."

"Just leave it running out front and turn your hazards on."

"No," he says, shaking his head. "I get ticket."

"Listen, Alexi—"

He looks at me through the rearview mirror and raises an eyebrow

"Oh, yeah, I got your name. And don't you pretend you don't know who I am, either! This town isn't that big."

"I know you."

"Yes, you do! You left me at the bottom of a hill, in a blizzard, with a ton of luggage. I have a feeling the Sitka Chamber of Commerce and the Department of Tourism would be very interested to hear about the way taxi drivers treat helpless female visitors."

He snorts. "I wait."

"Smart decision, Yeltsin. Let's end this Cold War."

He pulls up to Make Knit Work and I jump out.

Netty greets me before the bells have even stopped jingling. "Good morning, Fanny. Nolee told me you got a new job. She said you would be leaving us."

"*Oui,*" I say, smiling. "I was offered a position at Chanel."

"That is good news, but I am sorry to see you go. I really hoped we could work together to design some new garments."

"Maybe we can," I say, reaching into my pocket and pulling out an envelope. "I wrote down my contact information. Once I am settled, I will sketch a few designs and send them to you. If you like them, we can figure something out."

"I'd like that."

I hand her the envelope and she slips it into her apron pocket.

"I do have a favor to ask you."

"Me?"

"*Oui.*"

"What is it?"

"There is a check inside that envelope. I was wondering if you would mind cashing it and giving it to Nolee to pay for her tuition to Parsons."

Netty's eyes widen. "Are you serious?"

"*Oui,*" I say, smiling. "Please don't tell her it is from me. Just say you came into an inheritance and want to help her to fulfill her destiny."

"I couldn't—"

"Please." I gently squeeze her arm. "I wouldn't feel comfortable with her knowing I was her benefactor."

"Why would you help a girl you hardly know?"

"Nolee has talent."

"Plenty of people have talent. Why Nolee?"

Alexi honks the horn. I hold up my finger and mouth the words, "Just one more minute."

"I want to help Nolee because I see myself younger self in her," I confess. "My mother died when I was young, and my father was too wrapped up in his own problems to be a parent. Growing up without affection made me jaded and mistrustful. I don't want to see Nolee become hardened."

Alexi honks his horn again.

"You are a kind and generous girl," Netty says, patting my cheek. "Your mother would be very proud of you."

"Thank you." Tears flood my eyes. "Nobody has ever said that to me."

"Well, they should have."

Chapter 36

Filling the Hole

Text from Vivia Perpetua Grant:
Coco Quote: "How many cares one loses when one decides not to be something, but to be someone." Bisous.

I am standing in Chanel's light-filled atelier at 31 rue Cambon, just above Coco's old apartment, when I realize I have made a huge mistake. One minute, I am snapping photos of the *petits mains* putting finishing touches on a collection of garments designed exclusively for Kate Middleton, Prince William's stylish wife, and the next minute I am locked in a bathroom stall, silently sobbing into a wad of toilet paper.

I should feel deliriously happy. I spend my days conversing with the most skilled couturiers in the world, surrounded by garments so beautiful they could hang on the walls of the Louvre. A million women would kick off their Jimmy Choos and walk barefoot over scalding coals and broken glass to have my job. I realize, with painful clarity, that I am no longer one of those women.

My colleagues have been warm and welcoming. We've even gone out for drinks after work. Véronique, my boss, is the best mentor I have ever had. The work is challenging, but not so challenging that I feel like a piece of elastic that has been stretched to its limits.

Yet I can't help feeling like what I am doing is frothy, fluffy nonsense. If the world is a carnival, couture is the cotton candy. Have you ever watched cotton candy being made? Sugar is poured into this big heated drum that spins and spins until fine strands begin to form. Sure, they add flavoring and food color, but it lacks any real substance. It's a lot of work for something that lacks substance.

I've never liked cotton candy.

The work I did with Each One, Teach One had substance. A group of strangers came to me to be educated, elevated, and enlightened. I didn't teach them how to split atoms or conduct brain surgery, but every time we met, I made sure they left my classroom with at least one new skill.

I miss feeling truly useful. I miss falling into bed at night happily exhausted. I miss fresh air, towering trees, and quiet. I miss hearing Laney strum her ukulele. I miss...

...Calder.

I miss Calder so much I feel like someone reached into my chest and ripped a part of my heart out. I can't eat. I can't sleep. I just want to hole up in my room in my father's apartment and sleep away the pain.

I have emailed him and tried calling him, but my messages go unanswered. I sent flowers to the hospital for Angus and spa certificates to Fiona so she could feel tended to, as well. Fiona sent a lovely thank you card, but she didn't mention Calder.

What if every breath, every step I took before Calder was just so I could reach him? What if my destiny was to love and be loved by a cocky Scottish cowboy, and I blew it?

My chest tightens. My breath lodges in my throat. The bathroom stall suddenly feels too small, as if the walls are moving closer together to crush me.

I open the door and walk out of the bathroom, wad of toilet paper still clutched in my hand. I walk through the atelier, down the stairs, and out into the sunshine. I try taking a deep breath, but the air feels heavy, polluted, smothering.

And so I start walking.

I walk and walk and walk. I walk through the Tuileries Gardens, past the freshly planted tulip beds and the children tossing coins into the Bassin Octogonal. I walk around the Place de la Concorde, past the stalls that will sell trinkets and treats once the weather warms. I walk to Les Caves du Marais and purchase a bottle of champagne.

I walk until I am standing in front of my father's apartment building. I walk into the elevator. I walk out of the elevator. I walk into his apartment and into my bedroom. I pop open the bottle of champagne, drink the contents from the bottle, and then climb into my bed without taking off my clothes, pull the covers over my head, and go to sleep.

* * * *

Text to Vivia Perpetua Grant:
I am miserable. Too miserable to talk.

Text from Vivia Perpetua Grant:

Of course you are miserable. You are in the city of love without your lovah. Forget high fashion and go after that cowboy. You look better in Wellies than Louboutins anyway.

"Fanny?" My father knocks on my bedroom door. "Fanny?"

I pretend to be asleep because I am not ready to listen to him lecture me about how I have made colossally bad career choices and how I have wasted my education and ruined my professional reputation. Blah blah blah.

He opens the door anyway. Bright light floods my room. I groan and pull the covers over my head.

"Fanny?" He walks close enough for me to smell his cologne, an expensive scent made exclusively for him in a perfumerie in Grasse. "Vivian has called three times this morning. You can't keep ignoring her."

"Tell her I am sleeping."

"*Non, ma puce.*" His voice is low and firm. "She said to tell you if she doesn't hear from you in the next hour, she is booking a seat on the seven twenty-six TGV from Montpellier to Paris. I could not tell if she was serious."

"You don't know my best friend." I push the covers down to my nose. "She was serious."

"You will call her?"

"*Oui.*"

He frowns and shifts his weight from one foot to the other. He wants to say something, but is hesitating. Odd. Hesitation is not my father's natural state. His mind is like a super-computer, processing data at lightning speed, free of passion or compassion. His super-computer brain helped him increase our family's fortune. It helped him survive my mother's death. Most men would have been catatonic with grief at losing such a beautiful and vibrant wife. Not my Papa. Her death was barely a blip on his screen.

"*Qu'est-ce que c'est, Papa?*"

"I am worried about you."

I snort. "Don't worry about me. After all, I am a Moreau, and we don't let anything keep us down for long. Not a lost job or a lost love. *J'ai raison, n'est-ce pas?*"

"*Non.*" He sighs and takes a seat on the edge of my bed. "You are not right, *ma puce.*"

Leah Marie Brown

He hasn't called me *ma puce* since I was a very little girl. I want to say that it means nothing, but hearing him use the term of endearment has the same effect as watching a thousand sappy greeting card commercials. I sit up, tuck my knees under my chin, and wrap my arms around my legs.

"*La!*" He shakes his head and clucks his tongue. "What your grandmother would say if she could see you now, dirty, disheveled, and dreadfully depressed."

"She would say, 'Fanny, *ma fille*, stop feeling sorry for yourself. Get out of that bed, take a shower, and go buy a pretty new gown.'" I try to laugh, but the sound that comes out is more bitter than joyful. "For *Grand-mère*, there was no problem or pain too great that couldn't be fixed with a quick trip to Dior, Lancel, or Chanel."

"Ah, be careful there, *ma puce*," he says, crossing his arms over his chest. "Do not confuse her *joie de vivre* with a lack of feeling. Your *grand-mère* had great depth and more feeling than anyone I have ever known. She just didn't believe in wallowing in pain."

"Is that what you think I am doing, Papa? Wallowing in pain?"

"*Bien sûr*," he snorts. "But you are wallowing in pain, *tu n'es pas?*"

"*Oui*, Papa! I am wallowing. This is what people do when they lose someone they love; they wallow and wail and stop washing. This is normal!"

I stop talking and look away from him, but I know he heard my unspoken words, my accusation that he is not normal, that the way he grieved over my mother was not normal.

"Do not speak to me of loss, Fanny," he whispers. "Your mother was the love of my life. That feeling—that someone reached inside your chest and tore your heart out—I have had that feeling every day since your mother died."

"You could have fooled me."

"What does that mean?"

"What does that mean?" I scoff. "It means you have filled your life with a quick succession of vapid, silly, shallow girlfriends."

"Pfft."

It is an utterly French, utterly dismissive expression. His pfft is akin to someone rolling their eyes and saying, "Puh-leez. Are you kidding me?" Yet that simple pfft is the most genuine, heartfelt thing my father has said to me in years.

"You don't want to spend your life like me, *ma puce*, aching for a love you can't have and moving from one relationship to the next because you keep hoping the next person will ease your pain and fill the hole in your chest."

His voice is soft and raw, and it hurts my already aching heart. I reach for his hand and squeeze it.

"But what can I do, Papa? I've lost him."

"You are my daughter. Losing is not in your genetic composition."

"I feel like a loser."

"Bah!" He waves his hand at me—a gesture I once loathed, but now find endearing. "What does Vivian call you?"

"Never, ever, ever quit Fanny."

"*Voilà!*"

"*Voilà?* What are you saying?"

"Don't quit, Fanny. Go to your love. Woo him. Win him!"

Chapter 37

Juju

Text to Vivia Perpetua Grant:
I am pulling a Vivia! Headed to the Highlands to woo and win my man. Wish me luck.

Text from Vivia Perpetua Grant:
Atta Girl! Muster that inner-Churchill and conquer that cowboy! You're Never-Ever-Ever-Quit Fanny and you GOT THIS ONE!

I appreciate my best friend's optimism, but I am not so sure I have this one. After my father's hole-in-the-heart confession, I took a shower, brushed my teeth, and packed a carry-on. I took a taxi to the airport and bought a ticket on the first flight leaving Charles de Gaulle for Inverness. I had a brief layover in Dublin and finally landed in Scotland an hour ago.

Now, I am speeding north on the A9 over a narrow two-lane bridge called the Cromarty Firth Causeway. A flat slate-gray body of water—the Firth of Cromarty—stretches out on either side of the bridge. Rolling paps covered in yellow gorse stretch out before me, my windshield acting as a frame for the stunning panoramic snapshot.

The GPS built into the console indicates I will arrive at MacFarlane Farm in less than twenty minutes. I reach into my purse, pull out a tin of Altoids, and pop several mints into my mouth. If Calder rejects me, it won't be because I have bad breath.

Make a left turn off the A9 onto the A862...take the second exit out of the traffic circle in Dingwall...travel 1.3 miles on the A834...and you will arrive at your destination.

I turn off the A834 onto the long gravel drive leading to Calder's farm, gripping the steering wheel so tight my knuckles look like white marbles.

What if Calder refuses to see me? What if Fiona, his loyal, doting sister-in-law, slams the door in my face? What if I have traveled all of this way just to be told I am a selfish, self-absorbed loser who puts her ambitions before her heart?

I pull all of the way up the drive and park near the barn. I pop a few more mints into my mouth and consider my options. I could back down the driveway and leave before anyone even realizes I have arrived. I could....

My iPhone blings. I know it is Vivian texting before I even look at the screen.

Text from Vivia Perpetua Grant:
Argh! The suspense is killing me. What did you say to Calder? What did he say? Did he pull you into his big, brawny, badass arms and declare his undying devotion?

Text to Vivia Perpetua Grant:
I haven't spoken to him yet.

Text from Vivia Perpetua Grant:
WTH? Why not? You arrived over seventy five minutes ago.

Text to Vivia Perpetua Grant:
How do you even know that?

Text from Vivia Perpetua Grant:
Flight tracker. Please tell me you aren't sitting in your rental car, trying to decide whether you should ring his doorbell or drive away?

Text to Vivia Perpetua Grant:
That is exactly what I am doing.

Text from Vivia Perpetua Grant:
Listen to the American. Resist your French urges to retreat. You've landed in Normandy, now storm that freaking beach!

I am about to type a suitably snarky response when someone knocks on my window, scaring the *merde* out of me. I look up to find Fiona staring at me, a smile on her pretty face.

I roll down the window.

"Fiona! What are you doing here?"

She laughs. "I live here, remember?"

"I know." My cheeks flush with heat. "I just thought you would be inside, taking care of Angus."

"He's napping," she says, putting her hand on my door. "I was making a pot of tea when you pulled up. I thought maybe you were a lost tourist. I am glad I was wrong."

"You are?"

She smiles and nods. "Now get out of that car so I can give you a hug."

I hesitate for only a moment before opening the door and getting out of the car. She wraps her long, slender arms around me and squeezes. Fiona was a psychiatrist before she married Angus. She has the quiet, compassionate nature of a mental health professional and the uncanny ability to read people. Vivian called it creepy mind-reading juju.

Fiona pulls away and fixes her gaze on my face. "You're here for Calder, then?"

I nod my head because a lump of emotion is clogging my throat.

"I am sorry, but he is not here."

A razor sharp pain lacerates my heart. I was a fool to think a man as sexy and wonderful as Calder would be waiting around for me to come to my senses. He's probably found some bonny lass and is making slow, sweet love to her right now. Tears fill my eyes and, to my utter mortification, spill down my cheeks.

"Please don't cry." She grabs my hand and squeezes it. "He'll be back in a few hours. He's fixing a fence in the north pasture."

It's ridiculous, but hearing that he won't be home for a few more hours makes me cry even harder. "I c-c-c-an't wait. I have to s-s-see him n-n-now!"

Fiona puts her arm around my shoulders and leads me toward her cottage, a charming two-storied stone house with smoke curling out of the chimney toward the flat gray sky.

"Why don't you come inside and have a cup of tea? We can chat while you wait for Calder to return."

I pull away. "I am sorry, Fiona. I can't wait."

"Okay," she says, kicking a tone with the toe of her shiny black Wellies. "Tell me your plan and I will help you any way I can."

A new wave of heat ripples over my face and down my body.

"I don't have a p-p-plan," I say, sniffling. "When Vivian wanted to win Luc back, she came up with this grand public display with flowers and music and candies and a ring. I don't have any grand public displays planned."

"You are not Vivia, my friend."

"No," I whisper. "I am not Vivia."

I don't tell Fiona that I wished I were more like my friend. I wish I had her big, open, expressive heart and her ability to let go.

"I am glad," Fiona says.

I look up, tears clouding my vision.

"You are?"

Fiona nods. "Vivia is awesome, but you, my dear friend, have captured my beloved brother-in-law's heart."

I sniffle. "I have?"

She nods.

"Still?"

She nods again.

I throw my arms around her and squeeze her hard. We stand in the shadow of the barn, dark ominous clouds swirling over our heads, and hug for a long time. It doesn't feel awkward or uncomfortable. It feels right. It feels like family.

"I can't wait, Fiona." I pull away. "I have to get to Calder. I have to tell him I am sorry. I have to tell him that I love him and want to spend the rest of my life with him."

"Yessss!" Fiona punches the air. "I was hoping you were going to say that."

"Can I borrow a horse?"

"That depends. Have you ever ridden a horse before?"

"Only once, but I have climbed sheer rock walls, hiked on glaciers, and cycled through two countries. I think I can manage a horse."

Fiona leads me to the barn. She gives me a crash course on riding a horse, a map, and points me in the direction of Calder.

I am so desperate to see the man I love, I don't even bother to change out of my pants suit and high heeled boots. Besides, I can't think of a better uniform to win and woo my man than a perfectly tailored Armani suit, a silk Italian blouse, and sexy leather f-me boots.

Chapter 38

I'll Be Your Sassenach

Less than an hour later, I realize two humiliating facts: one, wearing a tight tailored Armani pantsuit to ride a horse is not sexy. My pant legs are covered in mud and I am sporting an unsightly and painful camel toe. And two, I am as abysmal at managing horses as Vivia is at managing touring bikes.

The old nag won't move faster than a gentle stroll. I nudge her flanks, coo in her ear, stroke her neck, curse at her in French, but we just plod along. Finally, in complete frustration, I drive my heels into her sides and she takes off like Seabiscuit.

Unfortunately, she must not be familiar with this track, because she is racing in the wrong direction. I clutch the reins with one hand and pull the map out of my suit pocket with the other. The map blows out of my hands and flutters high in the air.

I squeeze my aching thighs against the horse's flanks and pull back on the reins, but the old nag is drunk with power. She snickers, tosses her head, and gallops even faster. In horse language, she just said, "Fuck you!"

"Listen, you swaybacked, flea-bitten glue factory candidate"—I lean low over her neck and shout in her ear—"I didn't come all this way to be beaten by a horse. Now turn around and head in the right direction."

I swear to God the nasty nag understood every single one of my words and increased her speed…in the wrong direction. She continues galloping wildly toward a dark copse of trees, finally resuming her slow plod just before we reach the forest. I yank on the reins and she stops. Just stops plodding, stands in the shadow of a giant pine tree, and flicks her tail.

I slide out of the saddle, my heels sinking in thick primordial mud, and toss the reins around the saddle horn.

"I know a chef in Paris who could turn you into a delicious *pot-au-feu de cheval*." I look the nag in the eyes, but she merely nickers and paws the ground with her hoof, sending a fresh spray of mud over my pant legs. "Oh, you just wait! I am going to eat you with a nice Chianti!"

The horse turns and gallops back in the direction we came, leaving me standing ankle deep in mud, my Armani suit wrinkled and splattered with sheep shit.

"*Putain!*" I turn my face to the heavens and shout. "Could this day get any worse?"

And the heavens answer.

Fat freezing drops of rain fall from the sky and land on my forehead, my cheeks, my chin. I pull my feet out of the muck, gritting my teeth at the wet, slurping noise my now-ruined Christian Louboutin boots make.

With dread, I realize I will have to wait out the rain before trying to make my way back to the farm. I move deeper into the dark forest, crunching pinecones underfoot, pushing back low hanging branches, until I come to a hill. I climb to the top of the hill, my feet slipping on the rain-soaked grass, and find a ring of standing stones. One stone has fallen sideways and is resting against another, providing a shelter of sorts.

I sink to the ground, rest my back against the stone, pull my knees close to my chest, and huddle in my makeshift shelter.

I don't know what I thought would happen when I finally tracked Calder down, but I didn't think I would be covered in mud and animal excrement, reeking of foul beast, and dripping wet.

The bitter irony of my pathetic situation is not lost on me. Last year, before meeting Vivia in Edinburgh, I binge watched *Outlander*, a television show based on Diana Gabaldon's romantic novels about a British nurse named Claire, who walks between standing stones, travels back in time, and falls in love with a Scottish warrior named Jamie Fraser. I fantasized about walking through some standing stones and finding my own Jamie Fraser. I don't read romance novels, and I don't typically fantasize about Scottish warriors, but Sam Heughan, the actor who played Jamie, was crazy hot.

What an idiot.

Now, remembering my ridiculous fantasy, hot humiliating tears sting my eyes and slide down my cheeks. I found my own Scottish hottie—a hottie who is way hotter than Sam Heughan—and I blew it.

I bury my face in my hands and sob.

"Why are you crying?"

I look up and Calder is standing over me, the light of the setting sun turning his hair a coppery hue. My heart skips a beat, and another, and another. He looks so gorgeous, so strong and perfect. It makes me cry even more because I realize what I lost, what I will never regain.

He squats down until we are nearly on the same level.

"Why are you crying, *banfhlath*? Are ye hurt?"

There was a time I despised terms of endearment, when just the sound of a man calling me babe, sweetie, or honey made me want to vomit, but hearing Calder call me princess in Gaelic is the sweetest thing I have ever heard. It gives me the courage to tell him why I have come to Scotland, why I risked life and limb on an evil horse, why I am sitting in the middle of ancient stones sobbing like a baby.

"I am crying because I like you. I really, really like you." I lift my chin and my bottom lip begins to tremble. "No, that's not true. I don't like you."

"You didn't?"

"No, I didn't like you." I bat the tears from my cheeks with the backs of my hands like a five year old. "I love you."

Calder grins. "Aye, I ken ye love me."

"You do?"

He nods and keeps on grinning.

I frown. "Because all the ladies love you?"

"Aye," he winks, "That, and because I love you something fierce, and I don't believe God would let a love like mine go unrequited."

"Really?"

"Aye."

He pulls me into his big, brawny, badass arms and kisses me the way only a big, brawny, badass Scot can kiss a woman, completely and with his whole being.

Epilogue

I am standing in my new boutique in an old Victorian in Strathpeffer, a turn of the century spa town a few kilometers from MacFarlane Farm, when my iPhone rings. I grab my phone and read the text.

Text from Vivia Perpetua Grant:
Have you changed your mind about having your wedding in Scotland? After all, Chateau de Caumont would be the perfect setting for a fairytale wedding, banfhlath. LOL

Text to Vivia:
Nope. Small wedding, only family and close friends, between the standing stones.

Text from Vivia:
Okay, but I might not be able to make it.

Text to Vivia Perpetua Grant:
Shut up.

Text from Vivia Perpetua Grant:
I am serious.

Text to Vivia Perpetua Grant:
If you tell me you have some assignment interviewing Zac Efron in Rome or partying with Prince William in London, you will lose your position as my best friend.

Text from Vivia Perpetua Grant:

LOL. There isn't an assignment juicy enough to keep me from being by your side as you shackle yourself to the Cocky Cowboy.

Text to Vivia Perpetua Grant:
What is it then?

I wait, but Vivia doesn't respond. What reason could she possibly have for missing my wedding? Vivia isn't the type to shirk her BFF duties. And then it hits me.

Text to Vivia Perpetua Grant:
OMG! Vivia? Are you pregnant?

Meet the Author

Leah Marie Brown has worked as a journalist and photographer. An avid traveler, she has had adventures and mishaps from Paris to Tokyo. She doesn't buy cheesy tee-shirts or useless bric-a-brac, but prefers friendships and memories as souvenirs from her travels. She lives a bike ride away from the white sand beaches of Florida's Emerald Coast with her husband, children, and pampered poodles. She is hard at work on the next novel in the It Girls series, but loves to hear from readers. Please visit her website at www.leahmariebrown.com. You can also visit her blogs: leahmariebrownhistoricals.blogspot.com and leahmariebrown.blogspot.com, and follow her on Twitter @18thCFrance and @leahmariebrown.